The Forwarding Agent

Also by Austen Kark

Attic in Greece

Austen Kark

THE FORWARDING AGENT

The Toby Press, *London*

First published in Great Britain 1999

The Toby Press *Ltd, London*
www.tobypress.com

ISBN 1 902881 02 8

A CIP catalogue record for this title is available from the British Library

Designed by Fresh Produce, London

Typeset in Garamond by
Rowland Phototypesetting Ltd., Bury St Edmunds

Printed and bound in Great Britain by
St Edmundsbury Press, Bury St Edmunds

For Michael Shaw, for Nina and our multi-layered family and, as a sort of tribute, in memory of Tosco Fyvel, Derrick and Traute Sington, Alexander Lieven, George Hardinge, David Holloway, Leon Garfield, Edward Blishen, Veronica Manoukian and Konrad Syrop, all in their ways fellow forwarding agents.

Chapter one

I

t's not that I've got anything against Armenians. I suppose I'd never really given them much thought as a people. One of my good friends was called Manoukian and when I was a kid we both used to cry over the stories her mother told us of the dreadful things that had happened to them. The chronology came through a touch scrambled but the sentiments were clear. I wouldn't say I was actively pro-Armenian either; just neutral. An observer, that's me; objective, disinterested—not uninterested, my school beat that distinction into me before I was ten.

I had been standing, observing, not really thinking at all, outside the hotel. There was a little old lady, well not that little and probably not that old, say 65 to 75, in black, limping, a cane in her right hand, and handbag and Groppi's parcel—pastries, sweetmeats, Cairo's best—in the other. One of those ID labels travel agents foist on you dangled from her bag: Armenian Church Tours, it said. I wasn't close enough to read her name. Suddenly she stumbled down the steps in front of the hotel and I caught her and set her properly on her feet while she clung on to me. She was making, I supposed, for the tour bus parked twenty metres away. I was just about to say something—Take care, Look where you put your feet—when I sensed a disturbance in the pattern, light, shadow; something flickered in the corner of my eye. It took a nanosecond, I couldn't really have registered much; a blur of a covered face, eyes, a gun barrel.

I threw the old lady on the ground and crashed down on top of her. I suppose I was trying to cover her, protect her. Afterwards I always said I thought she'd make a softer landing. I'm fairly tall and reasonably fit at 38, if not perhaps quite as acrobatic as I was as a young marine commando at twenty-something. And I don't like falling. So maybe both stories are true.

I thought the firing would never stop, bursts of automatic fire from two or three AK47s. It went on for years, centuries, the dinosaurs rose and fell. It must have been forty, fifty seconds. Beneath me the old darling was sobbing, silently but with great heaves. I nearly fell off her but clung on like a non-swimmer to a life-raft. I felt a sharp jab in my arm and thought she must have inadvertently stabbed me with her cane.

Then silence, awful, deadly silence, for several, long, haunting seconds, before the screaming began: dreadful screams full of pain and fear and loss. I somehow got myself and the little old Armenian lady upright. I remembered, as I started to push us up and into the hotel, that subconsciously I must have noted, before the hush, the roar of accelerating, getting away, motor-cycles. The terrorist guns had got the hell out. The coast's clear, I said, to cheer her up. They've gone. And then a black hole, searing pain, spurting blood. I felt the wetness of it and the pulsing; a jet, a fountain. I thought it was her and I'd let her down.

When I came to, I was in hospital, wired up, tubes everywhere. An Egyptian doctor was speaking to me in French. He looked rather like that surgeon who's always doing the difficult heart operations, quintuple by-passes on elderly Siamese twins; Maguib, something like that.

I couldn't really concentrate. There was a kind of deafening, obliterating pain, like having a ghetto-blaster next to your pillow, turned up full volume, only it wasn't noise: it was pain. I blacked out—redded out.

The next time I understood him. Of course it might only have been a few minutes later. A nurse was injecting me. Morphine, someone said: it should ease the pain.

It did, after a fashion. The pain went to the foot of the bed, sat on the black bar, grinned, grimaced at me. It was still excruciating.

They must operate, he said. *Aujourd'hui. Ce soir.* I was, he told me, very lucky. Lucky? It must have been a ricochet, otherwise . . . But it had done some damage. *Pas mal.*

Where, I said, small-voiced, light-headed? Where? Perhaps he didn't hear. Perhaps I hadn't made any sound.

We are going to operate. OK? Now.

Was this another occasion? Or was it what our sixth-form maths and physics master called a continu-um to rhyme with a Yorkshire hum? Or bum. Flashes and freezes, colour to black-and-white and back, like in a clever film. Then my being lifted up, rising like a hot-air balloon.

It was dark except for a small light near my head. A nurse was re-arranging me, and some pillows, plumping them up. My right side was sore and heavy and the shoulder was caught in something. I looked. It was a sling suspended from overhead and part of me was in a large plaster cast in the sling. And there, on the left, was Eloïse, clutching some wilting roses, her knuckles white with the strain. They weren't wilting: they were dead. She must have broken the stems, she was holding them so hard.

"I thought you were in Alexandria." I heard myself, a croaking, Dalek, artificial noise.

"Darlink," she said. She always said Darlink first. It was a not very private joke, from the old films; Greta Garbo being a comrade, Marlene Dietrich a fatal woman. "Darling," she went on, "darling, darling, darling." I tried to smile as she gathered her thoughts. "I thought you'd be dead." *Snap,* I croaked in my head. She was weeping, real tears, buckets of them, spilling out on to her skirt, the bed-clothes, the floor.

"I saw it on the news," she said. "Last night. I borrowed Gérard's Peugeot and drove, drove, drove to Cairo. It takes me all day to find what happened to you. The hotel said you were a hero. You had been shot, shot dead, they thought. I told them I'd rather you were a coward and alive."

Admirable sentiment.

She wept some more, patted my left hand which, as far as I could see, looked all right; at least it looked like a hand and it didn't hurt.

Eloïse. I was never quite sure about the name. I mean Abelard and all that: not the happiest of *affaires.* And was her father really French? She certainly spoke a good, educated French and a beautiful Alexandrian Greek, her mother tongue. But I rather fancied her father—who went off with a Lebanese waiter when she was five or six—was a cultured, French-speaking Egyptian. And why not? Eloïse Dieudonné; it didn't sound very Egyptian, mind you, and I eventually found out her mother had kept her maiden name, for both of them.

But what mattered, she also spoke a charming, accented English, was the whole, the glorious combination. Body *and* brains. Her long legs, her startling green eyes, her faultless light olive skin, her shining elbow-length blue-black hair, her elegantly lazy carriage, deportment, some such finishing school word. She moved with unstudied grace. She was a stunning, raving beauty. Except for the nose. It was a strangely off-centred, awry nose, not meant for that face. I loved it and her, a dear, dear girl, without perhaps much of a sense of humour but a great sense of fun and lots of intensity and passion; and sex. We'd probably get married sooner or later, as my Mum kept pressing and hers hinting, meaningfully, as though she wished she still had a husband, bisexual or not, to brandish the 12-bore. Anyway I adored the girl and wanted to marry her, even without a shot-gun.

Shot-gun! I bolted upright and crashed the agony barrier. The nurse used one of the many lines gouged into my veins to deliver another shot and as I began to drift, inside a soap bubble, everyone outside, remote, curved, just audible, there was my lovely Eloïse saying something about 26 injured and thirteen dead.

4

Thirteen, I said, THIRTEEN, and laughed. Or tried to.

"My father," I said, enunciating pedantically, like one of those ancient recordings of 1940s BBC announcers being brave in the Blitz, "my father would have . . ." and my bubble floated away, me inside; away from the bed, the hospital, Eloïse.

My father was obsessed with the number thirteen. Otherwise a not superstitious, if anything, a scientific man, thirteen bugged him. I remember once our all going to a hotel together. It was a quite classy establishment and when we got out of the lift and followed the bell-boy, porter, whatever he was, to the room, my father said, "No. No, we're not having that room." We returned to Reception. There were no other rooms available, except—the desk clerk looked at us, not quite smiling; mother, father and my eight-year-old self—the Bridal Suite. It was spoken, reverentially, in capital letters.

It cost over double the original room. My mother complained all the time. We couldn't afford it, she reminded us every other minute: it was madness. I rather enjoyed it. It had a sitting room and two bathrooms. Why, I wondered later, two bathrooms in a honeymoon suite? His and hers?

When I got Mum alone and asked her what all that was about, she said, "Your father has his little funny ways. About numbers I mean."

"But," I remember saying, "it was a nice number, grey and blue." I think I saw three as grey and seven as blue.

"I don't know what you're talking about," she said in one of those infuriating parent-to-child voices, all superiority and sanity. "It was room 337. And the numbers were in lacquered brass." And that'll squish you up, Sonny, with knobs on, is what she meant. You think it's not bad enough to have a husband who does his nut over funny numbers but a child that's colour blind as well?

It was a week or two before I thought about it again and realized it added up to thirteen and Dad had been posted to Northern Ireland by then.

"Thirteen dead," Eloïse was saying when I and my bubble floated back, "and you might have made the fourteenth."

Cheerful thought. Cheated death again, gentlemen. Third time over the top and saved by the bible in my tunic pocket. Talking about numbers, chaps, the bullet lodged in the holy book just hadn't got mine on it. Nonsense, my mother would say; As God Intended. She always seemed to have a private line to Him Up There. I was never sure whether it was to Yahweh the Ancient of Days or Christ the Redeemer. She'd had a double dose of religion, poor Mum.

Her parents were Ladino-speaking Jews in Salonika and they, like almost all the Jewish community there, were exterminated in the gas-chambers. Mum had escaped the death camps because an Orthodox priest had taken her, aged five, into his family. He'd found her inside his church, trying to light a candle, a small suitcase beside her and a battered doll. Her father had left her there, rightly fearing the SS and the Gestapo.

The Pappas had smuggled her into his house, joined her to his family, his children were all older than her, and had her baptized. Exit Rachel, enter Eleni. She must, he told her, beard fiercely jabbing the words home, forget all about Rachel. She was new-born in the love and grace of Christ the Saviour, Eleni. Did she know who Eleni was? She was the mother of the Emperor Constantine who made Constantinople the Christian capital of the world. She had brought back from the Holy Land a piece of the True Cross.

When Mum told me the story I was at school in England and not very interested in Greek priests. Emperors were different. I came to life with Constantine and told her proudly that he was first proclaimed emperor in

5

York in 306, won as Emperor of the West in 312 and became Emperor of the East, sole Roman overlord in fact, in 324. The only reason I remembered all this was the happy run of numbers.

What Mum remembered was the priest burning her doll. It had a little gold chain round its neck with a Star of David, also in gold. She howled for two hours, until one of the older girls told her that if she didn't shut up they'd put her in a coffin and close the lid.

In reality they were marvellously kind and brave. The Pappas could have been executed, his family dispossessed and imprisoned. She came to love them as they loved her. She stayed with them till after the Civil War, around 1950. All her immediate family had been wiped out but there was a cousin who for some reason or other had fetched up in Cairo, Cousin Sam.

He somehow traced her and after much argument took her with him. The priest was losing not only a much-loved adopted daughter—she had been with them for ten years, two-thirds of her life—but also a soul, a Christian soul, who would now return to the unredeemed ranks of the Christ-killers. Before she left, all of them in tears, he made her promise always to wear her baptismal cross around her neck. And she always has. Much to the consternation of Cousin Sam's other Jewish friends in Alexandria where he and my mother went to live.

"I wonder if your Mum ever met my Mum in Alex," I said to Eloïse but, when I looked, the room was empty.

I could feel the sunlight, warm, bright but not yet that hot, intense breath of high summer. I opened an eye. Eloïse was back, curled up in a chair, touching the bed, my left hand held against her cheek. her beautiful, curved, high-cheekboned face.

It was a lovely waking up. Then I moved and the rest of my body sang with pain. I looked at the plaster cast. Where the hell was my right hand?

I must have woken Eloïse up. It was not altogether surprising: I expect I'd shouted. A nurse was called and then more drugs, more remoteness, less pain. Back inside your bubble, laddy.

My father, a Lancastrian, used to put on Scots, Welsh and Irish accents, and words to suit. It was whenever he wanted to, felt he should, express some emotion. The "laddy" came with a light touch on the shoulder and an awful music hall Scottish patter. He was a shy man, very competent, very self-contained very controlled, which was just as well since he was a bomb disposal expert.

I used to say he was a captain when I was in England but he was really a WO1, the most senior Warrant Officer in the army, a much more special thing to be. He was quiet even when, very rarely, he'd had a few beers or scotches; quiet but you always, without his trying, heard every word. It was a soft voice but very clear, every syllable properly formed.

There was a voice speaking; insistent, harsh, loud. It was another doctor, telling me I must wake. The chief was coming. Now. Any moment. I tried to open my eyes. They closed again. I forced them open and saw him arriving, two nurses and another doctor in tow.

The operation had gone well, he said. It had taken three and a half hours. Quite complex, difficult. They'd got everything alien out. Alien? And put everything in its proper place. The plaster, or another perhaps lighter, we'll see, will have to stay on for four or five months. Four or five MONTHS? It looks good. Any questions?

Dozens. But I only asked one. What was the damage?

"The arm from the elbow down. The wrist. The hand. Some damage to nerves as well as bones, sinews, muscles, tendons. A problem with the ulnar nerve. Bits of metal embedded in tissue, muscles, joints and so forth."

Smashed to smithereens, I said to myself.

"And the prognosis, Professor?" This was Eloïse.

"Good, good. Pretty good."

Lousy.

"What does that mean?" Eloïse again.

"The elbow joint may be a little restricted in movement, stiff, the joint not fully rotating. The wrist will be weak. Not able to carry anything heavy. For a while at any rate."

"And the hand?"

"We'll have to see. Nerves should join up. Bones and muscles mend."

"Well that's the end of my tennis career," I said out loud. They all looked worried, except Eloïse who had retreated into a catatonic trance. "Joke," I said. "JOKE."

But I was thinking I'd miss the weekly doubles and zooming up to the net and putting the ball away, bouncing high so our opponents could never reach it.

"Oh," I said. "And my boxing, dammit."

This was the shock therapy Eloïse had been needing. Without convulsions.

"Stop it," she said. "Stop it, stop it, stop it. It's ghastly enough without you clowning."

I slid away. This time inside a large, transparent, orange balloon.

I got the details from the English papers that were brought in daily. The eighteen Armenians had been visiting the Holy Land. Some of them had come from the United States, Canada, Mexico, Australia; others from Europe and the Levant. An Islamist terrorist group had shot up their bus, it was said later, because they were thought to be Israeli tourists. It turned out that an Israeli group had booked the bus but their tour had been rescheduled. Apart from the thirteen dead, three others had been injured and another twenty bystanders, mostly Egyptian, six small children among them, were seriously hurt.

Most of the papers ran similar accounts. The English broadsheets reminded their readers of other attacks on foreign tourists; of the history of Islamist movements in Egypt, the significance of the Muslim League, the role of the essentially modernising Government. Here and in the Egyptian press there were questions on security. Why had the guards been withdrawn from the hotel? Particularly when Israeli tourists were expected?

The day I left the hospital—Eloïse was taking me to her mother's in Alexandria for a few days recuperation before we returned to my Mum's—the doctors re-appeared. They mouthed pious hopes and waited for praise.

I thanked them for doing their best. I'd praise them all right when, and if, my arm, wrist, hand etc. worked; after a fashion, at any rate. I wasn't asking for miracles.

"I am ashamed," said the assistant surgeon with the harsh, almost guttural voice. "I am a Muslim. These animals proclaim Islam but they are false, faithless. Enemies, not protectors, of Islam."

The senior surgeon raised one eyebrow and then the other.

"The Armenians," he said, "would have been guarded better if they'd stayed in Israel."

They shook, in reverse order of seniority, my left hand.

During the Suez Affair in 1956 when almost everyone made fools of themselves except the Israelis and the Russians, who were able to have their wicked way with the Magyars, Cousin Sam sent my mother, who was nineteen, to Cyprus; for safety. Safety from war and, I suspect, from licentious soldiery. So she went to Limassol, got a job as an interpreter with the British forces and met and married her own very proper soldier, my dad. I was born at the base hospital in imperial comfort. When I was seven we, or rather my father, returned to England. Mum and I were going for the first time. Dad was posted to the War Office and we had a large flat in Kennington over-looking the Oval. I was sent to a fancy prep school, as a day boy. I learnt some French, quite a bit of Latin, a little ancient Greek and lots of maths, cricket and soccer. And the King James Bible, not that I've opened it in years.

My Mum for all her baptismal cross got worried and sent me on Sundays to learn Hebrew and how to be a Jew. That didn't last long. I said why couldn't I be a Methodist like Granny-on-the-moors and she said that I was a Jew whether I liked it or not. Why, I said, why? Because. she told me gnomically, you've got a Jewish mother just as I had. So? So what?

I think my father was quite pleased with me. He didn't go much for religion himself. In his undemanding way, I fancy he hoped I'd follow his logical agnosticism. But then there was his number thirteen quirk. He gave me a lecture around the time I put aside Hebrew. I wasn't really paying much attention to what he was saying, I was hoping I could wheedle a new cricket bat out of him, but I must have filed it away. I remembered it the other day; it was on the value of doubt.

That's me all right, the doubter. He would have been glad: Chip off the old Block, Doubting Thomas and more so. But Dad never lived to see it.

When I was just twelve he went to Northern Ireland for his third tour. He was called out, flown by helicopter, to what they called an incident. Another bomb disposal expert was caught in a booby-trap, a major. Dad relieved him, took over from him, had him safely away, all the time keeping pressure on the gimmick that would otherwise have detonated. Then he tried to defuse the complex device. He had been working on it for three hours when a long-range sniper fired at him and hit his hand. It was a fluke, they said, for even the best of marksmen, at twilight. But that was it. The bomb went off and Mum got given Dad's George Cross and a stirring citation.

There was a whip-round in the regiment, and some grants; and a pretty miserly widow's pension. Mum hated the cold and saw no point in hanging around. We went back to Cyprus and bought a small hotel in Larnaca.

Funny, I suddenly remembered, it was Dad's right hand too that got shot. But I haven't got a bomb to worry about; just Mum, Eloïse, having in effect lost my job and getting my arm back into shape.

Back home in Cyprus, the day the orthopod at the Base Hospital cut off the heavy cast, x-rayed the remains and tried to get me to flex what was left, was the day I got the first letter.

It was from a lawyer in Toronto. The nub of the matter was that my dear little old Armenian lady had put him on to finding me. If I replied, I would hear Something To My Advantage.

I needed some advantage. The elbow hurt most of the time and would barely rotate 5%, as the physio told me in exasperation, adding of course that I wasn't really trying. How did he know, front-row of the scrum hearty? My wrist which had clearly been busted into splinters was unlikely ever to open a jar or hold a foaming pint. My hand had a working but weak thumb and first finger. The rest were dead, glued together, immobile, without sensation and a rather disagreeable pale, greyish white.

The second letter enclosed a cheque for $5000 US.

The third didn't come through the letter-box. It was delivered by hand. By her son.

10

Chapter two

Larnaca, Cyprus 11

am, Cousin Sam, was my mother's idea of a real man. Strong-featured—heavy brow, heavy nose, heavy chin, iron grey hair cropped short, teeth like grave stones, yellow grave stones—he wasn't my notion of the romantic hero. But Mum thought him glamorous, a bit of a mystery man and certainly he attracted the girls. The ones he appeared with were never less than internationally photographed models—with copies of *Vogue* to prove it—and barely older than his granddaughter, if he'd got round to having acknowledged progeny. And skinnier by the year. He had a good laugh though, a way with him, said Mum's friends, and a shy, surprising smile that even Eloïse, who once said he reminded her of a Jewish Dracula, responded to. Some of his mates, the ones from the Alexandrian shul (synagogue to the un-Bar Mitzvah-ed), called him Shmuel. Most people thought he was a spy.

And, talking about Bar-Mitzvahs, Cousin Sam grabbed me as soon as we got back to Cyprus having buried what was left of Dad.

"Young man," he said—he was given to that sort of phrase, it used to embarrass the hell out of me, I didn't know where to put myself – "Young man, you have a birthday soon. You know what birthday it is?" *Did he really think I'd forgotten?* "You will be Bar-Mitzvah."

"I say," I said, fresh from my prep school, "I'm not . . ."

"Not what?" he interrupted me.

I looked into the sky. There were no clouds and no help. I said nothing.

"Not a Jew," he said, "or not Bar-Mitzvah?"

I looked at the nearest tree. It was a Judas tree, symbolic. I kept mum, stumm.

"You are and always will be," he said. "And your Bar-Mitzvah will be in a fortnight's time."

He was a powerful fellow, Cousin Sam; not so much tall as solid, more muscle than fat, with a barrel chest, strong arms, hairy body.

"Yeah," I said. And crossed as many fingers as I could behind my back.

I was done at the local shul. It was dire, traumatic. Full of these funny old men wearing hats and draping themselves in large white wraps called tallisim, and all of them praying out of sync, and out of tune when it came to singing, and sort of bowing rhythmically. You remember those ducks that went on dipping into the water as though they'd patented perpetual motion? That's what the praying was like. And then I was called and had to go up, in front of the Ark where the scrolls of the Torah were kept. I knew the Greek words better: Pentateuch, Genesis, Exodus, Leviticus, Deuteronomy. There hadn't really been time to give me a crash course in cribbing and my Hebrew wasn't up to it. So I looked a right Charlie as someone else, Sam I suspect, read my piece and I just about mumbled the blessings.

Afterwards all these strangers congratulated me. Mum shed a basin or two of tears. I wondered what she had done with her baptismal cross while all these shenanigans had been going on.

Cousin Sam said, a smooth baritone: "You know what Bar-Mitzvah means?"

I remember thinking I've just gone through an hour and a half of purgatory, and made a big, big fool of myself and he believes I don't know. I fixed on a point in his left eyebrow where the black was interrupted by a burst of wiry gray hair sticking out like a shrimp's whiskers and tried to look solemn and interested.

"It comes from the Hebrew," he said.

What did he suppose I thought it: Hottentot?

"It means, literally, son of commandment, man of duty. Now in the eyes of the congregation you are a man. Bound to obey the Law and responsible for your deeds."

12

I nodded my head and looked at my Mum. She was crying again.

We went and had a sort of party, at a restaurant. Cousin Sam had said I could ask whoever I liked. After a quick trawl, in my mind, I'd decided on the only safe two but O'Callaghan was playing cricket and in any case, he said, his mum wouldn't let him come, she being a strict Catholic and all and not wanting him mixed up in any of these heathenish ways. So Chuck came on his own. He was a barrel-load of fun, a great help. He looked at all the weirdos, straight-faced, storing it away for later, for school. He didn't say a word till he stuttered out his th-th-thank-you. To be fair he made a very funny story out of it but if he hadn't been my best friend—and still is, for that matter, and now my business partner too, we call ourselves forwarding agents—I'd have killed him. It was, as Cousin Sam said, A Great Day.

I had, you might say, an ambiguous relationship with Cousin Sam. Which was why when he suddenly appeared in Larnaca shortly after I got the kilo-dollar cheque, I smelt a rat, a cousin-rat. Particularly when Mum went into exaggerated greetings. What a lovely surprise. You should have told us you were coming. (So why had she been cooking since sun-up – Imam Bayeldi, the Imam Fainted, for the ignorant, on account of it being so bloody marvellous, the aubergine, tomato, garlic, olive oil thing, and chicken and lamb cooked slowly with apricots, figs, and pine nuts – his favourite dishes?)

"It's been such a long time," she purred, hugging him and stroking his face at the same time. He smiled and patted her head, good doggie, pat-pat.

After lunch – at least he was a drinking man, so the best single malt was out and some drinkable wine – we had a man-to-man. We walked down to the sea and the fishing boats where a young boy was doing something nasty in the way of flagellation to an octopus.

"So, you've been in the wars," he said percipiently, lighting his pipe and making disgusting sucking noises, "damaged your hand, I see." The wind blew out his lighter and he gave up, tapping the bowl on the heel of his shoe and emptying the revolting dottle on to the sea, just one more dollop of pollution.

He saw my expression. "It's biodegradable."

"Yeah," I said just to be friendly. "So's the sewage."

Sam made me feel adolescent and rebellious. Of course, I should have grown out of it but it had become a habit. I shrugged my shoulders and stood tall, a field officer, a leader of men. He too had been reflecting. The time had come to be serious. He put on a solemn face to announce the fact.

"Just who are these Armenians who are so free, your Mother tells me, with their thanks and their dollars?"

"Not that free," I said, irked. "I suppose you could say I saved her life. Five Ks are handsome but not exactly munificent. Not for a life. Mind you she was quite old." I looked at his glacial blue eyes: he was just as old. "Mikoyan," I added quickly. "That seems to be her name. But the Canadian lawyers are called Stephens, Plaister and three other names, along the lines of *Private Eye*'s Sue, Grabbit and Run."

"Very funny."

I don't think he'd ever seen the *Eye* but you never could tell with Cousin Sam.

"And why did they send you US dollars?"

"Because they're worth more than Canadian ones?"

He muttered something in another tongue, along the lines of God give me strength.

"What's that?" I said.

"Judaeo-Spanish."

You can tell what sort of man he is. Judaeo-Spanish! Forsooth!

"Oh," I said, "you mean Ladino."

"That's what some people call it."

"Yeah," I said. "Like Mum."

"I do wish you wouldn't call Your Mother by that childish cockney abbreviation. How old are you?"

Of course he knew; he could work it out from the Bar-Mitzvah.

"Thirty-eight," I said.

He shook his head several times, muttering, probably in Judaeo-Spanish.

"Let me know if you hear from them again. At once please. You understand?"

"OK," I said. "Why the sudden interest in who I meet? Anyway, where will you be?"

He ignored the first question. "Paphos the next few days. The office there will find me after that."

"Where have you come from now?"

"Here and there. There and here."

At lunch he'd been talking about Eilat, and Jerusalem, and Mersin, and Istanbul, where he'd been born. Some people thought he was Shin Bet or Mossad, others CIA, a few MI6 and one ex-EOKA enthusiast reckoned he was KGB. I thought he was a pain and a tribulation; big mystery man, Cousin Sam.

He wasn't there, of course, when I could have used him, when the real live Armenian turned up; unannounced, unexpected.

He was wearing a beautiful mid-grey silk suit. It was the first thing I noticed. It rippled in the breeze, glinting and minimally changing colour, light and shade. He was a little shorter than me, say six foot or a shave under. He had thick dark hair expensively styled, a very white shirt, crisp collar, sincere dark eyes, a little, mobile mouth, small hands and feet. He was thin, slender but well-rounded, handsome; all that. Eloïse, who was there when he arrived, said he was very, very good-looking, very, very sexy. It was all I needed.

I had finally got around to asking her when she thought we should get married. I was thinking of October. Thereabouts.

"Oh, I don't know," she said. "You'll have to give me some time to think it over."

Time? We'd been living together for five years, that is when one or other of us wasn't away. And discussing the pros and cons of marriage for at least two. Mind you, I'd been a bit worried lately about Eloïse. Since my mishap, or rather, since my semi-recovery. She didn't much take to my dead fingers. She said they were creepy. Love-making had been a bit strained in the circumstances, if not constrained, the wounded arm always getting in the way. Could she mean she was thinking not about *when* but about *whether?*

It was shortly after this unsettling exchange that the white Mercedes convertible drew up and Mr Mikoyan Jr. got out; slinky suit, neat fancy shoes. My father would have sussed him out as a foreigner instantly. I was just a touch envious and, of course, inquisitive. But that was before I knew who he was.

He spoke with a soft North American accent. There were none of the Canadian "ou-ow" give-away vowels; out, about. Otherwise I might have twigged at once. He said he'd been wanting to meet me. He'd heard so much about me.

I was sitting on the veranda, thinking about Eloïse, as I quite often did even when she wasn't there. Had she meant what I thought she meant? Shit. She probably had and still did, I wouldn't wonder, looking across at

15

her. She was sitting on a swing seat about as far away from me as she could get, without falling off the stoep.

Then this chap, carrying a soft, black leather, despatch case, this man I didn't know at all, started talking to me, and climbing up the steps. I got up, not much of the Alexander technique there today, heavily, clumsily. He stretched out his right hand and I thrust my left firmly into his.

"Do I know you?" I said, quick with the one-liners.

"What happened to your hand?" He was trained in a similar school.

"An accident," I said. "At work."

"What kind of work ?"

"I'm the high wire man at the local circus," I said airily.

He gasped.

"He's not," said Eloïse. It was the first thing she'd said for hours.

He looked at her, went over and said how did she do and returned to me.

"I'm sorry," he said, "I must seem very impertinent. Forgive me. I know now how you hurt your hand."

What was he talking about? Hurt seemed somewhat unimaginative, inadequate.

16

"I fell," I said. With emphasis. *Tout court.*

"You fell, I believe, protecting my mother."

He smiled, a sad smile but it did, for the first time, remind me of my little old lady.

"It was an accident," I repeated. "Your mother happened to be beneath me."

"Yes." he said. In the tone of what-sort-of -fool-do-you-take-me-for. "You saved my mother's life."

Eloïse got up and said she had some exam papers to mark. We both watched her glide down the steps; magical. I expect he was thinking, "Pity about the nose." But I, with the usual sharp jolt that came with watching her leave, knew I adored that nose and the face and the girl that went with it.

I swallowed and returned to young Mikoyan, offering him a beer. He said he'd rather have a Perrier water. He had a long way still to drive. He'd brought me a letter from his mother and he wanted me to read it carefully but not now. We sipped our drinks. I'd explained we were right out of Perrier at the moment so he'd have to put up with a cool Cyprus lemon juice and I'd join him. We sat companionably enough. He told me his mother was in fine fighting spirit again. She had taken back the reins of her corporations which he had been looking after for her and she was locked in a new round of union negotiations and enjoying it.

That rather changed the image. *OK. So what's a corporation?* Family rug and carpet business and a staff of twenty, thirty, forty at most.

"How many employees do you have?"

"Thirty thousand in one. Twenty-three thousand in the second. And maybe twenty-five people in the third, the investment wing, a shell."

Gob-smacked, I thought for a moment he'd said Shell; with a capital S, Royal Dutch, Petroleum, OIL. But the happy vision faded. He looked at his watch, a very decent Patek Phillipe, and said he had to go. Please would I read the letter most carefully. He would be back in two days time. Perhaps we could have lunch together. He would pick me up.

I waved a languid hand and went and poured myself a whisky; good old faithful, reliable, smoky Laphroaig. The envelope, which he had left on a wicker-work deck chair, was large, stiff and legal looking. It had one of those arrangements with string wound round two miniature cardboard wheels and sealed with wax. With an imprint. A tiger? A cat? Swimming on heraldic waves. A Lake Van swimming cat? I refilled my glass, a smaller slug of Laphroaig with ice added to suit the climate. It was, as some of my Greek friends say, hot, hot. Midsummer was a-cumin in and the thermometer read forty-one.

Chapter three

I

Cairo, Egypt

was back in Cairo much sooner than I had intended. It seemed hotter and more stifling than ever with the dust, traffic, and crowds of people, last estimate eleven million; the city a perpetual building site. I got out of the airport arrivals scrum, bedraggled and sweaty within seconds, feeling the heat rising from the concrete and the dust clogging my nostrils like a physical assault. I knew it was a mistake to return but Mrs Mikoyan and her son had made it difficult for me to refuse. The run of obligations, hers and mine, supervened. In the letter, she said she had left me in her will a property in Philadelphia. I was getting a bit mystified by the Canadian/US transition: clearly she was a real transnational. In the meantime, till I inherited the freehold, I would receive the rent. Just sign on the dotted line, list bank account and sort code, and a more than moderate competence would be deposited quarterly.

New paragraph. A request, an entreaty; perhaps I would be kind enough to listen to her son's proposal. He was, she added, unmanned by the senseless slaughter of his aunt and uncle and cousin, and coming so soon after the tragic (natural) death of his father, her husband.

I hadn't known that three of the family had been killed in the attack;

her sister, brother-in-law and nephew. I suppose no one had thought to tell me. Her son, she now confided to me, was an only child: the weight of family responsibility on him. He wanted to, needed to, see where and how it happened. Could I please help him? Take him there, describe the massacre, exorcize his wilder imaginings? She was she knew heavily in my debt but if I could just add this little extra service, air tickets (business class) and folding-money (dollars) enclosed, just a short trip, perhaps less than a week, if I could possibly spare the time, her gratitude would be eternal.

Heavy words, and behind them lay duty, respect, do-as-you-would-be-done-by. Devil you do, devil you don't. So I arranged to meet him at the Hathor Palace Hotel in ten days' time, Thursday for a late lunch. He would book me in.

"Where's that?" I had said. "Never heard of it."

"Near the Nile Hilton," he had answered, with the total insouciance of one who had never been to Cairo. "A friend of mine uses it regularly. Says it's quiet, comfortable and discreet."

"Sounds like me," I said.

As I was looking to see if I could find a reasonably equipped taxi—brakes, taxi-meter, vehicle with only 800,000 kilometres on the clock, one driver and no jokey co-pilot—an aggressive bout of hooting made me jump. I looked round and it wasn't a zealously entrepreneurial cab but a private car, a moderately new Peugeot. I recognized it; the one Eloïse had borrowed from her cousin, Gérard, in Alexandria. And here he was, throwing open the passenger door, telling me to jump in, he hadn't got all day, and what was I doing in Cairo anyway, and where could he drop me, not too far off his route he hoped, and why didn't I just throw my case in the back, instead of standing there like *mia stili*, a pillar or whatever we called it in English. And then he stopped long enough to see my arm in a sling and remembered. He jumped out, wrenched my case away and opened and closed the boot with a slam, got in and just before I closed the door, took off with a great shriek of burning rubber and an explosion of filthy exhaust.

"So it's still pretty useless," he said, "I wondered why Ellie has a new tennis partner. I'm told he's pretty good too. *Formidable.* I ran into her mother yesterday, *non*," he hit the horn a couple of times in irritation, "*l'avant-hier*, I must be going senile. Alzheimer's. Premature Alzheimer's."

"You can't have premature Alzheimer's," I said. "Alzheimer's disease is premature. That's what it means. *Senium praecox.* Middle age not old age.

19

When you lose your marbles in the fullness of time it's senile dementia not Alzheimer's. Everybody gets it wrong."

"*Mille remerciments*, old fruit." He didn't like me and I didn't like him but we normally kept our behaviour within polite limits of distaste.

"Sorry," I said. "Pompous remark. Uncalled for. By now it's probably changed its meaning, anyhow."

He smiled forgivingly, an amiable alligator biding his time, waiting for the next small boy to put his foot in the lake.

"So where's it to be then?"

I explained I had an appointment at the hospital on Sharia Higaz but he could drop me anywhere in the centre where there were taxis. But no, the hospital was fine; he was going that way. He delivered me to the front door, even getting out to open the boot and hand me my case.

Perhaps, I thought, I've misjudged the man. There was too much history in my appreciation. It was Gérard who had crashed his new motorbike with Eloïse on the pillion when he was eighteen and she fifteen. Hence her broken nose. It was Gérard, who was I think a first cousin once removed, the generations having slipped out of kilter, that her mother had picked early on as a suitable husband for her daughter; a lawyer with private income. It was years before the disappointment came into the open; not only was Eloïse living with me but Gérard had devoted himself to a series of young live-in boyfriends. And Gérard had never made any bones about believing me ill-suited to be his cousin's lover, let alone anything more permanent.

Then, to bring it up to date, I hadn't much taken to the jibe about the new tennis partner.

The Professor would see me in two minutes; well, ten as it turned out. Had I, I wondered, known he was a proper Professor? No I hadn't. It wasn't that I was losing my marbles. Eloïse called all consultants *Professeur* and when I'd been an in-patient I'd had other things on my mind: pain, shock, fear.

We recognized each other. He admired the hinged, light-weight removable cast the army orthopods had rigged me up, with Velcro fastenings. He examined the arm, the elbow, the wrist, the fingers, very delicately and then put the joints through excruciating contortions. I was shaking with burning pain. Actually when I looked more closely there weren't any contortions. He was just very gently and minimally rotating what were meant to be highly mobile working parts.

He said he didn't think much of the physiotherapy I'd been having.

He then started pushing the palm of his hand against mine, a sort of wrist instead of arm wrestling.

"Not much strength there. Push, push. *POUSSEZ. Encore. POUSSEZ.*"

Outside, patients must have thought the good professor had metamorphosed into an obstetrician.

Then out came the blunt needle and he traced the paths of the nerves. I felt more pricks than I had expected and he was pleased. He grunted something to the effect that the nerves were joining up and three of the affected fingers were doing well. I examined them, I'd been rather giving them a miss, and they even looked a little less dead to me, less grey. Then he gave me a lecture about exercise and trying all the time to do a little more.

"Look," he said, quite fiercely, "there is every chance that you will be able to use your hand for most things quite normally. Not perhaps the tennis or the squash but more than I ever imagined when I first saw you. It's up to you. You must get a little rubber ball and play with it in your hand, all the time, squeezing, rotating, moving it from finger to finger to thumb to finger."

I thanked him properly and said what a good job he'd done, almost with conviction.

"I want to see you," he said, "in another three months. OK?"

"OK," I said. "I hope so."

"And I want to see much, much more improvement."

He got up came round and shook my left hand and ushered me towards the door.

"And how's your lovely girlfriend?"

"Fine," I said, "just fine."

"Remember me to her."

As we got to the door, I paused.

"Any news?"

"No," he said, "they arrested the usual list of suspected al-Jama'at people and known Mulsim Brethren and are, I suppose, in the process of releasing them. No evidence. Anyway, it wouldn't be them."

A wry, sad grin. He opened the door and patted my shoulder. "Be careful." He meant it. He had invested time and skill in me.

I collected my suitcase and wheeled it out to the entrance. I was lucky; a taxi was depositing a visitor and I grabbed it. We made it to the Hathor

21

Palace in record time, with no more than half-a-dozen heart-stopping near-misses. It was, as Mikoyan had said, not far from the Hilton.

I paid him off, checked in and got a bell-boy to take my cases up to the room. The hotel looked vintage, comfortable, well-run. It had the air of a stately Edwardian bordello, almost Parisian, with dulled gold pillars, marble floors, high windows framed by deep, faded rose curtains tied back with gilt tassels. A single large medallian of Hathor – the ancient Egyptian cow-goddess, with a sexy human body, and horns and bovine ears, annual lover of Horus, patroness of music and jollity, equated by the Greeks with Aphrodite – was visible in the lobby, high on the wall. There was no sense of hustle, not a sign of a tour, no hint of a package deal. These would all be full paying customers. I had a good hour in hand so I went to the newspaper shop to get some papers and see if I could find a convenient rubber ball. After some rootling about in a stores cupboard the obliging, if short of breath, shopkeeper came up triumphant, a small packet with three balls, one green, one red, one yellow. Left over from some special kids' offer, he said chuckling, as he dusted the plastic with his hand, and wafted garlic in my direction. A merry fellow with both incisors clad in imperishable gold.

By the time I got to the top, the tenth floor, I had dropped the yellow ball twice in the lift and was still bent down retrieving it when the doors opened. I just got out before they closed again. I was noticing that the ball felt soft and malleable in the left hand but hard and unresisting as a billiard ball in the right, as the Prof. would say I had a long way to go with that hand, when I saw the bell-boy coming out of my room. He recognized me, held the door open and gave me the key.

A nice enough, comfortable, if strangely proportioned, rather narrow, room, well-made reproduction furniture, good quality, near-new, unstained carpet. I opened the curtains. It was not a bad view, mostly of the back of the Hilton in the distance. The air conditioning was turned up too high but that's par for the course. There was a writing desk and even a box full of two kinds of writing paper and cubby-holes of different sized envelopes. Not bad at all. The bathroom was better still with proper large Turkish towels, plumbing that seemed to work and shower and bath big enough to use without hitting one's elbows and knees. I tried the bed, comfortable but firm.

As I lay and looked at the ceiling I awarded nine out of ten to Mikoyan's unknown friend. Mind you the air conditioning made too much noise and there was another hum. I got up to investigate. Television was off. Radio was off. To hell with it. I stripped and showered the dust of Cairo down the drain.

Putting on a clean shirt, still a difficult, having-to-be-thought-about, manoeuvre with my right arm, I heard the hum again, sounding like distant voices. Perhaps it was the TV from the next door room. I could almost hear what was being said. I moved across to the bed and the noise disappeared. I moved back towards the window and started to put my trousers on and I could hear it again. It seemed to be clearest near the cupboard with sliding doors. I opened them. It was a deep walk-in cupboard, with a rail with heavy duty wooden hangers on one side, drawers and trays ahead of me, up to waist height, then a polished top awaiting a pair of military hair-brushes to match the clothes brush and long-handled shoe-horn already there. Above them was a large oval looking-glass. The voice seemed to be coming from there. It was American, mid-west, educated, a touch hectoring.

"You'll have to forgive me," it said, seeking no forgiveness, "if I tell you what you already know. Such, for example, as upward of 900 people died 1992–96 alone. From Islamic attacks, that is, and, I would emphatically add, from Husni Mubarak's government's responses to them. Note I say Islamist, whatever the hell that might be taken to mean."

"But . . ." said another voice, unsuccessfully trying to abort the flow.

"You might ask are we talking classical terrorism here, violence to provoke fear to engender a political change? Or something destructively different; amorphous aims, woolly ideologies, seeking bloodshed and publicity in equal measures? Random, illogical, inconsequential. No, forgive me, let me continue."

Eavesdropping, I could visualize the long, bony hand raised to quell insubordinate interruption.

"If we don't get off on a straight path here, now, we'll never climb the mountain. And by God it's one hell of a peak. You'll remember hearing about Muslims and the holy book, the people of the book, the bible, all that? Forget it: it's gone. Christians, Jews, Hindus, heathen, all the same. They're infidels, without faith, without The Faith. Only the Jews are, you might imagine that, at the top of the hate pile. The Cross-worshippers come a close second. Islam is the One True Faith. The object is not to deter a tourist or two; to change a government – although both would be deemed desirable side-effects – but to change the whole goddamned world. To create the City of Faith, Dar al-Imam. Islamic rule, Islamic rules – the Shari'ah, hand-lopping for theft, stoning to death for adultery – for the world. That's it. That's what they want, whoever the hell they are. Now as to that, let me tell you a cautionary tale or two."

I tapped the mirror gently, trying to find out why I could hear the conversation so clearly, and there was a slight click and a small circle suddenly appeared, of one-way glass, showing me part of the next room; disappointingly I could make out only the bed and a table with a bottle of water on it. I clicked the mirror back to normality and was turning round to find my shoes when I heard the counter-explosion.

"STOP," the second voice said, and I was slowly, stupidly, beginning to recognize whose it was. "You can tell me all this later when my colleague joins us. I dare say he knows more about it than I do. Now what about that report I asked for?"

"I've got it right here, nicely printed out for you, with punctuation and all, Arabic spellings checked. I can tell you there's not much that's sexy, barely interesting."

"I don't want any hard copy being left around, incriminating me," said the other who, it sounded, was less than admiring of his interlocutor's style, or sense. "Just tell me what you found out."

I imagined, perhaps half-heard, the opening of an envelope, the rustle of paper. I thought I might as well wait and hear the rest.

"OK. Here it is, Bill. You mind me calling you Bill?"

"William," said my Armenian buddy, William Mikoyan, fiercely.

"OK. William. You understand I didn't find anything out. I sent a signal or two and this is what I got back. Can't swear to it personally, you understand, but the boys are good. I'll read it to you. Benjamin Martin Bolton."

Hey, that's me.

"Born Cyprus, British Sovereign Base Area Hospital, 6 December 1957. Father David Bolton, WO1 – they tell me that's equivalent to Sergeant-Major – bomb-disposal expert, born Leeds, Yorkshire, England, 20 May 1934. Died October 1969 result of IRA sharpshooter. George Cross for bravery. I guess that's quite an honour. He was defusing a bomb at the time. Mother Eleni, earlier Rachel, Massarano. Born Thessaloniki, we call it Salonika, 23 April '35. That's St George's Day, should have called her Georgina. Jewish parents and grandparents wiped out. SS concentration camps, Poland. Holocaust. Tough for the child. Lives at Alasia Hotel. New to me, that; pronounced Alásia. Seems it's what Cyprus was called, late bronze age, say fifteenth–fourteenth centuries BC, by Ancient Egyptians and Mycenaeans. Didn't know the Cypriots were around then. Live and learn."

"I've visited the hotel," said William. "Get on with it. He'll be here in a few minutes."

"OK, OK. I'll summarize. Good grades at school, England and Cyprus. Good at cricket, for God's sake; boxing, lawn tennis (is that the same as hard court, regular tennis?) swimming. University entrance to LSE (I guess that's the London School of Economics, yeah it says so). Drops out after one term. No explanation. And then a lot of nothing very much."

"When was that?"

"Christmas 1975, thereabouts."

"A long time doing nothing very much. What did he live on? Got anything else?"

"Trips abroad. UK Cyprus. Cyprus UK. London New York London. Cairo. Tel Aviv. Beirut. Washington DC. Seattle. Johannesburg. Accra. Nairobi. Athens. Ankara. Cyprus. Istanbul. Athens. Salonika. Rome. Prague. Munich. Cyprus. Hong Kong. Cyprus . . ."

"OK skip the travel details. Anything else?"

"Not a whisper. Till late 1993. This looks more inviting. Specialized travel agency, Norwich, England. Staff or partner query. Here's something else again. Mother's cousin; Sam Massarano, free-lance. That means intelligence. Contacts: Mossad, British SIS, oh hell, CIA."

By now, I'd gone through the possibilities. The discreet hotel with voyeurs accommodated in adjacent rooms; spy-view and audible accompaniment available. Perhaps the other room had been the bridal suite. If mine was narrow, William's might well be half as wide again as a normal room. And certainly the bed had been big enough for frolicking. But why had I been given the viewing and listening room? Had William set the whole thing up? Was I meant to hear his conversation? But how could he know I'd get there early enough to make it interesting? The housekeeping staff might have unlocked the mirror gizmo, however it worked, to clean it and then failed to lock it up again. Of course, the rooms had been booked as a pair; but so what? The cupboard must have obtruded into his room and, of course, if his cupboard doors had been open too then it might have been a coincidence that I was able to overhear them talking. But I don't much believe in coincidences.

I left everything as it was, slid silently out of my room – who knows what reciprocal arrangements might lie on the other side of the cupboard?

– and went down to the lobby. There was an internal phone near the desk. I asked to be put through to Mr Mikoyan's room. He answered at once; he must have been waiting for it to ring. I said I'd meet him in the bar or come up, whichever he preferred. He was next door to me, he said, so why didn't I drop my things and come along and join him. The Taittinger was on ice, waiting.

And so it was. I'd made bustling noises in my room, run a tap or two and then gone outside and knocked at his door. William was pouring the champagne.

"Ben," he said, and waved towards his companion, "meet Cy Drucker, from the Embassy."

I had been expecting a tall, lean, sharp-faced man, in preppy Brooks Brothers rig. About the only thing I'd got right was the button down shirt and quiet patterned tie. Drucker was tubby, round-faced, with rosy glistening cheeks and light brown curly hair, wearing a crumpled off-white cotton suit and a piece of tissue on his chin where he had cut himself shaving.

"So you're the famous Ben Bolton," he said, sweaty palm, small pudgy hand outstretched.

26

"Famous?" I said, raising an eyebrow or two.

"William told me about his Mother," very much the capital M, reverential. "How you saved her."

I sipped the Taittinger. It was not bad, not bad at all. Cy sipped his and looked at me. William looked at Cy. It was going to be a sparky occasion. I could feel it: electric.

"What's the latest?" I said, trying to get a ball rolling, which reminded me to take out my little yellow plaything and roll it around my beslung hand.

Cy looked bewildered. It hadn't said anything about that in his briefing. Hey, what have we here? Psychosis? A latter day version of Captain Queeg's brass balls? I thought I'd better explain, put him out of his misery.

William looked bored, vaguely sympathetic but bored. He flopped down in a chair and said, "Yeah, of course. So what did the surgeon say?" as though he had something else on his mind.

He rang room service and asked them to bring up the lunch he'd ordered.

"Cy's kindly come along," he said, while waiting for the food, "to give us an update, a general briefing."

That was all he needed. Within seconds we were into the history of the Party of Allah, or Hezb-Allah as he preferred to call it; Ayatollahs; Sunni; Shi'ite; Saddam Hussain; Carlos the Jackal; Arab student organizations in the US of A; Anwar Sadat's assassination and Faraj of Holy Terror who, he asserted, master-minded it. Then there was the role of the Cold War in providing a sturdy American lobby in favour of Islamist fundamentalists over against pro-Russian Commies.

"Mr Drucker," I said.

"Cy," he said, between munches of smoked salmon sandwich. "Call me Cy."

"You make it sound as though the whole of Islam is like the Taliban and all Muslims terrorists; bombing, maiming, stoning adulterers, suppressing and covering up women. Whereas . . ."

"Yeah, yeah, yeah. All that." He flapped a hand. "As your compatriots would say," he put on an exaggerated English accent, "grarnted, grarnted. They're all peace-loving. They love non-Muslims. They're kind and just and they've a great positive programme of affirmative action to promote their womenfolk."

"Come on," I said, "you're overdoing it. Prejudice, bias. Where's the diplomatic objectivity? The cool, factual analysis?"

William's eyes had long glazed over. I reckoned he was asleep, or wishing he was. Perhaps Cy had got the message. He emptied his third glass, wolfed the last sandwich, and then looked at his watch, got up and said; "That's it, you guys. I've got to head back to the office. Meet with the Ambassador." Capital A, pause for obeisance. "Let me know what more you want. Anything we can do to help. Good hunting! Don't do anything I wouldn't . . ."

He saw himself out.

"Who the hell was that?"

"Mother knew someone in Washington who knew someone at State who nominated Cyrus Drucker the third. Cy Drucker II was something big in Duponts back when. His son, as you rightly observed, doesn't take after his old man. Talks balls."

"Talks and talks and talks," I said, "and tells us nothing. Maybe it's a clever ploy. What's he meant to do at the embassy?"

"Attaché," William looked at the visiting card he'd taken from his pocket, "Inter-Arab Affairs, US Embassy, Cairo."

"Yeah, well," I said, "press-culling dogsbody."

"Mother thought he was CIA."

"Don't you believe it," I said. "Even their worst enemies wouldn't reckon they're that down on their luck."

"So what do we do now?"

"Well," I said helpfully, "what do you want to do?"

"Find the bastards that killed my aunt and uncle and nearly killed my mother." Pause for gravity. "And you for that matter." An afterthought.

"Whoa there," I said. "Hang about. That's going a bit fast for me. I don't remember either your mother or you . . ."

"No, she wouldn't have. And I was just thinking it over back there in Larnaca. But now I see what I've got to do. And for the moment you're here with me. My best hope."

"Not for long, I'm not. Even if I'm your only hope. I'm going to have a good, long siesta. Then we'll see."

I slept for an hour and a half, had a bath, thought, exercised my hand, checked the cupboard door was properly closed and phoned Freddie.

Frederick Ericsson was very tall, six foot seven. He had light, almost white blond hair and still lighter eyebrows which even in his early seventies were barely touched by any change in colour. His father, Bo Ericsson, had been an SOE hero, in and out of occupied Norway, by parachute, submarine and fishing boat. On one of his trips he had smuggled out, against orders, practice and precedent, his twelve-year old son who was then sent to Eton. After Oxford, Freddie joined the *Manchester Evening News* as a trainee reporter. Two years later he got into the BBC. By the time he left, a quarter of a century later, to join Reuters, he had been North African Correspondent, Paris Correspondent, Cairo Correspondent, Middle East Correspondent, Rome Correspondent.

He was a friend of my father's, I think they first met in Cyprus, and as luck would have it Freddie was in Northern Ireland when the bomb went off and he covered the story. He was a part of my life as far back as I can remember. He used to take me to the Television Centre, to Broadcasting House, to Bush House, to the envy of my English school-mates. We had always kept in touch. When he retired as Reuter's chef de bureau in Cairo, he decided to stay on and mount his own small, developing nations, operation. I don't think it made any money but it kept his press pass and membership of the foreign correspondents' association intact; and him happy. His wife, Tamara, born in Harbin of Russian parents and brought up variously in Tientsin, Tangiers and Bromley South, was a magnificent cook, a fluent demotic Arabic speaker and had become an assiduous, observant, deeply religious Copt.

Freddie had a disconcerting habit of producing a tube of toothpaste from his pocket whenever he was thinking and squeezing small amounts into his mouth. It was not your average Colgate but something called Euthymol with a medical, disinfectant sort of flavour. He used to import it by the case. Apparently you couldn't get it in Eygpt. He was sucking it now, I could hear, as I explained my predicament.

"Kerr-rist," he said, "you daft bugger. You don't do it by halves, do you? Why didn't you let us know you were coming?"

They'd been in Zaïre and Rwanda when the shoot-up took place and I didn't know whether they knew about my little mishap. So I rehearsed the tale, interspersed with more sucking on toothpaste and grunts from his side.

He was hurt because I hadn't told him the first time I was coming but as I pointed out he and Tamara were already in Kigali. That's what the answerphone had said when I tried their number.

"I thought we had this fool-proof system that you set up with your mates in SATIS, or whatever you call it."

"That's it. Special Arrangements Travel and Information Service – SATIS by name and SATIS-factory by nature. But you weren't there so I couldn't use our carefully worked out passwords and coded messages. Could I?"

When, around 1992, Ginger O'Callaghan and Chuck Levendhis, my two best mates from school, and I all reckoned we had finished, or were finishing, the first phase of our respective careers, we decided to form a partnership. Ginger had been badly burned in the Falklands and had later married one of the nurses at the East Grinstead burns unit, where he spent a couple of years on and off, having skin-grafts. Jane was a Norfolk girl and they had gone to live in the outskirts of Norwich, in what had been her parents' house. Chuck, who was an accountant, was fed up with Cyprus, sold his practice and made a bee-line for England where he set himself up as a computer consultant in Hackney. When Ginger offered him office room in his large house, Chuck moved to Norwich and I suggested SATIS, with myself as the courier, guide, escort, leader, fixer, gopher, out on the road. We had appointed Freddie as our Middle East contact, agent, whatever.

It wasn't a big business but it was highly specialized, go anywhere, do anything, deliver, recover whatever (not drugs, not arms, not explosives or deadly viruses), act as forwarding agents and feed information. We were doing all right until I had my accident which rather invalidated, for the moment at least, a large part of the operation.

Ginger had become an expert on air, sea, road and rail travel. Chuck had contributed a very sophisticated computer programme that took care of everything, including invoices and tax and tickets and background information on every city in any country we'd ever heard about; and timetables and hotel and restuarant lists; and emergency lawyers and doctors and dentists. And I had conducted some pretty hairy visits to unlikely spots, sometimes retrieving property, sometimes liberating people from undesirable situations, sometimes escorting parties in and out of illiberal states but also planning, accompanying, stage-managing many more comparatively straight-forward trips. It was a neat little organization and we had been showing a small but comfortable profit.

"All right," said Freddie. "I'll see what I can dig up. Bring your Armenian along for dinner tonight. Eight o'clock-ish. Tamara will be tickled pink to see you."

Chapter four

The taxi took us through what seemed miles of poured concrete, jerry-built apartments, houses, shops, wooden shacks, mountains of plastic bags, end-to-end traffic, jostling crowds of people and then suddenly, towards the old Gezira Club, there was a little enclave of older houses. On top of one of them was a balcony, green with shrubs and bright with flowers, and a flag-pole with a Union flag hanging limply. It was the Ericssons' flat.

Freddie greeted us in a white sharkskin suit, tube of toothpaste showing in front of a yellow handkerchief in top pocket, and an MCC, full colours, bow-tie. He offered us some Arak which he swore had aged for 25 years in stone bottles in a wadi which no one had ever heard of.

"Don't touch it," said Tamara. "It'll send you mad, or make you blind."

I nodded and asked for some beer.

"Bloody prole," said Freddie. "This your Armenian friend?"

I introduced William to them both. He made the right noises.

Tamara was looking marvellous: dark hair drawn back in ballerina fashion; simple, black, silk shift with a dramatic, large, antique silver Coptic cross round her neck. She was in very good shape for her 70-plus years, with an attractively husky voice—she gave up smoking when she was 65, she claimed—that vibrated breathily whenever she spoke.

There was a Coptic cleric with fierce black beard and calm, contemplative eyes who said grace before we ate. He said little more and I assumed he was retained as Tamara's confessor, or domestic chaplain. The remaining guests were a man from the British embassy, Jeremy Sims, and his somewhat younger and red-haired Australian wife, Katie, who sat on my right.

"I was going round the world," she said in reply to no question of mine, "starting with the States and moving eastward towards home, home being Darwin; Darwin, north Australia?" I nodded. "I'd got as far as Ankara. Phew. I met Jerra and never looked back."

She was heavily freckled, had a little retroussé nose which was blistered and a pair of engaging dimples. She also had the loudest voice in the room; a shrieker.

"When was that?" I said.

"When did we get married, Jerra?" A shout across a crowded railway station.

"Four years ago, come August." He spoke so quietly, we all had to strain to hear him.

"Yeah. That'd be about right."

Freddie tapped his glass, calling the meeting to order. Even seated he looked a giant. He said he could only get decent clothes in Hong Kong or Savile Row. Of course, they had to be made to measure. Except when he was actually on the air, or recording a piece down the line, Freddie spoke extremely fast, syllables tumbling over each other in a race to the finish. If your attention wandered, you missed the next chapter.

"It might be," he said, starting off at a lick, "some of you have other notions. Interrupt. Speak. Intervene. Or hold your peace. For me, there are three lines. One, it was a random attack. Any tourists would have done, as long as they weren't Arab or Muslim. Two, it was planned as an anti-Israeli massacre but their intelligence was adrift and they killed the wrong people. Three, it was carefully contrived. Someone, or some group, on that bus was to be killed: the other deaths were to obscure, confuse the real motive; i.e. amongst those murdered were those intended to be murdered.

"I've spoken to my police contacts. Useless. Nothing relevant known. No real clues. No proper suspects. Nichevo. My one line to the secret police, used to be called the Mukhabarat in Nasser's day, has gone dead. I tried my fellow correspondents, my successors, BBC, Reuter's, and the AFP man and the AP chap. Duck's eggs. My considered bet is choice One—random, senseless slaughter. Senseless to us that is, not to those who want to establish the City of Faith. On earth. Here. Now. And, thereby, a poke in the eye for the Egyptian government and Mr Mubarak."

Jeremy, from the embassy, spoke. Again we all strained to listen. "No word," he said, "has reached our sensitive ears, either."

Pompous, little tick, I thought.

Tamara harrumphed. "Enough of that. This, my loves, is a dinner party not a post-mortem." She turned to William, on her left. "Appalling for you. I'm very sorry about your family. Terrible, terrible tragedy." She paused, took his hand, looked into his eyes, and then dismissed the topic. "Now," she said, brightly, "I know very little about the Armenian church. You must educate me."

William was finding it hard going. "It's very ancient, our church," he said, giving the matter his full consideration.

"As ancient as the Coptic Church?" asked Tamara in what passed for gentleness. "I don't think so."

Katie, from Darwin, confided in me. "I was an entomologist, specialized in dung beetles. Lovely, rewarding little beasts. Jerra didn't think it suitable for a British diplomat's wife."

Her husband meanwhile was engaging the priest in conversation, or rather he was talking to the priest. In return he got smiles, nods and bows but no words. Perhaps the man of God was shy about his English.

In one of those sudden, universal silences that overtake ill-assorted dinner tables, I found myself speaking across the void, asking what any of them made of Mr Cyrus Drucker at the US Embassy. Three of them spoke at once and then deferred to each other.

Freddie: "Not even a mini-spook. Arabist manqué. Not really a career diplomat. Not really anything very much. Bit of a shit. Don't trust him."

Jeremy: "Don't underestimate him. His Arabic's good, much better than he lets on. He's got private money and a book full of contacts. I find him dangerously ambivalent."

He looked at me. Meaningfully. "For you," he said, "bad news."

Why, I wondered, should Drucker's ambivalence be bad news for me? What was he talking about?

The third voice was the priest's, mellifluous, in precise English. "His mother was a parishioner, a communicant, of our church. She was born a Muslim but converted to Christianity in America when she married his father. In recent years—she has now died—when she lived in Cairo with her son, she always came to my church. Islamists, of course, considered her an apostate. It may, in part, explain her son."

Towards eleven, Freddie poured out large brandies and made it clear these were stirrup cups.

"Jeremy, dear boy," he said, "would it be too terribly tedious and out of the way for you and Katie to drop Ben and William off at the Hathor Palace, *poli konda sto* Hilton?"

William and Katie sat at the back of the Rover while Jeremy drove and talked, or rather mumbled, non-stop: about Egypt being a pressure-cooker; exponential population growth, overwhelming unemployment and poverty; Mubarak juggling too many balls; disastrous economy, relying on international hand-outs, US, Saudis, whoever; the slow follow-up to the Oslo peace talks; Rabin's assassination, and the apparent growing Israeli intransigence . . .

I slid away and re-tuned to the conversation in the back. It was louder, easier to hear. William must have said something about his mother being brought up in Philadelphia.

"Ah, City of brotherly and sisterly love," Katie was saying. "You know I met three Quaker sisters there who lived in a large white house with vast grounds and bred Samoyeds. Do you know what they are?"

"I don't think I do," said William.

"White, long-haired, beautiful sledge-dogs, entirely white. Real beauts. Faith, Hope and Charity, those are the three sisters, bred champions. Enormous kennels. Suddenly, while I was visiting, Hope, must have been in her mid-forties, dropped down dead. An asthma attack. Never had asthma in her life, they said; nor had they. No one in the family. A well woman, too; strong, competent, entered sledge-dog competitions, won many of them, they said. She, Hope, the middle one, had, the doctors said afterwards, developed an allergy to Samoyed hair, dander, all that; out of the blue. And dead within minutes of the first wheeze. The others, shocked rigid, you know, sold all those beaut dogs and bitches and puppies within the week, closed the kennels, turned the house over to the poor and terminally crook, the ill and flaking. Retreated to good works, they did, after a quarter of a century of breeding the most beautiful dogs in the world."

She finished on a rising inflection; many of her sentences did, as though she was always asking for confirmation. Jeremy was still muttering on about GDP, lowest per capita income in the universe, or something, and then suddenly, without any change in tone or rhythm or speech pattern, nonsense.

"Profeau," I heard.

"Baroness Orczy escapade."

"You're rumbled."

I began to understand. It must have been "Prof. O".

"Not perhaps the gunsels," he was saying, "not the goons who took out the tourists." *What sort of books had he been ransacking?* "But known nonetheless," he said.

"Be he in Heaven, be he in Hell," I said out loud, "That demned, elusive . . . I didn't think anyone of our generation had read the Baroness. Except me."

"It has been known," he said prayerfully, while he drove into the Hathor Palace drive, "and anyway I'm significantly older than you."

When I got to my room, someone had searched it. Not very expertly. Nothing seemed to have gone but a few things were disturbed. It might have been the cleaners. In any case there was nothing incriminating to be found there, except perhaps if you were an ardent Muslim. What made me suspicious was a little rearrangement of the book in my bedside drawer, next to the Gideon Bible thoughtfully provided by charity. Or rather it was the postcard which I use as a bookmark. It was at the right page but not quite aligned with the first line of text as I always leave it and it was upside down and face down, looking towards the end of the book.

It's the Courtauld Adam and Eve by Lucas Cranach the Elder; a wondrous painting. She, just emerged from pubescence, deliciously nubile, a convenient tendril covering her pudendum. He, scratching his head and taking the fruit of disobedience from her, a larger leaf covering his presumed larger genitalia. Wild animals are seated calmly around the tree, unaware of the calamity. Not, I supposed, at all theologically endearing to those who ban representations of the human form and would strongly object to the near-nakedness as being lewd.

So an inexperienced searcher. Low-grade. Perhaps the card had fallen out as s/he leafed through the book—expecting to find what?—and s/he hadn't wanted to touch it. Pop it back quickly. Unclean.

The Cranach made me think of Eloïse. I telephoned her. It rang and rang and rang. Out or away? I felt a frisson of jealousy. The new tennis partner? I rejected it and tried to go to sleep.

Chapter five

I was shaving when the bedside telephone rang. It was William. He'd ordered breakfast for two in his room and it would be up shortly. I joined him a few minutes later.

"I want to ask you two things," he said, munching his cornflakes. "I got up early this morning, found a church and went in to pray."

I poured myself a large, black coffee.

"I lit candles," he said. "For my aunt; for my uncle; for my cousin; for my mother, too, even though, thank God, she's still with us. And then I made a solemn vow. I'd find whoever was responsible and kill them."

Just like that.

"In turn," he said, in case I hadn't got the idea. "Hunt them and kill them."

I groaned.

"Well," he said, "will you help me?"

"And the second question?"

"Why were you in Cairo? What were you doing when the massacre took place?"

"I'd been commissioned," I said, "to do three weeks marine archaeology, underwater photography in the ancient harbour of Alexandria. And I'd come to Cairo to say I'd finished the assignment, to hand back my pass to the ministry and to give them their copies of the pictures I took. And some of the films."

It was sort of true. No; it was true as far as it went but not perhaps exactly, in its entirety, the whole truth.

"And will you, will you please help?"

"I don't know," I said, in as kindly a voice as I could muster at breakfast-time. "I promise you I'll think about it but I shouldn't think so. Not if I've got any sense, I won't. Tell you one thing in return. I'm flying out on the next plane to Cyprus. I think you should too. We're not going to get anything more here; except trouble. My room was searched when we were at Freddie's and to be honest the hairs on the back of my neck are bristling. Come on, we'll go and see where the attack took place and then we'll pull out."

William wept a little when I showed him the step on which his mother had stumbled and the parking place where the bus had been. There was nothing to see, not even a bunch of flowers; just an extra pair of policeman. My memory was of smells of gunfire and death and of cake and biscuits which must have come from the Groppi's parcel that Mrs Mikoyan was carrying. Now there was just the dry scent of builder's dust and the ranker smells of rotting rubbish and hot, sweaty people.

William took the next flight to New York. He said he had a man he wanted to see. I wondered if this was someone he thought might help him in his search and destroy mission. I feared not. It sounded as though he was reposing all his hopes in me. I was bothered; no, embarrassed. A present, however handsome, is no more than a present. It doesn't lead to further obligations, or indeed any obligations. This was her, Mrs Mikoyan's, way of saying thank you for what she saw as, and may well have been, my saving her life. So have I got to nursemaid her son for ever thereafter? Do I have to become an aide to his desire, his need, for revenge? No: clearly I don't. And yet . . . and yet . . . I cannot entirely rid myself of the notion that I am grappled to this family. Have I not done enough? I came to Cairo. I showed him the site of the massacre. I asked questions. Have I done enough? I have done enough.

The Air Cyprus plane wasn't too full. I had the business class to myself. About halfway through, the captain came to have a chat. He said he'd seen me in Alex a few months back. I'd been in a bar on the harbour having a beer with all my scuba gear and wet suit around me.

"Yes," I said. "You did." *You and how many thousand more prying eyes?*

37

"Is that how you did your arm in?" he said sympathetically.

"No," I said. "I got in the way of a terrorist."

"Tough," he said, moving on. "Have a pleasant flight. Mend well!" It wasn't the sort of thing that airline pilots want to hear. He went to see whether the wing had fallen off or whatever air crew do when they peer ominously and single-mindedly out of the passenger windows.

My underwater archaeological stint in Alexandria had, of course, nothing to with the Armenians but a lot to do with Jeremy Sims's "Prof. O." Ali-Akhbar Osman was a leading light of the law school at Cairo University. He was also a liberal; a progressive. He deplored what he saw as the deep night into which the fundamentalists were taking his and other faculties at the university, and his country, and his religion, for the Prof. was a good Muslim. But he dared to speak out. He renounced, as being contrary to Islam, and wrong, the killing of members of other faiths; the throwing of acid in the faces of young girls accused of lax dressing and insulting the blood of the martyrs by not having their hair fully covered. He had quoted an Iranian *mujtahid*, a recognized expert on Islamic law, with similar views to his own: to the effect that there was nothing amiss in men and women being together and that the *hijab*, the hair covering, did not come from Islam.

The professor was attacked and traduced, then condemned by a religious court and finally proclaimed to be an enemy of Islam, faithless, a follower of Satan. Being no longer a Muslim, he was therefore also an adulterer, and worse, since he was still living with his wife. She, as a Muslim, it was asserted, could not be married to an apostate. As a loyal Muslim, she must divorce him, or suffer a similar fate to his. Death threats abounded. She refused to divorce or leave him. Sentences of death were passed on both of them. They went into hiding.

Around this time, a humanitarian organization in Stockholm approached SATIS, our travel agency, and asked if we would undertake a highly sensitive operation which had to remain confidential. They wanted us to get Osman out of Egypt, alive. They had another plan for his wife. I came up with what I thought was a workable but complex and rather expensive scheme. They bought it and I spent the winter planning and perfecting, as near as I could, Operation Primrose.

I chartered a sea-going fishing boat and its crew, owned by another school-friend, Stavros, who captained it. I bought two large, blow-up rubber dinghies with high-powered outboards, wet suits and scuba diving equipment and, the key to it all, one of those miniature two-man submarines which I arranged to be converted with lights and cameras for underwater exploration. Then I set about getting licences for a short burst of archaeological underwater photography around the recently, and as it turned out in the end wrongly, prospected site of one of the seven wonders of the ancient world, the Pharos, the light-house of Alexandria. I cultivated the Egyptian embassy in Nicosia and wrote endless letters to officials in Cairo. I sold the idea of a photo-journalist feature to the *National Geographic* to lend additional verisimilitude and to clock up a few more dollars against a rainy day.

My team of six trained on and in the sub, in and out of scuba equipment, in and out of the dinghies. The plan depended first on the Swedes getting Osman to Alexandria, he being an outcast whom it was any decent Muslim's duty to exterminate like a rabid dog, and second on our being sure we had a wet-suit to fit him. My assumption, which worked, as it turned out, was that with seven of us around everyday, all wearing the same wet-suits distinguished with a single, primrose yellow, stripe, and rapidly fading and indistinguishable ID cards behind obscured, scratched plastic slithers, a stranger in the same rig would be unnoticed. We got him into the sub with me at the controls and I took it further out than we normally did, to our larger craft, some miles beyond the harbour. They lifted the sub out, on the side hidden from the shore, removed the Prof. and I then returned with another member of the team in the sub, almost running out of power by the time we returned to harbour. Osman was away at sea by then. Mission, as they say, accomplished. A week later we all pulled out and I went to Cairo to sign off. And, as it happened, get shot.

39

I spent the rest of the flight exercising my wrist and hand and playing with the little yellow ball. I kept on thinking how silly it was that after all these weeks I still couldn't use my right hand properly. Suitcases were a problem. My much-loved red Triumph Stag was still in the garage near the airport where I had parked it six months ago. I still couldn't drive it. As I stood in the immigration and customs queue, I was feeling decidedly sorry for myself. I wheeled my case out to a taxi, there was only a short wait thankfully, and then went back inside to reclaim the attaché case I'd left in a locker.

It's a rather special little case, looking like one of those hard, rectangular, black cases that many travellers and businessmen carry. But this one is, as we say in the trade, secure. It has an eight-digit tumbler lock and then you have to carry out a sequence of button releases. Any mistake and a time lock comes into operation for a delay of four minutes before you can try again. After three consecutive failures, it locks for ever and screams. Sitting in the back of the cab, being jolted a bit, I mucked up one of the digits. So four minutes' frustrated delay and then try again. This time I got it right and dug out my cellphone.

No answer from Eloïse. Where the hell was she? I tried my mother. No answer. OK it was Saturday, maybe she'd gone to the market and dropped in on a friend. But I phoned the desk at the hotel, anyway.

"Oh Mr Ben," said the receptionist, "Miss Frosso wants to speak to you. I'll put you through."

Frosso was Manageress and Housekeeper and Mum's strong right arm.

"Ben," she said, "where are you?"

"In a taxi on the way in from Larnaca airport," I said.

"Thank God," she said. "Brace yourself. Bad news. Eleni's in hospital. Eloïse is with her."

"Which hospital?"

"The town."

I re-routed the taxi. Getting there was the longest twenty minutes I could remember. I gave the driver some extra money and asked him to take my suitcase to the hotel. I kept the attaché case with me. It took some more minutes actually getting into Mum's ward. There was a policewoman outside. Eloïse was sitting by the bed, holding Mum's hand, but Mum was sleeping or unconscious.

"What happened?"

Eloïse looked up, her eyes red and tearful. She got up and hugged and kissed me and wept.

"I found her," she said. "I couldn't get an answer all evening. So after dinner, about 11 o'clock, I drove over to her bungalow. The lights were off and no answer to the doorbell. Then I saw the door wasn't properly closed and went in. Turned the lights on and Oh God Benjy . . ."

I held her tight. After maybe a minute's sobbing, she controlled her breathing and whispered in my ear, her head resting on my shoulder.

"Oh Benjy I don't know that I can tell you straight, it was so horrible. There was blood and broken vases and furniture turned over. Your Mum was sitting in a chair, her blouse ripped apart and her left breast out of her brassière. It was wounded, burnt terribly. Cigarette burns I think. Can you imagine? Her feet were on the table, tied together. They were trussed with wire. It was biting into the flesh. And her left foot didn't look like a foot any more. It was more like one of those slabs of shapeless liver you see in the boucherie. They'd hit her foot, beaten it, with electric wire cord. It was there, all bloody, with bits of skin on it. Oh Ben, I couldn't do anything. At first. I called and called to her but she was too weak, perhaps unconscious. I got Frosso out of bed and she rang ambulance and police."

Eloïse paused, still clinging to me. Brave, good, loving girl.

"What could I do, Ben? What could I have done? Where were you, Ben?"

"You did well, my darling," I said. "Marvellously. And I was in the wrong bloody place, as usual. How is she now? What have the doctors done?"

"She's sedated. They've given her morphine for the pain. They say the foot is in a terrible state. They've dressed the burns on her breast. But, Ben, she hasn't spoken. Not one word. Not even a moan or a cry. As they carried her to the ambulance, before they gave her the pain-killers and sedatives, she was pressing my hand. I think she knew who I was. But now, nothing."

"She's asleep," I said. "You need some sleep too."

I persuaded her to lie down on the other bed and I sat beside Mum and stroked her arm. Terror, horror, pain, fury, sadness. And guilt. What had my poor mother ever done to deserve this? I settled into a cold, determined anger.

There was a cage over her body. There were drips attached to her veins and every half-hour a nurse looked in and measured her blood pressure, took her pulse and temperature and listened to her breathing. Now and again a young doctor did much the same thing but also rolled back her eyelids and peered with a torch into the back of her eyes. I kept on asking questions but he said I'd have to wait till his chief came along. When would that be? Later: as soon as he could.

Early on in my vigil I phoned Cousin Sam's number in Paphos. Julia, his long-time secretary answered. He wasn't there.

"Get him," I said. "Tell him to ring me on my mobile. Now."

He rang back in ten minutes. "What's it this time, Boychik? The police arrested you for drunk in charge of a donkey?"

"Eleni's been attacked. She's been badly hurt, tortured," I said. "So get your fat arse over to Larnaca General and see if you can do something useful for a change." Maybe I was being unfair but I didn't care.

Mum was sleeping quietly. It was a gentle, rather serene face. And beautiful, though tonight she looked older. Pain and fear had engraved lines

41

around her mouth and bruised and darkened the semi-circles under her eyes. I tried to concentrate on the pain, the almost unimaginable pain of being burnt by a lighted cigarette end on the breast, of the bottom of one's foot being beaten to a pulp, the torture called bastinado. But all I could see was the little, frightened girl, left alone in the dark Greek church while her parents waited for the transport to hell.

"*Obscænus*, you filthy little boys," Mr Miller, Chalky Miller, our Latin master used to say, "means ill-omened and not what your dirty little minds hope it means." Englished, Chalky reminded us, in a locution he favoured, obscene gravitated from inauspicious to disgusting, abominable, loathsome.

Shakespeare's "So heinous, black, obscene a deed" rang in my ears, resonated, deafened. *For God's sake, let us sit upon the ground and tell sad stories . . .*

Whoever did this obscene deed to my mother must have meant it as a warning. To warn me off, I supposed. But this was savagery not warning. This was obscenely beyond anything rational. It was an abomination, the insane act of a sadist, a psychopath. And who would use a psychopath as a messenger? And warn me off what? What could he or they have thought Mum could have known? Why torture her?

This surely could not have been—in revenge for Professor O.'s disentanglement, for example, I had been thinking—the act of any normal, sane Islamist political group, any Muslim religious organization. It was not their way, was it, to treat an individual, innocent woman, even if Christian or Jewish, with such wanton cruelty. She had broken no law of the Shari'ah. Death, yes; perhaps, an incidental death, as with some of the other tourists in Egypt over the years, but not torture. But what did I know about the inward thoughts of the Islamist opposition in Egypt; how they thought; how they felt and reasoned, and acted? I was a simple bloody marine, not a foreign correspondent.

But this, I kept on telling myself, had to be something else. A psychopath, certainly, but working for whom? To what end? It can only have been intended as a warning. I came back to this over and over again. A warning to whom? To me. Keep away. Stand back. Lay off. Or else.

Chapter six

A

t some point I had persuaded Eloïse to go home and have a bath and a meal and a proper sleep. So I was alone when the senior doctor finally arrived, accompanied by the junior doctor, a sister and a younger nurse. He shook me by the hand and then said he was going to examine my mother. Perhaps I would rather leave the room. I said I'd rather stay.

"It may hurt her," he said, a balding, plump man who moved lightly on the balls of his feet, a good dancer. "I'll be as gentle as I can. Of course, we'll give her more painkillers afterwards."

He was extremely careful and delicate but as he gently lifted the dressing from her breasts, the full, appalling wounds, highly coloured and oozing, made me gag. He looked up and I shut my mouth and bit my tongue. Her foot was, in a way, worse; like something, as Eloïse had said, on a butcher's slab.

"She won't be able to walk on that foot of hers for a month or two," the older doctor said. "We'll x-ray her tomorrow and see how much reconstruction will be needed. The burns are less bad than they look, thankfully." He paused and then added in case I'd thought him callous; "Horrible enough and painful enough, God knows. But they're not third degree. We can treat them."

"Is she conscious?" I asked.

"She's asleep. With a heavy dose of morphine. She's not in a coma, if that's what you mean. I haven't allowed the police to see her yet. There'd be no point. If she has an uninterrupted night then perhaps she'll be able to talk tomorrow. Today there's too much pain and shock."

About four o'clock in the morning, she stirred, opened her eyes and looked at me. She squeezed my hand, tried to smile and began to speak very quietly, something between a whisper and a croak.

"I'm so glad you're here, darling," she said. "Do you remember when we went on that holiday to Dubrovnik? Long before all the troubles there? And I tried to get a Serbo-Croat dictionary. And the girl said not Serpski-Hrvatski but Hrvatski-Serpski. Didn't I know we were in Croatia, not Serbia?"

And she was asleep again.

Earlier I had been musing, trying, I suppose, not to think about what had happened to Mum. Before William had left me to book his flight to New York, he had said that on reflection he didn't give a damn who was behind it, he just wanted to kill those who had killed his aunt and uncle. A simple, uncomplicated chap, our William. I hadn't wanted to have anything to do with his plans for revenge from the beginning, and I didn't now, but more than anything I wanted to make sure that SATIS was kept well away from him. This was not the kind of thing that SATIS was set up to tackle and my poor partners in Norwich had to be protected. Sooner or later they would have to be told what had happened to Eleni but that was another matter: both of them knew and were fond of my mother. And I had this recurrent, jabbing anxiety; what should I do to protect her? What should I have done? A bit late anyway, you might think. But if it really was a warning to me, perhaps I ought to get her away, away from Cyprus, Egypt or anywhere they might look for her. She was hardly in a state to be moved at the moment.

I must have drifted into a half-sleep. Suddenly I was awake. A tall figure in white was leaning over my mother. Training told, I was on my feet and restraining the hand that was about to pour something from a glass into Eleni's mouth, before a sound could be heard.

"What's that?" I said.

"Water," said a startled voice, thickly. "Ordinary water. She must be parched, poor lady."

It was a tall nurse, in a mask. *So what? It could have been a terrorist with poison, finishing off the job.*

"I was the duty sister in Casualty when she was brought in," she enunciated carefully in a precise English-as-a-Foreign-Language, "and having a few minutes off, I thought I should look in and see how she was progressing. You are her son? Or a policeman perhaps?"

"Son," I said. "Ben. Sorry if I hurt you."

"You frightened me a little," she said, taking off her mask. "I was not hurt. I understand, nonetheless. Do you know who they were, the assailants? Or why?"

"No," I said. "Did she say anything?"

"She moved in and out of consciousness. She was clasping a broken chain with a cross on it. It was silver I think. She held it so tight that it had made indentations in her palm and fingers, which had to be prised open."

"Where is it?" I asked.

She went over to the bedside locker and opened a drawer and took out the cross and chain.

"I'll try and join it up for the moment," I said. "She'll want it when she wakes up. It never leaves her." I used a paper-clip that I knew I had in my pocket. It had been driving me mad for days. Whenever I put my hand in the pocket, there it was, loose and purposeless and in the way. Now it had a temporary use.

"How bad is her foot?" I found myself seeking truth if not reassurance. "Will she ever walk again?"

"I cannot tell you," she said. "I just do not know enough to give even an uninformed guess. I have never seen anything like it before. But Dr Pappaioannou" (she pronounced it carefully, Pappa-Yo-Annoo, in case I found it difficult) "has a friend, I think he is an orthopaedic surgeon, in Athens. He worked with some of the victims of the Colonels' torture squads in the early seventies. Dr Pappaioannou is going to phone him later today to get some advice. They trained together at the John Radcliffe in Oxford."

"Don't suppose they saw many bastinado-ed feet at the Radcliffe," I said.

She ignored me and walked over and took my mother's temperature, pulse and blood pressure.

"I still think your mother could do with a drink."

She refilled the glass and very gently and slowly trickled some of the water into her mouth. I slumped back into my chair and drifted off.

"Ben. Ben . . ." It was my mother's voice, from a long way away. She was awake. I took her hand in mine.

"Go to sleep," I said.

"No. I meant to tell you this before you went to Cairo. When we were in England, you nearly had a sister. I miscarried in the sixth month and she died. They said she was perfect. Wasn't that my lovely baby lying in the sluice? That's what they said. Now, of course, they would have kept her alive. But then . . . Not possible."

Her lips quivered.

"Not now, darling," I said. "Another time. Sleep."

"It's very important," she cried, almost inaudibly. "I then had a bleeding, when I got home to the flat: a post-partum haemorrhage. They had to rush me to hospital in an ambulance."

"Where was I?" I said.

"You were staying with your Yorkshire Granny. You called her Granny-in-the-moor. There was a gynaecologist there, the registrar, and he hurt me rather a lot. No anaesthetic and he manually removed a piece of the after-birth that had been left behind. Women like pain, he kept on saying. He'd sit on the bed and tell me that and other things. How, had it not been for the Turks, the Armenians would have conquered the world. He used to use his hypodermic syringe like a dart and throw it at the bottoms of his women patients. Daddy thought he was a disgrace to his profession. He wrote a letter to his boss, the consultant. And he was dismissed. But Mr Frain, the chief gynaecologist said the Armenian had been a good doctor all the same. Had saved people's lives . . ."

By the time I asked her his name, she was sound asleep.

Now properly awake myself, I did what I should have done hours before. I began to think coherently about safeguarding her.

I phoned Vic Malone, who lived in the other bungalow about twenty metres beyond my mother's. The phone rang for a minute or more before someone picked it up, not unreasonably since it was something before dawn.

"Colour Sergeant Malone?"

"Sir." Or rather he made it sound like a sorrh.

"When did you get back?"

"A couple of hours ago, Major. The plane was very late leaving Gatwick."

"So you haven't heard about my mother?"

I told him.

"Christ Almighty, Major. What would you like me to do?"

I suggested he check the video cameras that he and I had fitted outside and inside my mother's bungalow and at the entrance to the hotel itself. Vic Malone was the only person around who called me by my rank but then he was virtually the only one who knew it. He had at some point been drill sergeant of the ceremonial Queen's Squad of Royal Marines. He was the senior trainer on the commando course I had sweated my heart out on and Colour Sergeant when I had progressed to and graduated from the officer's course. In fact he was the first person to salute me off the parade ground as, self-consciously, I walked around with brand new pips on my shoulders. Later, when he retired, he married a Cypriot girl half his age and now he helped out with the security at the hotel in return for a rent-free bungalow. Unfortunately he, his wife and twin babies had been visiting his sister in Plymouth, so my mother had been alone.

At sun up, and it looked as fresh a rosy-fingered dawn as springtime even though I knew it would turn into a flagging, soggy, ennervatingly hot day, she stirred again and opened her eyes wide.

"I've got your baptismal cross," I said. "The chain's a bit broken but I've fitted a jury rig which will serve till we can get it and you to a jeweller's."

I put it round her neck and she immediately fingered the cross, held it and smiled.

"You know he made me cross myself. Just to prove I was Orthodox, so he could hate me more."

"Who?"

"The Croat. He was RC of course and they cross themselves the wrong way round."

"How did you know he was Croatian?"

"There was another one and they were speaking Slav, Southern Slav. Serbo-Croat, or Croat-Serb, Hrvatski-Serpski. I told you all this before." She paused and thought. "Didn't I? But the Serbs are Orthodox so I knew he must be a Croat. The other two—I think there were only four—were Turkish. You know the way they have vowel congruity, assonance, whatever you call it. Makes a liquid, lightly sonorous language. Can be very attractive. You could sing it. It always makes me wish I understood it. The Turks were sent outside. The Croats tied me down and put something over my head.

Claustrophobia. I panicked. I couldn't see. I felt I couldn't breathe. Then I think the other one went out and the sadist was on his own."

"What did he want? What did he say?"

"I thought it was something to do with Cousin Sam. It wasn't. It was you."

She looked accusingly at me.

"Why had you gone to Cairo? How did you make your money? What had you done between 1976 and when you came back to Cyprus for good?"

"What did you say?"

"Not much. That's why he kept on hurting me. And I was trying to needle him. You understand."

It was a statement, not a question, almost an order.

"You have to hate your interrogator. Truly hate him. Otherwise you go under; you give him what he wants. I said he was a filthy Slav Catholic who'd helped the Venetians bring down Constantinople. I said he'd kiss the Pope's bottom rather than tell the truth. I said he was a Nazi. That the Ustashi were traitors who sold their mothers into prostitution. That was when he started to stub his cigarette out on my breast. He beat my foot. Oh God that was painful. That was when I said you'd done this and that. Freelance journalism. Travel agents' courier. And so on. And on and on and on. Repeating myself."

She glared at me. This part at least was self-evidently my fault.

"I didn't know any more, did I?"

I gave her some water to drink, propping up her head a little.

"Well, did I?" she asked, and then without pausing for an answer; "Have they cut off my foot? I can feel pain but no foot, no toes. They say you still feel pain and tickling and itching when they've been amputated . . ."

"No, no, no," I said. "You've still got your foot, both feet but one of them's not very pretty at the moment."

"I am tired now," she said. "Too tired for conversation."

This too was clearly my doing, tiring her out. I smiled, placating her.

"One more question," she said, her voice faint with exhaustion. "What were you doing all that time, all those years, that you couldn't tell your own mother?"

"I joined the marines," I said.

She smiled and went back to sleep.

*   *   *

She had never wanted me to go into the forces. Losing Dad was enough. She hadn't quite made me promise not to but she would have liked to. I knew she'd be upset, so I'd gone to LSE and pretended to be a student. But I hated it. I was quite clever but I wasn't an intellectual. I knew my limitations and I knew what I liked: weapons; target shooting, with rifles and revolvers; sailing; scuba and deep sea diving; and games: cricket, soccer, rugger, tennis, squash. Boxing I didn't really like but I was good enough at it: I wasn't very heavy, I had a long reach and I hit hard.

I knew I didn't suit LSE and I realized that great institution didn't suit me. So after a term, I walked round the block and enlisted in the Royal Marines. Not wanting to trade on Dad's George Cross, and perhaps also not wanting to alert the IRA that here was another Bolton waiting to be blown up, I asked if I could change my name. After huffing and puffing and a long time later, only after I'd volunteered for and been selected for Special Forces, and been commissioned, their Lords Commissioner of the Admiralty agreed and Bolton, B. was eradicated from the records and Lieutenant David Ditchling took his place, Ditchling being my English grandmother's maiden name. So what had started as not wanting Mum to know that I had gone into uniform became not wanting her, or anyone else for that matter, to know that I had gone into something a deal more dangerous. And at that point the Admiralty and I were at one in not wanting my antecedents to be apparent.

So that's what I'd been up to in my twenties, and part of my thirties too, come to think of it. If I had been secretive—careful and sensible I would have said—it was because it was a discipline imposed on us. Everybody has heard of the SAS, from Lady Thatcher in her prime ministerial days, if from no one else, after they'd marvellously stormed the Iranian Embassy in Knightsbridge. And of course, in rather more operational, if occasionally and properly fictional, detail from ex-members such as Andy Macnab and Chris Ryan, and to an extent from that highly distinguished soldier, General Sir Peter de la Billière. But not much has been heard of our lot, the SBS, except in fleeting allusions to Paddy Ashdown, leader of the Lib Dems, having been in it and, I fancy, a few, very few, references in histories by operational commanders such as General de la Billière. We were told to keep quiet, and we did. Originally the Special Boat Squadron, it's now called the Special Boat Service; I suppose to chime with the Special Air Service. Unlike the SAS whose members come from all sorts of regiments, the SBS is selected only from the Royal Marines. It's a small, highly trained

49

unit, an élite force with all sorts of useful, special and mainly maritime skills, with an HQ in Dorset although there's been talk of moving to Pompey, alongside the navy. I'd been promoted major just before Desert Storm and I'd retired to the reserve list eighteen months later. And that's enough of that.

It was light outside now and the night shift were bustling along, tidying beds and lockers, ready for the morning shift to do the same thing when they took over. They came in, tidied everything up without waking her, checked her drips and, very gently, her pulse. In the daylight she looked calm but careworn and pale. I knew (who better?) her toughness, her courage, her resilience. But could she live with that poor mangled foot, with being crippled for some long time?

The night had gone and I had achieved nothing, decided nothing. For a minute or two I wished I had a squad of marine commandos to back me up. There were so many things to be done. Protect my mother; get after the Croat; figure out what it was all about; get whatever evidence we had on camera to the police and to whoever else might be able to make an identification; and kill the bastards, slowly, painfully. I stopped myself: that way lay madness.

Instead of a couple of dozen young, fit, go anywhere, do anything, highly trained, well-armed Royal Marines, I had the 58-year old Colour Sergeant Malone, now much-married and domesticated, and my own impaired self. I had been a goodish shot but my marksman skills which had taken my team and myself to decent rankings at Bisley for several years running were not going to be much in evidence with my right arm intermittently in a sling. I hastily and guiltily got the little yellow ball out of my jacket pocket and exercised obsessionally with it for at least twenty minutes by which time the morning sister and her acolytes were smiling cheerfully at me and saying how well my mother was sleeping, wasn't she. It was a shame to wake her up. But it was time to see how she was feeling and perhaps give her a topping up of pain-killers. Anyway she must be lifted and turned a little so as not to get bed-sores. Why didn't I go and have a wash and a shave and get some breakfast while they did what they had to do?

The world outside Mum's ward looked casually busy and cheerful. A somnolent policeman sprang to his feet and offered to unlock a staff bathroom for me. A young nurse brought me a bath towel and a disposable razor. After showering and scraping the worst of my beard off, I felt marginally more presentable but my linen trousers looked as though I had spent several days rolling round the countryside in them. I was wearing a crumpled Burgundy and white striped short-sleeve shirt which clashed somewhat with the angry red of the rims of my already bloodshot eyes. *Ugh!* I pressed a strip of lavatory paper to staunch a nick on my chin. *Not the smartest of reserve officers today, young Ditchling.* And that was another thing I was reminded of when I looked at myself in the unflattering mirror; I was not so young any more. Nearer 40, much nearer 40, than 35. *And very much Mr Bolton, not Major Ditchling.*

I ducked the coffee and went back to the ward. Mum was asleep again and looked a touch more comfortable. The policeman sitting on his chair outside the room said he was due to be relieved at eight o'clock and was looking forward to his wife's *takhinóppita* and a long sleep. He expected the detective top brass would turn up around nine and want to question my mother. He added quickly that of course it would only be if the doctors thought she was up to being interviewed.

Vic Malone, when I got through to him, was confident that the security cameras would be of considerable use. There had been two running at the time, giving different angles, one covering the entrance, as people approached the bungalow and came to the door, the other a wide-angle, almost fish-eye lens fixed inside the door and covering and moving round the sitting room. Neither seem to have been spotted, admittedly they were miniatures and quite cleverly concealed. The approach videotape showed some of the faces very clearly. He had contacted a mate of his who was an RAF photographic reconnaissance whiz and was somehow trying to get a still of decent quality and then print it up. Vic didn't know how he could do this but reckoned it probably involved computer enhancement. We might have a print or two shortly. He'd bring them wherever—to the hospital, I said—ASAP.

"And bring a shirt and some trousers," I said, "if you can find any. I think there's a clean shirt in my suitcase."

He arrived, with both video cassettes, a shirt, a pair of chinos and two sets of three stills with quite clear and defined faces, a few minutes before nine o'clock. I changed clothes and stuffed the dirty ones, together with one set of prints, in my despatch case and locked it.

"Sweet Jesus," he said, as he looked down at Mum, her nightdress had slipped off her shoulder and her dressings and discoloured breast were in view.

"We'll find the bastards, sir," he said. "Pardon the language, ma'am."

My mother slept on.

"I doubt it," I said. "They'll be in Lebanon, Syria or Egypt by now."

"That's as maybe, Major."

I held up a hand. "No ranks from now on. And remember it's Bolton not Ditchling. I'm Ben Bolton here."

"You'd better call me Vic then." He grinned and then wiped it off his face: these were serious times. "As I was saying, sir, I think they were off of a ship."

"Why?"

"Well, *Mr* Bolton, *sir*, on one of the vids there's a small swarthy man with a duffel bag and a label on it. You can't read the label, mind, and Jack Callaghan sweated his arse off, if you'll pardon the expression"—he looked at my mother who was still fast asleep – "trying to bring it up on his computer. It looks a bit like the name of a ship and a berth number and letter. Maybe the police can do something with it."

"Even if we find the name and the berth, the odds are the ship'll have sailed."

"Never say die, sir. Don't be downcast. We'll get 'em, however long it takes. My word on it."

Whether he was an incurable optimist, an unredeemed romantic believing that right would miraculously prevail, or just wanting to ease my mind, Vic Malone standing straight and comfortable in his starched white shirt and shorts and highly polished black shoes, his brown eyes clear and unwavering, exuded certainty and determination. Perhaps we would find the ship. And the sadist. For no justifiable reason I felt a surge of hope.

Chapter seven

They all arrived together, arguing: Consultant's round, the chief, junior doctors, nurses; the police, a detective superintendent and attendants; Cousin Sam with men from the ministries—he could never do anything by halves. The consultant insisted on seeing his patient first. The police argued, entreated. Sam asserted, loudly, that he was close family. I let the medical team in, told the others to keep their voices down, the patient was sleeping, and shut the door. There was a deal of muttering in the corridor. Vic Malone said he'd better go out, hadn't he, so I suggested he give the videos to the police and explain that he'd just got back from England last night and had only heard about the attack this morning.

"Mr Bolton?"

It was the consultant. I agreed with a nod. I hadn't noticed the intrusive "r" before but it didn't seem quite the occasion to point it out.

"Your mother has had a reasonable night, I understand."

I nodded again.

"The burns look better this morning. They seem to be healing. I'm afraid there'll be some scarring and it's going to take time."

He smiled encouragingly at Eleni at whom this was all addressed. She looked wide awake; and not, it would seem, in too much pain.

"But the foot is another matter." He turned to her again. "I want to

53

call in two specialists; a British neurologist from the base at Dhekelia and an orthopaedic surgeon from Athens."

"Why from Athens? Haven't we enough specialists in Cyprus?" It was a low croak from Mum.

"He has er . . ." – the physician was embarrassed – "experience of similar traumata." He pronounced it in the modern Greek manner, *trávmata.* "You won't," he went on quickly, "be able to walk for a while, you know."

He looked at her, he looked at me; a job well done.

"Now," he said brightly, this was the easy bit, "the police will be wanting to interview you, Mrs Brolton. If you think you feel up to it."

She fluttered an assenting hand. Talking was tiring; she was conserving herself.

"I'll say they can stay for fifteen, twenty minutes only. Is that about right? You must not let them wear you out, Mrs Brolton. When you have had enough, ask them to leave. Just ring your bell. And remember you've had a very unpleasant time." *Remember? Was she likely to forget? Unpleasant time indeed. Oh I know, Dr Pappaioannou; a doctor's job is a difficult one and they don't teach you how to deal with the after-effects of bastinado.*

"You must take care of yourself. Plenty of rest. I'll look in later today."

He was moving towards the door as he spoke.

"You will stay with your mother while the police are here?"

"Of course," I said. "Somebody's got to be referee."

I went out with him.

"I'll tell Sister Katerina to check how your mother is, after," he looked at his watch, "a quarter of an hour. Your mother will find it exhausting."

The others were variously sitting and leaning. There were only three chairs and the detective superintendent and the men from the ministries had bagged them, leaving Sam with a stool, which was really a table, to sit on and the helots with a wall to lean against. They were drinking coffee and smoking. Dr Pappaioannou gave them their orders in a firm, no nonsense, the doctor-knows-best voice. Eleni was badly hurt. She had been attacked and her injuries were horrific. She was traumatised. She could not, they would understand, take much stress, lengthy interrogation, insistent questioning. After you, she will see nobody for several days. No journalists. No cameras. No microphones. No police follow-up. OK? Her recovery comes first. Her health is the number one priority. The Superintendent muttered that catching violent criminals was important too, particularly ones that beat up women.

Seated he looked tall and stringy, with a long, narrow head, high forehead and scanty, dark black hair and sloping shoulders. When he stood up, he was thin to the point of discomfort with long legs that seemed to bend backwards at the knees as he walked. He introduced himself as Stavros Angeloglou (the g hard as in get), Superintendent CID.

I gave him the blown-up prints and told him that my mother hadn't seen them. I added that I didn't recognize any of them. I also warned him that Eleni might have a violent reaction to seeing the faces of the men that had assaulted her.

I had been trying for some hours to think myself back into the role of disinterested observer. Of course, it wasn't really possible but I made all my statements neutral. It was assault not torture. This was Eleni not Mum we were talking about, even though I had to refer to her, from time to time, as my mother.

Angeloglou, followed by a detective inspector and a uniformed policewoman sergeant, went into the room, I went with them. Or rather I tried to but Cousin Sam stopped me.

"Not now," I said. "There are too many people in there already. Thank you for making such good time."

"I was in St Petersburg" – it had stung him – "at a conference. I had to deliver a keynote paper. I got away as soon as I could."

"Well," I said generously, "it didn't make any difference. There was nothing much could be done until she came round and perhaps could identify the assailants."

I made to re-enter the ward. He restrained me.

"These" – he pointed to the men from the ministries – "are two colleagues from the foreign ministry and the interior bureau." He lowered his voice conspiratorially. "What is this really all about?"

"Later," I said. "I'll tell Eleni how concerned you've been."

Inside the ward, the superintendent was making polite noises and edging gently towards a question.

"Now that your son is able to be with us, Mrs Bolton, and if you're reasonably comfortable, I'd like to start the tape recorder." Eleni waved a hand. "Rather than ask you questions, at this stage, I want you to tell us, in your own time, what happened yesterday evening."

And in a small, rather throaty voice, she told him.

I had heard most of it during the night but this account was more detailed, more coherent and somehow more shocking thereby. After a few minutes I poured her a glass of water and stayed nearby, holding her hand, the veil of disinterestedness wearing pretty thin. Even objectively it was a dreadful tale to listen to, and the police were noticeably affected. The policewoman, a comfortable and comforting matron in her late forties, had wept. Eleni seemed not to focus on them but to be replaying the horror film in her private cinema.

It had taken ten minutes, an almost non-stop solo performance with maybe three prompts, and I could feel that she was drained to the point of exhaustion. I told Superintendent Angeloglou that I thought she was very tired. She squeezed my hand.

"Of course," he said, "I don't wish to tire you any further, Mrs Bolton. But I know you would want to help us find these men; to stop them committing more crimes of outrage and violence."

Eleni said nothing but she squeezed my hand again.

"You may find this disturbing," he said, his English good and clear, though accompanied by unexpected gutturals. "We have photographs here that perhaps you will recognize. Will you look at them?"

She nodded her head. He got up, came closer to the bed and showed her the prints, one by one.

"Yes," she said, "that's the other Croat. And yes that's one of the Turks. Oh yes, yes" – and she squeezed my hand, her nails digging in so hard that they drew blood – "that's the Croat pig who tortured me. Get him. Lock him up. For ever." She lay back, her eyes closed and tears squeezing out and running down her cheeks.

The ward sister came in, looking anxiously first at her watch and then at her patient. I said I thought they ought to go now and leave Eleni to sleep. In fact she might already have been half-asleep. She neither opened her eyes nor showed any sign of having heard me. Out for the count I reckoned. They left quietly as Sister Katerina, a stately Nordic blonde, started to take her blood pressure. I waited until she gave me a reassuring smile.

"Up a bit," she whispered, "but not dangerous."

"I should hope not," I whispered back. "Are you staying with her for a few minutes?"

She nodded and I went out to see what was going on. Angeloglou was briefing the two suits in Greek. Sam was listening to what sounded like an emotional account, in English, from the policewoman. The detective inspector, notebook out, prints of suspects in hand, was quizzing Vic Malone.

The superintendent and the men from the ministries were much of a

size but Angeloglou was darker skinned and gave off a tang of the land and
of the ancient world. His face was that of a benign Satyr. The government
men from Nicosia were smoother, cosmopolitan, contemporary. They had
been to university (one to Athens, the other to King's College, London, they
told me later) and there was something about the way, every so often, they
smiled at each other, which made me think that they were criticizing the
policeman's Greek. It was too rustic perhaps; the tenses were wrong and
the verb-endings common, vulgar, whatever. I warmed to him. And their
clothes were too well-cut.

This could not have been said of Cousin Sam, who was jacketless,
tieless and adorned with springy grey curls which issued like some primeval
cladding from his open shirt. He joined the Greek-speaking trio, made a
few muscular gestures, asked a question or two in fluent but not flawless
Greek and waited for their answers which, not surprisingly, came in good
standard English.

I found myself yawning. I was groggy with unslept sleep. I shook
myself awake.

Suddenly the colours become vivid, the scene finely focused. I fix on a hair
in Superintendent Angeloglou's right nostril. I feel I could snip it off with
a pair of long-handled shears. It's as though everything is in close up, seen
through a telescope, finely adjusted. Perhaps this is what it's like before you
have an attack of epilepsy. I look at my watch. Hours surely have passed;
the day nearly over. In reality, it's just gone ten a.m.

Sam is eying me. Colour Sergeant Malone, sorry, *Vic* Malone, just
beats Sam to it. He wants to get home. Is there anything else he can help
with? I can't think of anything. I can't think, period. He's told the inspector
that he reckons it's a ship with berth details on the label. The police will
get their boffins on to it. Over and out.

Sam has gone back to his coffee-klatsch. Time must not be wasted.
He sees me momentarily unoccupied and walks over.

"So, again, what's all this about?"

"You want to see Eleni?"

"To level with you, Ben, I can't take women, girls, in pain. Particularly
ones I'm fond of."

Funny fellow, Sam; always a surprise. Who'd have thought he was
squeamish? Still it's quite touching, the tough guy with a chink in his armour.
No, a bloody great hole. He doesn't often call me Ben. It's usually You, or

Boychik or Nudnik; playing out the joke of Jewish ecumenism, a Sephardi using Yiddish.

"But," I say, "you heard the details of what he did to her?"

He puts up his hand.

"I didn't want to hear anything. Imagination, my imagination, will supply the blood and mess. I don't suppose I'll get to sleep tonight."

I let the pause lengthen, wait for him to listen to his words, feel ashamed. He doesn't. He picks up his thread.

"They," he indicates the suits and Superintendent Angeloglou, "were talking about international dimensions; Croatians, Turks—were they Turkish Turks or Cyprus Turks?"

"Eleni had them down as mainland Turks."

"How would she know?"

"Hell's bells, Sam. She's lived in Cyprus long enough to recognize the sound of Cypriot Turkish."

"I suppose," he says, grudging, doubting. "Anyway, why was she attacked?"

"She thought it was about you, to start with. Then it turned out to be me. Why had I gone to Cairo? What had I been doing? They didn't like the answers, and she told them all she knew, so the Croat, no name but she recognized the photo, beat her foot to pulp."

He shudders, looks away.

"I don't want to know."

"So don't ask."

"Any clues, pointers? What they really wanted to find out?"

"Something to do with the killing of the Armenians, perhaps? I honestly don't know. Something I'd seen, heard, figured out. I've cudgelled my brains. I can't think of a damned thing."

"What gives with your Armenian buddy, Molotov?"

"Mikoyan," I say, laughing.

"Of course, Mikoyan," he says, slapping his head. "That wily old Armenian, haven't thought of him in a million years. He tried to stop Khrushchev sending the missiles to Cuba." He slaps his head again and then remembers something that may explain his lapse. "Both of them, Molotov *and* Mikoyan, mind you, were involved in the massacre of Polish officers at Katyn. I'm getting old, Ben, getting old."

I know Sam's getting on but I don't like to hear him calling himself old. It's out of character.

"William's in Washington," I say, putting senescence on the back-burner. "He's trying to think up ways of finding the killers and executing them."

"Not good, Boychik. Stay well away. Not your business."

"My line, to a T. Not my business."

But as I say it, I perceive a change in myself. The professed objectivity has gone. I have flipped a switch: or maybe, more starkly, I have just flipped, full stop. The notion of personal revenge has become something visceral: it is now clamorous and demanding. Along the way, I note with interest, I've accepted it as a possibility—not, of course, politically correct, not ethically to be recommended but possible all the same. The moment of clarity passes. I'm slow and muzzy and fighting my way through a cloud of feathers.

"Sam," I manage to say. "What about protecting Eleni? They could try again. I don't think they will but now that she's recognized three of them there are other reasons . . ." I tail off. I don't want to contemplate the consequences; not right now; but I press on. "I could try the Sovereign Bases medics. Any better ideas?"

"I could take her to Israel. They've got the best doctors, surgeons, hospitals. The very best. She'd be safe there."

By the time I arrived home, and reorganized myself, I was full of energy and catalogues of things to be done. Sam had said he would stick around at the hospital until Julia or someone came to spell him. I looked in on Eleni but she was deeply asleep. No prospect of Sam's sitting at her bedside.

"I am," he had said, finding another explanation, "allergic to hospitals, to ether, disinfectants, doctors, bed-pans. To illness. Blood. Pain. And," he added, *sotto voce*, "Death."

The diplomat had offered me a lift. His colleague from the ministry of the interior came too.

"The Cyprus government is appalled at what happened to your mother," said the man from the foreign ministry. "We wish," added his colleague, "to convey the government's and our sympathies to you and your mother and to say that the Cyprus police will do everything they possibly can to apprehend these abominable, international criminals. There seems," he said, with obvious relief, "to have been no suggestion of Cypriot involvement."

I nearly said well that makes a change, after rumours of a police, drugs and murders scandal; but I didn't. I smiled reminiscently.

Having got that out of the way, they introduced themselves; Achilles Christodoulou on the foreign side, large brown eyes, small nose, small mouth, downbeat, and George Grivas ("No relation," with a smile) from the home department, large hook nose, small eyes, big grin, widely spaced teeth. Grivas was the one who had been at London University while Christodoulou had gone to Athens to read philosophy and ancient Greek. But Achilles also knew the UK well, having spent three years in London *en poste*.

It had become very hot, damp and enervating and the sharp cool blast from the Xantia's air conditioner was as good as a shot of adrenaline. Just before we got to the Alasia, Achilles, who was driving, turned to me and said: "What are your thoughts?"

"Something to do with the Armenians killed in Cairo."

He nodded.

"Someone thinks," I went on, "I saw something incriminating. God knows what. It's a pretty lame theory and I'm not convinced but it's all I've come up with to date. And you? Any *lumières?*"

"Nothing so far." He stopped the car.

While I was grabbing my attaché case and shaking hands, I asked: "Either of you figure what this Croatian psychopath and his Turkish side-kicks are doing together? And, if I'm right, what's their Egyptian connection?"

I got out. The pavement felt like a large furnace concentrating on my feet. The air was still and dusty with only a remote whisper, more an act of belief than of sense, of sea and salt. Even the trees drooped and the flowers wilted, though there was rapidly drying evidence of widespread watering and spraying. It was the run up to high noon, in high summer, in a heat wave.

"I think you should ask your cousin," said George the Interior. "He knows about that sort of thing." He laughed. "Or used to."

"Last week I too was in Cairo," said Achilles the Exterior. "I was talking to an acquaintance of yours; Jeremy Sims. He's coming over, today, tomorrow, I don't remember. He's got some business with the High Commission in Nicosia. Said he might look you up."

I pulled a face representing, in intention anyhow, mixed resignation and dismay.

"No, no. You've got him wrong. He's clever, sensitive, efficient. I admire and like him. Not my closest friend but a good colleague. You can bet your bottom dollar on it that if he wants to see you, and I'm sure he does, he'll find you."

"No doubt," I said and waved them goodbye.

"Be seeing you," said the one.

"Be in touch," said the other.

"A word, if I may" – this was the home office speaking – "leave it to the police, eh. They know their job."

My bungalow had been swept, cleaned and dusted. But it smelt stale. I unlatched a pair of shutters and threw open the windows. The sunlight rushed in and, with it, a wave of heat. I shut the windows, closed the shutters and wheeled out the portable air conditioner I'd bought the year before and never used. I had to open another smaller window so the elephant's trunk could thrust itself into the outside world and discharge hot air and drips of water. Miraculously, it worked first time. After I'd had a proper shower, washed my hair and unpacked the suitcase, the living room almost felt cool.

When something goes massively, painfully wrong, there's a kind of fragmentation, a dissolution of the bonds that hold the centre together, the world flies apart. For the last several hours I had been trying to hold together what seemed like a giant centrifuge; not very successfully. Things were spinning off the turntable even as I watched. And when I turned my back?

61

I headed my list "NO MORE INTROSPECTION!" and went on to enumerate more activities than I could manage in a week. First, ring Eloïse. I was surprised not to have heard from her. Her answer machine was on. Perhaps she had gone to the hospital. I left a message, saying I was at home and would love to see her. My answerphone was flashing lights. The artificial voice said I had four messages. I slid the switch to play.

"I hate these bloody things" – it was Freddie – "and I've mislaid your confounded fax code. This'll have to be *en clair*. The US embassy have contacted your Armenian chum to say the Egyptians have found one of the assassins. I can never say the damned word without thinking of the original hashshashin, hashish-eaters, those Muslim fanatics at the time of the Crusades, sent forth by the Old Man of the Mountain to murder Christian leaders. Rather appropriate to your case, don't you think? The authorities say he, Mikoyan, can interview the suspect. You can't, despite your wound: you're not family of the deceased. Or a Corsican Brother."

The second was from Eloïse's mother saying how sorry she was to hear about Eleni's "accident". The third was from my dentist's receptionist saying I was due for an inspection. The fourth was from someone trying to sell me a solar-powered cooling system.

Chuck Levendhis had equipped me with a reasonably high-powered PC and various programmes he had worked up himself. He had also recently shipped me a flatbed scanner. I used this to send him, via computer and modem, the stills of the Croats and Turks and asked him to see if he could trace any of them; particularly the older Croat. I told him that Eleni had been attacked. And left it at that. It wasn't quite as easy as it sounds. Chuck's encoding programme was time sensitive. It changed every ten minutes so it was essential to keep the computer's clock as accurate as possible. The time of encoding was recorded on the message. It meant checking, against a telephone or radio time-check, every time you turned on the PC. I had a large message on my screen: "CHECK THE CLOCK!"

Superintendent Angeloglou rang and said they'd made some progress with enlarging the label on the duffel-bag; but not enough. There seemed to be C or O, and a 3 or 8. They were checking the names of all ships that had occupied C3, C8, O3 and O8 berths in the last 48 hours. The name of the ship, if ship it was, could not be seen clearly enough to make out any letters with any degree of certainty. As soon as he had any more news, he would be in touch.

I telephoned the British High Commission in Nicosia, thinking I'd get in first. Were they expecting Jeremy Sims today or tomorrow? He had arrived last night. Would I like to speak to him?

"Sims," went the quiet little voice.

"Ben Bolton," I said.

"I've got an appointment at the Sovereign Base Dhekelia tomorrow morning. Shall we lunch? Would that suit?"

"Come to the Alasia," I said. "Around a quarter to one. We'll go out and eat some fish."

"Very good," he said and put his phone down.

I was amazed. Not quite the non-stop, loquacious Sims of our last encounter.

I rang the hospital and was put through to the ward sister. How was Mrs Bolton? She'd had some food and was now sleeping. Eloïse had not been in to see her. *Strange, that; after all she had done for Mum the day before. Where* was *Eloïse?* Julia, Sam's PA, was with Eleni now. And Sam? He had gone. Dr Pappaioannou wanted to speak to me later. When was I coming in? I said I'd be there between five and six.

I sent another encrypted (I hoped the damn thing was working) message to Chuck in Norwich, asking him to pass it on, in whatever secure method he had arranged, to Prof O. Chuck was the only one of us who knew how to contact the professor, on the need to know principle. My question was a one and a half liner: what were two Croats and two Turks doing asking questions in Cyprus about me, presumably as witness to the tourist massacre in Cairo? I signed it Your Forwarding Agent. No names, no retribution. Of course he would know that there was another possibility: that they were on to me because of him.

I had just e-mailed the message when Vic Malone came and showed me the list of the four ships which had occupied the likely berths. Three of them had sailed this morning. The fourth had left last night. Two were Panamanian flags, one was Liberian and the fourth was Syrian, home port Latakia. I sent yet another signal to Chuck asking him to find out from Lloyds List, or wherever, anything he could about whither and whence in sailing histories, about cargoes and crew, and who owned what.

I made an appointment with the army physio for tomorrow morning, hurriedly exercising with my little rubber ball the while, and lay down and slept for three-quarters of an hour.

Chapter eight

I was waylaid as I arrived at the hospital. The receptionist said that Dr Pappaioannou was ready to see me. I was shown to his room. It was hung with large modern sea paintings, vivid with colour and light and somehow rather daunting.

"I have spoken at length," he said, "to my old friend and colleague, Peter Haralambopoulos, in Athens. We were at the Radcliffe together." I nodded. "He worked with Lady Amalia Fleming in looking after victims of the Greek Junta's torturers. Many of them, Inspector Lambrou is one name that comes to mind, used the bastinado. So he knows much about feet badly injured like your poor mother's. Tomorrow the English neurologist will examine her. We will study the x-rays again with an orthopaedic surgeon and if we all agree, I should then recommend that we fly her to Athens and put her in the immensely skilled hands of Peter."

"I wonder . . ." I said.

He put up a hand. "I know you must be thinking, 'Is this the best way to look after Mrs Brolton?'"

"Well," I said, "I was rather . . ."

"But what is a better alternative? I do not propose that we move her till we are sure that she is strong enough. An air ambulance will be arranged and two of our nurses will accompany her. Peter is, I am sure, the most experienced orthopaedic surgeon in this small specialty. Luckily there are not all that many calls on this particular skill."

It was almost a joke. He smiled.

"Your cousin Sam, I understand, thinks she should go to Israel. Their doctors and hospitals are amongst the best in the world. But have they much experience in feet like this? I do not think so. And there are now very good facilities in Athens. Very modern and well-equipped."

"But . . ." I said.

"If you were worried about the expense, and I dare say it will be very costly, do not! Insurance will pay and perhaps the government will chip in; who knows?"

"What about . . ."

"Don't give me an answer now. Tomorrow evening let's talk again." He got up and shook me by the hand, ushering me towards the door. "It's been most helpful talking to you. Thank you for hearing me out. Of course I take note of what you say, your hesitations. And now," he looked at his watch as though I had been detaining him, "your mother will be pleased to see you." He walked me some way towards the ward.

Eleni was sitting up in bed, a blue-green silk stole round her shoulders, her hair combed and brushed and a lipstick in one hand and a Victorian silver hand mirror, which belonged to Dad's mother, in the other.

"Not bad," I said as I kissed her. "Expecting anyone special?"

She wiped away any lipstick that might have got on to me with a Kleenex.

"No. Just you, darling. It was Eloïse who suggested it. To make me feel better. And she was right. I feel a new woman; a new, crippled woman. You know I can't stand, can't put any weight on the damaged foot. And the pain is" – she drew breath – "hellish." Her hand went to her chain and cross round her neck. The paper clip was still holding it together.

"Shall I take the chain and get it properly mended?"

"Not yet. Wait till I'm up and about. Then we can go together to Mr Hadjijosef's shop. He's always so kind and clever at mending things."

Rather than think about how long that was likely to be, I shifted tack to another area of anxiety.

"When was Eloïse here?"

"She's still around somewhere. She's just gone to find a vase for the flowers she brought. What a lovely girl she is. A jewel." I nodded. "Why don't you do something about her?"

"Like what?"

"Get her to marry you, fool."

"I've asked her."

"Not often enough, not romantically enough, not intensely enough, I bet. You probably just slipped it in at the end of a shopping list. I know you. You're worse than your father at putting emotions into words. Suitable, acceptable words."

There was nothing wrong with Mum's mind. It was back on track.

"Right," I said. "Glad to see you've recovered your spirits."

Eloïse came into the room with a large vase of yellow roses and Arum lilies which looked glorious but, in these temperatures, probably wouldn't last the night. Eleni's face lit up as she saw them. She had Eloïse try out several different surfaces for them; tables, locker, window-sill, the swinging table-tray over her bed. She settled for the locker, away from the window.

Eloïse hugged me, fiercely. She looked tired, wrung out, bruised under the eyes.

"I've had a dreadful day," she whispered, *"mia apaísia méra."* The Greek *apaísios* is a punishing word; you can really thump down on that second syllable. Awful, atrocious, that sort of thing, but with more of a punch to it.

"Why? What happened?"

"Not now. I've got to go in a minute. See you this evening?"

"Yes, please," I said. "Mine or yours?"

"Mine," she replied, firmly. "I'll get something for us to eat. Nine, nine thirty?"

I nodded, kissed her on the end of her endearing nose and then more determinedly on her lips. She squeezed me hard, went over and kissed Eleni goodbye and left.

"Handle that all right, did I?"

Eleni didn't bother to reply. She was looking out of the window.

"Anything else you'd like me to do?"

"I'd always hoped to have grandchildren about me as I grew old." She hadn't turned round. She was still staring at an unseen outside world. "I can barely remember what my grandparents, my father or mother looked like. I've lost the sense of ever having had parents, grandmothers, grandfathers. I know they existed and I have my two precious photos. But I don't really believe in them, the people, my family, any more. I can't smell them or touch them in my memory. I don't know them at all. I've lost them.

They've gone." She gave a stifled sob and wiped her eyes. "I thought I'd replace them in a way with my own descendants, a crowded young family. And all I've got is you, childless and footloose. I think you're probably a selfish old bugger. Or as your father used to say, because he didn't like me picking up the nasty words of his mates, a nasty old b-b-bachelor."

She laughed, turned round and smiled at me.

"I don't suppose I really meant all of that."

"No? Didn't you?"

"Well, most of it probably. To be honest."

She drifted into a light sleep with a sense, I thought, of satisfaction. She had spoken her mind. Of course I knew I hadn't exactly turned out an ideal son and, on top of it all—no daughter-in-law (though Eloïse did well enough in the role) and no grandchildren—I had, in a manner of speaking, ruined her life, turned her into a cripple.

A little later, she woke up, smiled at me and said, "It makes you laugh, doesn't it? I remember your father always saying, when he was putting someone down, *Tell it to the marines!* And that's what you decided to be: a *marine*. I don't know what your father would have said."

"Probably tell it to the marines," I said but she'd chuckled herself back into a snooze.

67

Julia's sister, who also worked in some unexplained capacity for Sam, turned up to sit with Eleni for the evening shift. She was a widow in her early sixties, originally from Bradford, and had stayed on in Cyprus after her husband, an Ordnance sergeant, had died from a sudden tumour on the brain. She brought her knitting with her.

"I do hope your poor mother won't be disturbed by the clicking of my little needles."

She appeared to be making very small socks; for an imminent grandchild, she explained. I decided it was time to leave.

I got back to the Alasia. The answerphone was flashing. I turned on the computer and summoned up Internet mail and there seemed to be messages galore. The phone first. It was Freddie again. Mikoyan had arrived, would be seeing the suspect tomorrow. "None of them incidentally," he said, "mentioned al-Gamaa al-Islamiya, who, of course, claimed responsibility for the Christmas '93 attack on the Austrian tour bus and other atrocities.

"You bet they didn't," he said, "because this incident was odd, unlike.

No chanting of Allah Akbar before the shooting. Holmes's dog that didn't bark. Severely atypical, one off. Think about it."

The mail messages were from Chuck and had to be decrypted. It was only eight o'clock, so I reckoned I had time enough to wash, read the messages and get to Eloïse's before nine.

There were three quite short notes. Query on-passed. Shipping lists and histories tomorrow. PAY=DIRT, in flashing heliotrope, Chuck was keen on startling computer typography, ON CROAT PSYCHO. With a PS in black, heavy italic: "*Think I'll fly to Cyprus.*" The third said, "Will advise arrival, time, flight, tomorrow."

I called a taxi, changed my clothes, washed in a hurry and arrived at Eloïse's flat as the nine o'clock news came up on a neighbour's television set. The door was on the latch and I could hear she was on the phone, speaking angrily and fast in Greek. I know Greeks often sound as though they're shouting in anger when they're just having a normal conversation but this was positive fury. I suspected she was talking to her mother.

I walked in. She gestured at the long, waist high, iron and glass table. On it stood a pitcher of iced brandy sour, sliced lemons floating in the dark gold and Angostura adding pink streaks. The glasses were frosted from the fridge and the rims dusted with sugar. I poured us each a full glass and took them over to the phone. She was wearing dark blue linen trousers and a light forget-me-not silk shirt hanging loose. Around her neck there was a thin silver chain and a small antique carved jade pendant I'd brought her back from Hong Kong; a bird on a piece of bamboo, a phoenix, very Chinese, symbolic, beautiful. It always pleased me to see her wear it. She smiled at me and held out the telephone so I could hear the squawking voice at the other end of the line. And then enough was enough. She erupted into rapid automatic fire and put the phone down. It had been her mother.

"Darlink," she said, reaching up to kiss me, "the old bat's gone mad." And in case I hadn't got the point, she repeated it in Greek. "*Trelí eínai.*"

Carrying our glasses, holding hands, we moved over to the sofa opposite the balcony, looking out towards the sea. She sipped, I swallowed, the very good brandy sour.

"I needed that," I said.

"I needed my mother like a hole in my tights."

"What's it this time?" I refilled my glass and topped hers up.

"My father."

"Your *father*?"

"She wants me to go to Athens. To meet my father." She pouted outrageously. *"Mon père adoré* who went off with the waiter when I was a child. She says he wants to meet me and get to know me. He's sorry. SORRY! What about her? *She* sensibly won't take the risk. I think she's frightened of him. Why, I don't know. But for me it would be interesting, educational. Roots. Surely I wouldn't wish to stay *déracinée?* Don't I want to know, to find out, something more about my father, his family, his strengths and weaknesses? Would it not be natural to have such a curiosity? Should I not acquaint myself with things like that before I find myself having children with unsuspected traits? What a monster she is!"

By now she was sitting on my lap, arm round my shoulders, alternately licking my left ear and sipping her brandy.

"But why you? Why not her? She married him." A husky, breathless voice issued deep down from my oesophagus.

"She gives off fear. Do you think he used to hurt her? I ask myself if he really was gay," she searched for a more precise word, and ended, as so often, with the Greek "a *poústis*. That is," she laughed, "if he wasn't more likely a *kolombarás*." (A *poústis* is the generic word for homosexual but more specifically it means the "female" partner whereas *kolombarás* is the "male".) "In a funny way, you know, he begins to fascinate me. The idea of a mysterious father intrigues me. This magnetic Egyptian."

"Egyptian?" I said "I thought you told me he was French."

She wriggled into a closer embrace.

"I don't know where you found that idea. They were married in Marseilles, I think she told me, but that doesn't make him French. A civil ceremony at the *mairie*. I can't imagine what the aunts said."

"Surely the fact that he wasn't a Christian," I said, largely thinking of my own anomalous status, "must have worried them more than a civil marriage."

"I suppose so but I don't think he was very religious then. Maman said she met him when he was a student. Very romantic, she said. Charismatic. A student leader."

She squeezed my hand, almost absent-mindedly.

"But now," she paused and stroked my cheek, *"un vrai Musulman*, she said. A veritable Pasha. Intriguing."

She kissed me, giving her lips and tongue the sort of concentrated intensity that made my scalp tingle.

She broke off to say, "I should worry. I've got my own Pasha, if I want one. But don't you dare."

She kissed me again.

"Yeah," I said in a throaty whisper. "Well," I said. "Perhaps bed. More comfortable."

We didn't quite make it. Not first go. There was a large white flokati rug just inside her bedroom. It made a softer landing than the marble we'd been rolling about on. Later there was the bed and half-sleep and more leisurely love-making. Still later Eloïse sang, a high keening song of love and despair; very Greek. And then stopped abruptly.

"Do I always sing that lament afterwards, when I'm happy?" Her laughter trilled up and down the scales as she played with the matted hairs on my chest. "I am wicked," she said, still laughing. "Immoral, erotic . . ."

"Yeah," I said, eyes closed, "keep it that way."

Paying no attention, she went on, "I'm pleasure-seeking, sybaritic, multi-orgasmic. Perhaps we'd better get married. Whatever . . ."

"Yes. We'll get married," I said, sleepily, contentedly. I did love that girl. And she had a great sense of fun. "Whatever what?"

"Whatever your strange life as a travel courier." *Cour-ier*, as in the French. She made the words sound like counter-jumper or petty-criminal or drug-dealer, and then added, making it rhyme. "Does it pay?"

I woke at six. Eloïse was in the shower, the windows were open and the sun was colouring and brightening the morning sky. A few birds were singing. I picked up clothes, hers and mine, folded them as neatly as I could, nobody could say I wasn't house-trained, squeezed some oranges, put on the coffee, shaved and showered, and felt ready to face the world.

Chapter nine

I ran rather than jogged back to the Alasia and changed quickly into uncrumpled clothes before going to the base hospital. Apart from swimming every day, when I could, for an hour or so, I had not been taking all that much exercise and I was missing it. The kilometre and a half was just enough to get my muscles aching and pulses throbbing. Another two kilometres, I don't believe in overdoing it, would have done the trick, ironed out the creases, set me up for the day.

Eloïse had been bubbling with ideas at breakfast. She would accompany Eleni to Athens. That would save a nurse. She could make sure that Eleni was comfortable and properly looked after in the Greek hospital. She made the new Athens medical centre sound like some bush hospital in equatorial Africa, pre-Schweitzer. Then she would summon (her word) her father. She would stay with her aunt in the larger of the two flats they owned in Skoufá, the one overlooking the fashionable church where all the weddings took place. Perhaps I would join her there when I had finished whatever I was doing in Larnaca. She would like me to meet her father. It would only be proper since we were now, she supposed I would agree, affianced. Had I a date in mind? What about October? Lovely month. Should she tell her mother? Mine? She rather thought she would.

She smiled at the imminent epiphany. "Your Mum will be so pleased.

And mine? I don't know. A mixture of pique, lots of I-told-you-so satisfaction, that's-what-comes-of-mixing-out-of-your-own-circles. Lots of I-knew-as-soon-as-you-started-taking-up-with ... And turning-your-back-on ... I-don't-know-what-your-grandmother-would-have-said-but-thank-God-she's-not-here-to-see-the-disgrace-you've-brought-upon-the-family. But secretly she'll be glad it's settled. And with me not even being pregnant. Grab that! She'll be able to tell me you're too old for me, not good enough for me; wrong stock, religion, education; poor." She tried the word again for size, stretching out the vowel. "Poor. Well, not wealthy anyway. I'll have to reassure her that the children will be baptized Greek Orthodox. She'll weep and say it never would have happened had I had a father when I was growing up. She'll have a lovely time. Tears, rage and laughter. And wedding clothes to think about. Good thing I'm going to Athens."

She kissed and hugged me happily as I got ready to leave. "We won't really be poor, will we?"

"No," I said, with all the confidence born of a young, clear, breezy summer's day and the expectation of years of happiness ahead. But I was no longer in even the second flush of youth and I was plying, it would seem, a risky trade.

"I expect," I said, "your mother really did have a bit of trouble with her family, marrying an Egyptian, a Muslim and all."

"I think she did," Eloïse said. "But she never spoke much about it. And from what she says now he wasn't all that keen a Muslim, praying five times a day and all that. Not when he was with my mother. More of a free-thinker. Her parents were much put out because they thought he was some kind of Arab. They meant dark-skinned and long-nosed."

The physiotherapist was a dour, laconic, Ulster rugger player in his early thirties. He seemed to have esoteric ways, perhaps military and contact sports physios take a special graduate course, of making my muscles and nerves shriek from the shoulder down. I concentrated on Eloïse; Marriage; The Future; Growing Up; being 40.

"You've been exercising the wrist now," he said with a bare hint of approval. "But not enough. Mind, it's showing some improvement."

"Could I drive do you think?"

"Don't see why not. No racing round corners. Gently-gently. Give it a try."

"What about lifting small weights. Will I do any harm to the wrist?"

"What sort of weights are you after?"

"A light automatic, say."

"Probably."

I went to the range, drew two hand-guns and some ammunition, and put on ear protectors. Even the lighter one, the .22 Berretta which someone had donated, hurt like hell. To start with, using only the right hand, I could barely lift it to a firing position. I rested it a bit, tried again, rested it a bit, tried again and eventually fired off some not badly grouped clusters. But I couldn't keep it up. My hand wobbled and the wrist felt it was about to collapse. But it was a beginning. Just for the hell of it I fired off the rest of the ammunition with my left hand. It was pretty wayward but not totally ineffective. I'd have winged the target, and wounded several friendly bystanders.

I got a lift part of the way back, with a nurse going off duty, and ran the rest of it, playing with the little yellow ball and full of good intentions. It was actually getting too hot to run or, rather, too hot to run and wear a shirt and trousers. Back at the bungalow I had another shower and then played back e-mail and answerphone messages. Chuck was catching Cyprus Air flight 327. Would I meet him at the airport? Prof. O. had replied; he'd bring the message with him. The voice of Jeremy Sims repeated that he would be with me for lunch, a bit before one. A strangulated Freddie said something about damning all answering machines and went off air. It reminded me that I had yet to tell him about Eleni. He and Tamara would be horrified. And was it sensible on an open line?

I phoned the hospital. Eleni was, they said, in good spirits. Would I like to speak to her? I would; and found she was in remarkably good heart, looking forward to going to Athens, delighted that Eloïse was going to accompany her, bubbling away. I said I'd come to see her after I picked Chuck up from the airport. More bubbling; what a lovely treat to see Chuck again. No mention of weddings yet: I'd leave it to Eloïse.

I rang Freddie. He wanted to tell me about Mikoyan and the suspect. I cut him short.

"Some rather bad news," I said, "about Eleni . . ."

I heard him say, "God Almighty" and Tamara cut across with a "Must you always blaspheme?"

"She's OK," I said, "but she's in hospital."

"What happened?"

"She was attacked and badly beaten by some thugs."

"Sweet suffering Christ . . ."

Tamara shouted something about she'd had enough of his always Taking-the-Name-Of-The-Lord-In-Vain and he shouted back, hand over the telephone, that Eleni had been attacked and was in hospital and if he felt like calling on the Deity he damned well would do so.

I told him that she was going to Athens to see a specialist and she'd probably be in hospital there for a week or two. And left it at that. He was shocked enough as it was.

"Poor lady," he kept on saying. "What a dreadful thing. Poor lovely lady."

And he didn't know the half of it.

Chapter ten

Sims drove up, on time, in a British racing green Rover with tinted
windows. He lent across and threw open the passenger door. The air conditioning was on full blast and I shivered involuntarily as I got in. He turned
it down and said, in what I wrongly thought was a continuation of his new,
spare, laconic style, "Where shall we eat?"

"Zíyi."

"Thank heavens," he said, "you don't go in for that awful anglicization:
Ziggy."

"Well," I said, "they see it in capitals. ΖΥΓΥ. And they know the
funny letter between the Ys is a Gamma, so they say Ziggy. Does it matter?"

"Did you know that Howell in his Foreign Travels of 1642 was already
noting that in some parts of the Peloponnisos—of course he called it the
Morea—the locals did not distinguish between the sounds of the Eta, the
Iota and the Upsilon? Anyway wasn't it one of the Retained Sites?" I grunted
assent. "Where the BBC had its transmitters? Or to be precise where we
had our transmitters carrying BBC programmes."

"Our," I said, "meaning the Foreign Office?"

"And Commonwealth, dear boy. Never forget the Commonwealth.
You know I was here in one of my early postings, in the seventies, well
before the partition, the Turkish invasion, call it what you will."

I muttered something appropriate. "Take the next right and second left."

"I was reminded," he said, "when I went to the Sovereign Base this morning, of an extraordinary kerfuffle at which I was present. We had a very small, neat High Commissioner and a very large C-in-C and Governor of the Sovereign Bases. Extravagantly tall, I remember, and wide with it. Outsize moustaches too. I rather think he was an Air Marshal. The High Commissioner, of course, was clean shaven. Total contrast. Each of them as proud and jealous of their preserves and privileges as any medieval prince. So to the matter of the flag. In Cyprus at large, the High Commissioner represented Her Majesty the Queen. As he went abroad about his business in his Daimler—I don't *think* it was a Rolls but I can't really remember—the car flew a rather large union flag as his official standard. In Nicosia, the capital, and wherever else in the republic, His Excellency the H.C. was, to all intents and purposes, the Queen."

I said we'd do better to cut inland to the old main road, which runs parallel to the newer expressway, because the coastal road peters out. It means going in and coming out again to the shore, two long sides of an elongated triangle, to gain a short base line along the sea, but it's better than getting bogged down in the sand. So we turned off to Mazotós, joined the B1 and turned left through Psematisménos to Zíyi.

"But," said Sims, untroubled by any such travelling considerations, "back at the so-called Sovereign Base Areas, the C-in-C was Governor and Queen. So there was I sitting beside, and dwarfing, my master, and I'm hardly a big person but he always made me feel like some freak suffering from gigantism, with overlarge hands and feet and everything getting in the way, and we enter the Sovereign Base Area of Episkopi. Our car gets stopped by the Military Police. The High Commissioner goes white, incandescent with fury. He, the H.C., says: Do you know who I am? Yes, sir, says the Sergeant, reading from a piece of paper. Elsewhere in Cyprus you're Her Majesty's Representative. But here in the SBAs, sir, you're just another civilian. So please lower your flag, sir, before the C-in-C eats me for lunch.

"The flag was taken down. The meeting, and the repast that followed, was conducted with icy politeness—of the after you, Sir Gordon, no after you, Sir Clive variety—and I think I spoke more than the two principals taken together."

"No surprise there," I threw in.

"I wasn't loquacious in those days," he said rather sharply. "Far too young and tentative. Bloody nonsense, anyway; shaming nonsense. Two grown men fighting over whom should be called H.E, and whose car wear the standard. I nearly resigned from the service right then and there."

"Why didn't you?" I said.

"Because at the same time I was slyly amused. By the game, I suppose. By its being played so seriously. And what it really betokened: the difference between the diplomat's approach to Cyprus and the soldier's; and, of course what mattered, whose advice was being listened to back in Whitehall."

We were coming into the small port of Zíyi by now and I directed him down to the old customs house by the jetty where I'd booked a table at Apovathra, the acknowledged best of the half-dozen fish-tavernas.

"I'd no idea," he said. "It's become quite a little resort. You know, of course, it was founded to ship out the carob pods. The name . . ."

". . . means scales, balances, weighing machines," I finished it for him as we were shown to our table.

He rattled on inconsequentially as we chose our main dish, and ordered some meze and a dry white from a small vinery near Ayía Mávra, a ruined monastery close to Limassol, while they grilled the probably recently unfrozen fish. There was a bit of a dearth of your actual, leaping, sparkling, bright-eyed, iridescent, scaly fish, just out of the sea, but we didn't over-publicize the fact to our visitors.

He told me that there was no movement on the Cyprus front; little hope of peace talks between Clerides and Denktash; or Greece and Turkey for that matter; that the EU negotiations were stalled; the UN initiative petering out, and the US power-broking proving futile. So what was HMG doing about it? Not a lot.

He was drinking liberally, we had got on to the second bottle, and I was a touch worried about his being the nominated driver but he seemed sober enough. The wine had, to be fair, turned out to be rather decent and the fish could almost have been fresh and local; perhaps they were, but I expect they came from Iceland.

He suddenly dropped his voice and said, "I've brought you a transcript of what the young suspect has admitted to. Quite interesting. Your friend, Cy Drucker the third, says he's got a lead for you but he wouldn't tell me what it was. He wants to see you in person. Only for your ears." He harrumphed.

"I'm not going to Cairo," I said. "And I don't trust him."

I paid the bill which he made no attempt to share.

77

"You do him wrong. Deeply unattractive as he may be, he has, I've decided, a kind of tarnished, vestigial truth about him."

"So has the Nile crocodile," I said.

We got into the car and he retrieved his despatch case, black leather, well worn, with the royal cipher just visible, unlocked it and gave me a file. It was indeed a transcript, translated into English, of an Egyptian police interrogation. I skimmed through it, keeping half an eye on the road, as he drove us back perfectly competently to the hotel.

"No," he said, "I won't come in. I'm flying back to Cairo tonight and I've got a few calls to make."

"Would Drucker come here?"

"I expect so. If you asked him. Do you know anyone in the US Intelligence community? If you do, ask them to check him out. I'd wager he's on the side of the angels."

"Whose angels?" I remained unimpressed.

"Incidentally, another friend of yours, Max Bedell," stress on the last syllable, "has been asking about you."

"No friend of mine," I said. "I think he once tried to recruit me for something secret or other, probably SIS, MI6, or whatever it's calling itself these days. And I let him know I wasn't interested. Anyway, I thought he was in London."

"He is."

"Thanks, nice to know he's still keeping tabs on me. I realize I'm out of date but perhaps you'd know if there's a Special Forces Liaison set-up in the Middle East? Anyone I can contact?"

"Not that I'm aware of." That sounded about right. The SAS controlled most things from Hereford and kept its Director at the MOD. There weren't many outlying units except operational ones. The SBS kept to itself at Poole.

Just as he was starting the engine and beginning to pull away he leant out and said, "Katie's gone."

"What?" I said. I might just as well have said "Who?" I had temporarily forgotten his Australian wife.

"She's left . . ." he said and drove off, swallowing the final syllable of his lament, ". . . me."

Chapter eleven

One of the advantages of having an hotel as home is that you can always borrow, at short notice and little cost, a car from a friendly hire firm. I thought I'd try a small yellow Fiat which had taken my eye, as a first attempt at driving for several weeks, but I couldn't easily fit into to it so I upgraded myself to a slightly larger royal blue Opel and drove to the airport to wait for Chuck to come through immigration, baggage-reclaiming and customs. The plane was actually a bit ahead of itself and I'd barely been waiting five minutes when he appeared.

As usual, he looked as though he had slept in his suit, the shirt was coming out of the trousers, one shoe lace was undone and threatening to trip him up and he had a duffel bag slung across a shoulder while a suitcase trundled creakily behind him, like an arthritic dog on a lead. He had a round, slightly baby face, strawberries and cream in colour, which showed little sign of maturing, let alone ageing, a wide mouth, often grinning, an unlikely small button nose, a full head of curly chestnut hair and a pair of large, deep-set, blue-grey eyes, a sort of marine colour, deep and unfathomed, glaucous, as in Shelley's *Under the glaucous caverns of old ocean.* He was a great bear of a man, six foot four and probably 16–17 stone, like a wrestler going a bit to fat. He still stammered and occasionally stuttered, under stress, embarrassment or shyness, and from childhood till now remained my best friend.

We went to see Eleni first. On the way I got Chuck to read the Cairo police transcript. It was a simple and sad enough tale, even in police-speak. The suspect, aged seventeen, the sixth of eight children, and the fourth boy, was born and brought up in one of the camps for the Palestinian dispossessed. In turn each of the boys disappeared into one or other armed group. The older two had been killed in an explosion in "occupied Palestine"; so too, it was understood, had some Israeli civilians. The third son had come back to recruit his younger brother for a special mission. He had been promised honour in this life, paradise, houris and an Islamic hero's welcome in the next. He had been trained to use automatic rifles. He had been given better and more food than he was used to, a sense of excitement and purpose, and with a slow-burning, angry, zeal, the aim of wiping out, he said, by whatever means, the Jewish state. He came to realize, he added, his people, his family, had been deprived of their land, their home, their work, their being. Now, he said, he had been shown what to do about it.

On the day of the incident, the two brothers had been driven into Cairo in a fruit lorry. The third man, the leader of the group, had met them at the market where they were dropped off. All three wore the same keffiyeh, chess-board black and white. Like Arafat he said and the interrogator reported that he had been unsure whether this was a statement of fact, of pride or criticism. They had walked to a house with a large courtyard. Where? Near a mosque, he thought. Which mosque? He didn't know. He thought they were in Cairo. And then? There were two motor-cycles. His brother got on to one of them and the other man, his brother referred to him as The Turk, examined the guns and ammunition. No he certainly wasn't a Palestinian, or a Lebanese, or a Jordanian. He didn't think he was an Arab at all, and not an Egyptian. The Arabic he spoke sounded a bit like an Iranian he had once met.

He had sat on the pillion behind his brother, holding three AK 47s, wrapped in a dirty cloth. He thought The Turk had extra ammunition inside his pockets and clothes. They set off at a steady pace, The Turk leading. They saw the hotels and the bus from some way off. His brother dismounted and went forward to take a closer look. He came back and reported that the tourists were getting into the bus. And then added that they didn't look like Israelis to him. The men had no hats and the women were wearing black dresses and crosses round their necks. The Turk swore. By now they had wheeled their bikes close enough. They stood them upright and walked a few yards towards the bus. His brother, who had good eyesight and could read quite well, both in Arabic and American, said that the bus said it was for an Armenian Church Tour. They'd made a mistake, he said. These were not the Israelis they'd been promised. By then each of them had taken his gun and was carrying it, loosely covered by his djellabah.

The Turk said, "If they aren't Jews, they might as well be Armenians; the next best thing," and gave the order to fire.

The police note added that the older brother had been killed two weeks later in an incident in the Gaza strip and that no one had identified the so-called Turk. He was not, they were convinced, Turkish. Or Egyptian. At no point had the name of the suspect been given.

There were other unexplained lacunae. Why were they sure the ringleader was neither Turkish nor Egyptian? Merely because it was convenient? The young Palestinian hardly sounded an expert linguistic witness and the bit about they might as well be Armenians called to mind a certain kind of Turk. Had they any further evidence? Perhaps I should have asked Sims but if he'd known anything else he surely would have told me.

I had a certain amount of difficulty parking the Opel. The hospital car park was untidily full, the Opel was without power steering and my wrist was aching. Chuck gathered everything, including his bags and my briefcase, and we made for the ward.

He stopped a yard or two short of the door, plonked down his load, and said: "Can she handle this?"

He was unpacking one of his reticules, distributing socks, underpants, shirts around the floor, and feeling around its recesses. With a triumphant mutter, as it might have been abracadabra, he extracted a stiff plastic folder and handed it to me. The cover page said "Former Yugoslavia: Indictments for Crimes Against Humanity: Before International Court of Justice, The Hague." Inside was a list of names, one of which was starred and marked with fluorescent green ink. Next came three good, clear, large photographs of the one indictee, Eleni's torturer. A large, slab of a face, slightly wider-eyed than he had looked in the earlier computerised blow-ups, thin lips, a spreading nose and strangely, sinisterly, little ears without lobes.

"Sure she can." I said. "She's been looking forward to seeing you."

With Chuck still shoving everything back into the bag and my carrying the rest of the gear, we went in. Eleni whooped with pleasure. Chuck was appalled by her foot, which she showed him, and by what she told him of her ordeal. He went quite pale. She meanwhile was flirting outrageously with him, he had always been her favourite among my friends, telling him he must lose weight otherwise soon no girl would want him, too much of a health risk. She identified the pictures at once, said they were much better likenesses than the ones she had been shown by the Cyprus police. She listened attentively when Chuck said that the Croat had been indicted for war crimes.

"Killing and torturing Serbs," said Chuck. "He was running one of those dreadful death camps; ethnic cleansing. Mostly it was Serbs torturing and killing Bosnian Muslims. This time it was a Croat doing the same thing to the Serbs. He was notionally working under a Bosnian Muslim officer—who has also been indicted."

"I hope to God they catch him," said Eleni.

"We'll try," said Chuck, who had never been on the hunt of anything larger than a cockroach in his life.

"He should be strung up and left to die," said Eleni, thus dismaying Chuck who had her marked down from fifth form as the only mother against the death penalty.

He quickly adjusted himself to a less pro-active role. "Expect the local police will come up with something."

Eleni laughed, whether at Chuck or in disbelief. We took our leave. I picked up the photographs and the folder, put them in my briefcase and threw it on to the back seat of the car. I dropped Chuck off at his mother's house. She was in England and he wanted to sort out her mail and retrieve a few of what he called his real hot weather clothes, which he'd left behind, having little use for them, he had thought, in East Anglia. He would spend the night there but would get a taxi and come over and join me for supper.

It was getting dark by the time I got back to the hotel. I parked the car in the courtyard and was just leaning over picking up my briefcase when I heard the soft voice of Vic Malone.

"Major, sir. Sorry, sorry, sorry. *Mr* Bolton, I mean. That policeman, the superintendent, is waiting for you in your bungalow. I thought you'd like to know, rather than be taken by surprise."

He must have been standing silent, motionless in the shadows.

"How long have you been waiting, Vic?"

"Thirty–forty minutes, sir."

"Thank you," I said.

"Everything all right, is it then, sir?"

"As far as I know."

"I'll be around. Within earshot."

Quite what he though Superintendent Angeloglou was going to do to me was a mystery but it was a comfort all the same to know that Vic was nannying me.

The superintendent was sitting in the Parker-Knoll chair when I opened the door, a reading light illuminating his cadaverous face.

"Excuse me for coming in like this. Your housekeeper, Kyria Frosso, let me in. I wanted to see you without curious eyes or ears."

"In that case," I said brusquely, "we'd do better to talk outside. The bungalow is probably bugged for a start."

He looked startled. "OK. You may be right. We'll go for a drive in my car."

He took out his mobile and tapped in some numbers. I ushered him out and double-locked the front door mortice; not that it was going to make any difference if the pass-key was being used every time any Cypriot plain clothes policeman, or passing hippy disguised as one, was going to ask Frosso to let him in. By the time we had walked to the courtyard the police car was drawing up. Superintendent Angeloglou and I got in the back seat and the car set off on a scenic tour of Larnaca south shore by night.

"So what's all this about?" I said.

He held up his hands.

"Apologies, apologies. It won't take long." He smiled, showing long. sharp, yellow teeth.

"Your mother's assailant. We think the ship he's on is returning to Cyprus; tomorrow morning, docking at Limassol. Of course, he may have jumped ship. Equally he and his friends may have taken over the ship." He chuckled. It was an ominous sound. "We know nothing for sure. I've got Customs and the Harbour authorities to co-operate."

However doubtful the outcome, he looked pleased with himself and I dare say the joint planning was difficult to achieve.

"The ship is being shadowed by shore and ship radar and by tracking from the air. Mind you," his face went lugubrious again, "it may not be the right ship. And then it will all have been in vain."

"Was it a tip-off?"

"Yes: what we call," he smiled, "Information-from-a-Usually-Reliable-Source. But," he added, "you never know if it's true."

I had brought the folder with me and I gave it to him.

"You'll see," I said, thinking I was showing the dog a juicy rabbit, "it looks as though he's the same man who's been indicted by the War Crimes Commission on Bosnia, at The Hague."

"That's nothing to do with me. Nothing to do with us," he said hastily, thrusting the folder back at me. "Cyprus has no standing in the matter. It is none of our concern."

"It is," I said. "Crimes against humanity involve everyone. But never mind. That's not what I wanted you to see." I took out the photographs. "It was these. My mother has identified them. She says they are much better likenesses. I thought you'd want to have them copied and circulated."

He took them and studied them, turning on a map light. So much for security.

"Yes. They're much clearer. Thank you. Now for tomorrow. The uniformed police won't go in till after the ship has docked. Customs will already be on board and Harbour officials. My plain clothes detectives will be in place early but will wait to go aboard. If you want to come with me—and no weapons, no heroics, no independent action, understood?—we'll meet at the dock gates at 0745."

"Can Vic Malone come too?"

"As long as he behaves himself."

"He will. And one more please. Charles Levendhis."

"What's he got to do with it?"

"He brought the photos from London. And he's my partner."

"OK. Nobody moves without me, says anything, does anything. Understood? This is a police operation. Under my command. You are not constituting yourselves as a private army; a revenge detachment. I'm making a great exception, granting you a great favour. You understand?"

I nodded.

"You realize," I said, "that if he knows he's been indicted as a War Criminal, he'll be desperate to keep under cover till he gets back home where he knows he can find protection. But at least now we've got a good likeness and a name."

"Perhaps," he said. "See you at a quarter to eight."

The driver dropped me off outside the Alasia and shot off towards the north.

Chapter twelve

T

he port at Larnaca is comparatively small and barely used nowadays as anything more than a yacht marina with the adjunct of a minor commercial harbour for a few freighters. Limassol, the second biggest town in the island, is far and away the largest port, with a constant traffic in container ships and a rich variety of freighters, tankers and ferries. Larnaca is hardly renowned for its civic beauty but Limassol doesn't even make pretensions. It is hard-nosed commercialism with a lot of ugly tourism added on top. It also has a restored Byzantine-Venetian-Turkish castle, some mosques, a covered bazaar, the Sovereign Base Areas of Akrotiri and Episkopi and the KEO brewery, distillery and winery. And sailors and red-light districts and night clubs and British soldiers, not always well-behaved, and some pretty rowdy holiday-makers. Those of us who live in Larnaca don't rate Limassol high as a traveller's attraction but behind the town, behind the foothills, lurk the Troodos mountains and those are quite another matter.

The docks are no prettier than the rest. Not even on a fine late summer's morning bathed in golden sunlight. Utilitarian, unromantic.

Vic Malone decided to drive his own car with the inflatable dinghy on the roof-rack. Chuck had taken his mother's Peugeot 405 out of moth-balls and picked me up. I read the notes he had compiled on the suspect ship, which didn't amount to very much, as he drove us to Limassol.

The ship had been built in East Germany for the state trading company and launched in 1956 as the *Walter Ulbricht*. After eight years she had been passed on, in some friendship deal, to the Black Star line of Ghana and renamed *Kwame III*. By the 1980s, several coups and a few owners later, a small Franco-Syrian company had bought her and changed her name to *Pleiades* and her home port to Latakia. She mostly seemed to carry mixed cargoes around the eastern Mediterranean.

"I thought changing a ship's name was bad luck," I said.

"Let's hope it is." For an Information Technology whiz, Chuck had an endearingly commonplace approach to conversation. "In any case," he went on, "you couldn't live with *Kwame III*, years after Nkrumah had fallen, gone dotty and bitten the dust. Could you? That would have been asking for evil eyes and all round disaster. Wouldn't it? I mean if you'd been the ship-owner."

They had done their best to isolate the ship. She was being moored, with an empty berth on either side. A tug was still, and for no very good maritime reason, standing by, while a coastguard cutter was standing further out to sea. The *Pleiades* was being made fast with a mixture of rope and wire hawsers. She looked old, rusty, in need of paint, pretty dirty but marginally sea-worthy.

The creaking gangway which had been lowered into place some minutes before they shut down the main engines was taking a fair bit of traffic. Uniformed police, a drug squad dog-and-handler team and Angeloglou's CID group were lurking unseen in a warehouse, a sprint away. The superintendent himself was waiting to go aboard with the harbour-master's deputy. I would bring up the rear.

Suddenly, no word said, our procession of three moved off and climbed the gangway. On deck we were cut off by the captain arriving down from the bridge, a tall, bearded Syrian pirate, his white-ish uniform tunic open to the waist, four stripes visible on the epaulettes.

"Ah, Captain," said the deputy harbour-master hurriedly, "welcome to Limassol. I'm afraid we'll be having to make an inspection of your ship. This is Superintendent Angeloglou of the Cyprus police."

"We," said Angeloglou, as though intoning from his notebook, "have-reason-to-believe ... secreted-drugs-and-other-prohibited-items-

and-substances . . . aboard-your-vessel." He waved to the shore. "Customs officers, members of our drug squad and other policemen will be coming on board. Some have already been at work. We'll be as quick and discreet as we can."

Discreet? Rozzers and Customs Officers were tramping around like a herd or two of elephants before he had finished speaking. The ship's captain remonstrated in a loud, angry voice. I walked across the deck to the seaward, port side. Whether I'd actually seen someone moving or was preparing for it I'm not sure. But there standing still and silent, close by a stanchion with no guard rail attached, was a solitary man. He didn't look like a seaman. He could have been considering whether to jump. By now I was perhaps five metres from him. I had been moving quietly, wearing a pair of old black sneakers that made almost no noise. Elsewhere cranes were shrieking and whistling, cargoes being loaded and unloaded, men shouting. He could very well be the Croat but I couldn't be sure. His face was three-quarters turned away. He still hadn't seen or heard me. I thought I had to chance my luck; so I called out, "*Dobri dyen.*"

He turned round instantly. He didn't recognize me and I doubt if he'd looked properly at any pictures of me. But I had seen his photos again this morning and here, as certain as I could make it, was Eleni's torturer. Mind you, he was in partial shade and I couldn't see his lobe-less ears.

I rushed towards him as he turned back to face the sea, balanced himself momentarily on the edge and then launched himself into the water. I skidded on a piece of oily cotton waste, almost tripped on the wire of the abandoned guard-rail, and flopped inelegantly, and dangerously close to the side of the ship, into murky water. I could see nothing. In fact I kept my eyes closed. The risk of getting fuel oil in the eyes was too high to gamble.

I hadn't brought any scuba, or for that matter snorkel, equipment with me. The only thing I had put in my pocket was a pair of goggles and I had strapped my diving knife above my right ankle. I let myself come up slowly and quietly, close to the ship. When I felt air, I opened my eyes. There was a stirring in the water, ten metres away. It could have been the last gasp of the wash of some distant ship. It could have been the Croat making for the jetty. Another movement and this time a dark head.

I started to swim, underwater, putting on my goggles, keeping no more than a few centimetres beneath the surface and coming up every ten strokes to keep track of him. I was gaining but he was getting closer to one of those iron ladders set into the concrete. I put on a spurt. He got his right hand on to the lowest rung of the ladder which was just above the level of the water. I surged again, still below the surface, and caught his foot as he tried to lift it on to the ladder. He was wearing heavy walking shoes and he kicked at my face with the other foot. I got out of its way but had to let the first foot go. This time I shot up and out of the water and tugged and put all my weight on his body, pulling his arms away from the rungs of the ladder. We went down together.

He was struggling, butting with his head, kicking, punching, but I was still hanging on to him. Out of the corner of my eye, I saw a piece of old rope, amongst other flotsam and jetsam, moving with the stir but not altogether floating free. It was attached to something on the jetty. I grabbed it and put two turns round his nearest leg and then a half-hitch and then another. He kicked and strained and tore at the rope with his hands but it stayed firm. We were both running out of breath. I came up and breathed out and then, slowly and gently, breathed in.

He had not broken surface. I realized belatedly the rope wouldn't let him. His body was caught just below the surface.

So all right: he was most probably my mother's attacker. He would be better dead. But say he wasn't the man? Say there was a mix up with the photos? Say he was his brother? Or son? I was a civilized man, wasn't I?

All this time, I was back underwater trying to free his leg but the half-hitches had jammed and I couldn't work them loose.

I was killing him by mistake.

He had stopped moving. I remembered the knife, got it out and cut the rope, before I too passed out. His body floated up the few centimetres to the surface and I thought I saw hands pick him up.

When I broke surface myself, there was the inflatable dinghy with Colour Sergeant Malone carrying out revival drill. The Croat suddenly spewed out a gobbet of water and started breathing. Vic Malone moved round to where I was trying to find a handhold. He bent over to help me into the dinghy and at that moment I saw the Croat push himself to a kneeling position. Lazarus-like, returning from his near-death, or out of-body experience, he grabbed the boat hook and swung it at Vic's head. He couldn't have had much strength left in him but it was enough to thump Vic's shoulder and knock him into the water. The Croat fell on me and started trying to gouge my eyes out. Unfortunately I had taken off my goggles and he was raking, past my protecting hands, whatever part near the eyes he could get to. In a desperate twist, compounded of anger and frustration, I

88

flung away from the boat but he got hold of my hair and tugged me back. My eyes were watering, smarting with the pain, as he pushed me down into the water and held me under. I could get no purchase on the bottom of the dinghy and his fingers were tightly enmeshed in my hair. I was running out of breath, my lungs felt as though they would burst, my ears were popping although I was at no depth at all, my pulse was racing and my eyes seemed to be being pushed out of their sockets.

I never thought it would end like this, ludicrously, a few centimetres below the surface, a half-drowned psychopath holding me down by my hair. Lack of oxygen would affect me soon. Was affecting me now. Should have had a shorter haircut, Bright hair . . . Johnny so long at the fair.

I made one final kick, away from the dinghy. He was left holding a handful of hair, and some scalp.

I breathed and swallowed some filthy water. My head and face were hurting fiercely. God knows what the chances were of avoiding infection in the dock effluent. I was angry. I swam under the boat and came up over the opposite side pulling myself quickly into the dinghy. The Croat was still peering into the opaque water to see where he had lost me. But he turned in time to avoid my attack. We rolled together in the rubber bottom. He levered himself on top and bore down on me.

89

There's an awful intimacy in this sort of fighting. Why do I have to put up with it? Why do I have to breathe in his noxious breath, feel his body pressing down on me in a mock sexual clasp ? Because he's raking at my eyes again and because he's heavier than me and managing to stay on top.

I rocked myself from side to side, loosened his hold, freed my body and brought a knee up into his crotch. It had little force to it but it was enough to stop him attacking me for a few seconds. I punched him, a short, sharp jab in the solar plexus, making sure I used my left hand, and repeated the blow twice more. I reckoned that might keep him quiet while I helped Vic back into the inflatable dinghy.

OK I actually hit him as hard as I could. Several times. When he was down. But it wasn't revenge any more; that had seeped away. This was self-preservation, fury and an iron-clad resolve that he should suffer the proper rigours of the law, both Cypriot and War Crimes Tribunal at The Hague, for what he had done to hundreds of Serbs as well as to my mother. FIAT JUSTITIA.

We tied his wrists and ankles to the painter, revved up the outboard motor and tried to find some way of safely landing our fish. The iron ladder, I now saw, stretched up some four metres, at least, till it reached the level of the jetty and the dock roads. We could never push him, fighting, up that sort of vertical climb. We were invisible from the ship's deck. The tug had pulled away and was now making for the open sea and the coastguard cutter had disappeared.

"Never say die," said Vic, nursing his bruised shoulder and heading out to sea.

Our captive swore in Serbo-Croatian, Hrvatsky variant, and struggled and spat. I looked at him more closely. He had very small ears and no lobes. His eyes were full of anger and contempt. I tried to disengage, ignore him.

Despicable, sick, a torturer of women. I could tear him limb from limb. But I won't. I'm not like him; I'm not a barbarian.

The sun was beginning to beat down fiercely on us. There was no awning, no shade. He was suffering too. I resigned myself to a long journey. Trying to find a landing place for a dinghy in a deep sea port is like trying to find a chair for a doll's house in a furniture depository: the scale is all wrong. There was nowhere within sight where we could come alongside and be seen, let alone climb up and land ourselves and our prisoner.

No atavistic revenge. I just hated the bastard. And the sooner we got him ashore and in the hands of the police the better.

Chapter thirteen

Superintendent Angeloglou was not best pleased. I pointed out to him that it was his men (well the police, anyway) who made the arrest, and that he and they would get the kudos, not only for bringing in vicious international criminal Stjepan Zkrakovic but for nabbing the other Croat, two Turks and a decent haul of heroin.

His response was unfriendly. "You had to go off and do your own heroics."

"He'd have got away otherwise," I said.

"And Customs will claim the drugs." He focused on me. "You look a mess. You'd better get yourself to hospital and get those scratches seen to." He examined them more closely. "They can go septic very easily."

"Right," I said. "Thanks for reminding me."

I had underestimated Chuck. He'd gone aboard with the first wave of CID, had quickly checked that the police had seized the ship's log and the communications report, and had started looking for me. He then thought he'd see if there was a motor-boat or launch he could borrow and have a look round the ship from the outside. He left the ship, walked along the dockside and found a police launch with a full crew, standing by and looking bored, who were only too willing to take a short trip round the lighthouse for an outsize civilian they'd seen hob-nobbing with the superintendent.

It was some minutes before they had got under way and cruised round the ship, examining the barnacles, or whatever they thought they were doing, under Chuck's tutelage. But to give him and them their due, they spotted our dinghy zooming out into the harbour and gave chase at high speed, nearly capsizing us. They were our angels in police uniform. They picked us up and towed our dinghy in. They arrested and hand-cuffed the Croat. It was a good morning's work. We told them so. Angeloglou couldn't quite bring himself to praise them but Vic, Chuck and I went on thanking them so effusively that he was forced to acknowledge that they had saved the day; for us certainly and, indeed, for him.

By the time they'd finished with me at the RAF hospital at Akrotiri, my face was criss-crossed with those plasters they use instead of stitches if the wounds are not too deep.

The Sister said some of the scratches were horrifyingly close to the eyes. How on earth had I got them? Don't know, Sister. I was underwater most of the time. Ran into some loose bundles of wire before I saw them. Dark and dirty water. Ugh. I shuddered; and that was real.

"Why weren't you wearing a mask?"

Indeed, why wasn't I? "I'd forgotten to put it in the car," I said.

"You men are all the same," she said, "just big boobies, playing games."

It was hurting, smarting anyway, as she tidied up and cleaned the wounds. I let her voice wash over me. It was a cool mezzo sound, relaxing, calming, as long as you didn't listen to what she was saying. Switched off, I nearly missed her warnings about leaving the plasters on, about seeing a doctor within the next 48 hours and about the possible need for plastic surgery some time in the future. There were other dire forebodings but I relied on Vic Malone and Chuck to relay them to me later. They did; with some relish.

I slept in the car as Chuck drove back to Larnaca. I was a bit sore round the face but relaxed and refreshed when I woke up and found we were back at the Alasia. I said as much. It was a surprise.

"It's the air conditioning," he said. "It makes all the difference. Worth every penny. You'd be feeling stale and heavy with headache without it."

Nonetheless he came in with me, to make sure I was all right, could cope, that sort of thing.

There were three messages on the answerphone, all from Eleni. Wasn't I the sly one, not telling her myself and leaving it to poor Eloïse. *Why poor, all of a sudden?* Still I'd got around to it at last and that must be a good thing. So, well done! Two. October sounded fine but what was she going to wear? And what was she going to do about her foot? She wasn't going to hobble up the aisle at her only son's wedding. *Aisle? What aisle?* And all that dancing. With giant candles. And the priest. And those coronet things, chaplets of flowers, what-are-they-called, *stefania* is it? And then afterwards. At the reception. *What had Eloïse been saying?*

Three, much later. They had arranged an air ambulance for the day after tomorrow. Would I come and see her in Athens? When? And where was I anyway? Now, for example. Where had I gone? Why was I so secretive?

Chuck had been checking the fax and turning on the computer but he must have heard the messages. He didn't say anything.

"Yes, well," I said, "Eloïse and I finally decided we might as well get married."

"Marvellous," he said, spluttering. "I suppose it's for tax reasons." And he laughed and laughed.

"It's certainly not because she's pregnant, if that's what you think."

He continued to fall about like a twelve-year-old, collapsing with exaggerated laughter. Then he noticed an e-mail and summoned it up on the screen, said it was for me and printed it out. He brought it over, together with two faxes. He was still smiling.

"Congratulations, Ben. It couldn't happen to a nicer man. I've always fancied Eloïse, always wondered how you managed to avoid matrimony for so long."

Chuck had been married twice. And divorced twice. No children; plenty of alimony and still more acrimony.

The e-message was from Drucker, brief, cautious, pertinent. "Visiting Athens embassy," it said, "August 4th to 14th. At your disposal." It was signed Cy. Luckily for him he was the only diplomatic Cy I knew.

One fax was from Freddie in Cairo. Why no news? Why was I never in? How was darling Eleni? Should he come and see her? Tamara was driving him mad. Religion was one thing; religiosity quite another. And zeal! Ciao.

The second fax carried more of a punch. It was from William Mikoyan. He was flying to Cyprus. Imminently. He wanted discussions and plans for action. He would phone on arrival. He was relying on my help.

"Thanks a million, Mikoyan, old buddy, old buddy," I said.

"What's that?" said Chuck who was reading the messages as I finished them.

"Nothing," I said, "just the re-entry of the Armenians."

"That reminds me," said Chuck, fishing about in his trouser pocket. "I forgot to give you Professor O's reply."

He handed over a crumpled piece of paper. I looked at it glassily, thinking suddenly of the massacred Mikoyans.

"Don't worry; the original was encrypted," he said, misunderstanding my shocked expression. "And there are no give away addresses. I've kept this on my person."

"It looks like it," I said, trying to smooth it out enough to make it legible.

It was written in an unnecessarily elliptical style. The Prof had caught the secrecy bug.

"Tell my forwarding agent," it said, "two and two don't necessarily make four. Bosnia is most likely. Muslims were using Croats against Serbs. Turks were helping arm Bosnian Muslims and financing them. The Egyptians were sympathetic.

"I have also heard rumours of Kurdish connections and complications. Not all Turkish Kurds are at war with Turkish governments. Also there are alleged large scale criminals involved. Note Turkish, also Kurdish, drug links with Cairo criminals.

"I cannot vouch for any of this last. Not my milieux.

"There's always US, of course. But I doubt it."

I had been reading it aloud, in case the creases, or the syntax, misled me, and I said; "There's always US? What have the United States got to do with it?"

"U S meaning us, accusative of we," said Chuck authoritatively. "Pronoun. First person plural. Us meaning him and you."

"Oh," I said, "well I'm glad he's feeling reasonably confident. I'm no longer so sure. Perhaps we'll get something out of the Croat."

"Don't reckon on it," said Chuck. "I still have the feeling it's to do with the Armenians. Are you quite certain you don't have a glimmer of a memory. Something out of place? Unusual? Unexpected? Wrong?"

"Killing innocent old people with automatic weapons is wrong," I said. "Don't be silly. You're not a shrink and I'm not a patient."

"Not yet. Or perhaps you should be. Perhaps you've been so traumatised by what happened to the Armenians and to your mum, not to mention this morning's excitement—and it was lucky, I was there . . ."

"Yes, well thanks again, Chuck. You found us when we needed you."

He blushed. "I w-w-wasn't l-l-looking for p-p-praise."

I grinned at him and directed a loose punch towards his midriff, to show him I understood and, I hoped, to get him out of his stammer. Once started, it could go on for days.

"S-s-seriously though," he said, his voice strengthening, becoming almost confident, "we've got to s-s-suss out what this is really all about before they f-f-find you and f-f-finish you off."

It was a thought that had occurred to me.

Chapter fourteen

Stavrovouni monastery is supposedly the oldest Christian settlement in Cyprus—not the buildings, they were destroyed first by the Mamelukes 500 years ago and then, a couple of centuries later, by the Turks. The monastery was rebuilt in the nineteenth century. It is here, on an impressive, isolated crag, getting on for 700 metres high, that a sliver of the True Cross was deposited by St Helena, so the legend goes, mother of the Emperor Constantine, when she passed this way, returning from a visit to Jerusalem in AD 327. It was kept in a reliquary, protected by a community of monks, until destroyed, historians believe, in the fifteenth century.

The last time I'd been driven up the precipitous, and rather dangerously unsurfaced road, had been in a thunderstorm with my father. I could remember the dramatic views and the reliquary said to house the fragment of the Cross but, more likely, if it housed anything, according to agnostic Dad, it might have been part of the cross of the so-called Penitent Thief that St Helena, in the legend, was also, bringing across the sea. I remembered an elderly abbot and a solitary monk.

More than a quarter of a century later, the road had been paved and re-graded, the same abbot, apparently now a youthful 75 or so, was in residence together with some twenty or so youngish monks adhering strictly to a régime based on Mount Athos; fasting, praying, working hard in the fields and terraces, eating, when allowed, frugal vegetarian meals, and strictly prohibiting girls and women, or any female animals however young, within the confines. The views were still breathtaking. Even though I had expected something dramatic, they stunned me; a marvellous sky-filled panorama of sea and land as far as the eye could reach. Cross (Stavros) Mountain (Vouni) is the highest eminence in the south-eastern corner of Cyprus. The long, winding staircase also shook me a bit, though I took it at the double just to show the morning's activities hadn't sapped me.

I had brought Chuck along, partly because I didn't feel like driving and partly because his Greek was much better than mine. His father had always spoken Greek to him at home.

"It's odd," he was saying as we swung round the final tight bend approaching the monastery, "that every Costas and Eleni you know, the most popular Christian names throughout the Greek Orthodox world, come from St Helena and her son, Constantine."

"That's why we're here," I said. "Bloody inconvenient it is, too."

"Come on, it's the least you can do for your mum."

I wasn't really annoyed with Eleni, just a mite put out. I had gone to see her shortly after I had returned home and changed into clean clothes. She had swept into a great exclaiming about my face being covered in sticking plaster. What had I been up to? Silly boy, never looks where's he's going. She had said that she had a particular favour to ask of me and put on her quizzical face. I was meant to think she was wondering whether she wasn't asking too much of me.

"Fire away," I said patiently, folding my hands in my lap and smiling graciously.

"Take that silly grin off your face. You'll rupture all your scratches or whatever they are. You haven't erupted in some awful skin disease? Kreutzer's sarcoma—or whatever it's called? You haven't got AIDS have you? Is that why you delayed marrying Eloïse? Oh God . . ."

I told her not to be daft; that of course I hadn't got Kaposi's sarcoma or AIDS, and that I was still waiting to hear what she wanted me to do.

She took her baptismal cross off her neck and handed it to me, looking, I thought, decidedly sly.

"You see," she said, pointing, "I got Mr Hadjijossif to mend it as soon as I knew I was going to Athens. Hasn't he done it beautifully?"

It looked good; a strong but fine, new gold chain.

"The chain's new," I said. "He hasn't mended it. Isn't it funny having a new gold chain and an old silver cross?"

She chose to disregard me.

"I'd love to go to Stavrovouni," she went on, "to light a candle to my namesake, St Helena. But they won't allow any woman up there and with my foot it might be difficult anyway. But you could go and light a candle and get my little cross blessed. Touch it to the holy reliquary, get the abbot to bless it. Do what you can." She waved her hand airily. "I should feel quite differently about going to Athens if my cross had been renewed, re-powered."

"Mum . . ." I said, in exasperation.

"I thought you were never going to call me that again."

I went on, unmoved, "You're leaving tomorrow."

"Yes," she said, "that's why you'll have to go before they shut the monastery up for the night. Those poor monks go to bed early, rise before dawn."

"I don't understand your mother, Ben," said Chuck. "Which is she? Greek Orthodox or Jewish?"

"Both," I said, "and one or the other is temporarily uppermost, depending on where she is and what's happening. She's going to Athens for treatment, so it's back to priests, archimandrites and saints."

"I suppose," he said, thinking, "it's a perfectly practical approach in terms of benefits and protection; doubling the choice of guardian angels. But you'd have thought a conflict of beliefs might occasionally get in the way." He paused to consider this. "Anyway it obviously suits her. I haven't worked out much of a plan. Have you?" Chuck, I could tell, was beginning to enjoy himself. "We'll have to make a decent donation, you know, as well as buy an outsize candle. Leave it to me."

We bought and lit a candle, a fairly tall one. It would serve. There was no trouble there, but when Chuck asked to touch the reliquary, the severe young monk we were addressing, became surly and, in a religious way, bureaucratic. There was a faint, lingering smell of incense pervading the monastery. I wasn't really following all the Greek but I understood the drift. You needed special permission. Could we see the abbot? He was busy. Would he mind going and seeing? He went. The abbot was at prayer. We wished, said Chuck, waving a £50 note, to make a small donation and ask a very small favour. Would he perhaps be finished praying, he looked at his watch, in say five minutes? He withdrew the bank-note, substituted a visiting card and watched the monk unwillingly return to the abbot.

We had similar SATIS business cards, engraved not printed. Chuck's said Chairman; Ginger's Managing Director and Chief Executive Officer; and mine, quietly, Vice-Chairman (Operations and Activities). Last year I had been Chairman and Chuck, Vice-Chairman (Planning and Development). Ginger was always MD: he brought in the steady, business traveller and specialist, i.e. expensive, one-off, holiday, trade.

In the end, of course, Chuck's ploy worked. The abbot saw us for a few minutes, took us to the reliquary, put Eleni's cross against it and said some prayers . We thanked him, Chuck proffered the £50 note and he waved it aside, indicating to some acolyte that he should take charge of it. He blessed us both, wished Eleni a good, safe voyage and *perastiká*, get well soon.

By the time we got back to the hospital, the afternoon was well-advanced and Superintendent Angeloglou was talking to Eleni, telling her all four men were in custody and that he was arranging for her to attend an identity parade on her way to the airport.

"It will all be made quite easy for the wheelchair and a nurse is accompanying your mother. But we have to do it now before Mrs Eleni goes to Athens."

I nodded. Angeloglou shook everyone's hand and said he'd be there tomorrow in person. As soon as he'd left, we gave Eleni her re-blessed cross and she shone with pleasure.

"Well done, boys," she said, kissing us each in turn, and putting the chain round her neck."I knew it wouldn't be beyond your resources." Then she looked doubtful. "You did get it properly done? By the abbot? In my name?"

"Yes, yes," we said in unison.

"Exactly as you prescribed," said Chuck.

"You're sure, quite sure? You're not saying it just to reassure me?"

"Everything," I said, with conviction, "was completely kosher."

Chuck dissolved in laughter with Eleni gradually joining him till she too was crying as well as laughing. It was a good moment to leave.

As we drove back to the Alasia, Chuck said he thought he'd play around a bit, surfing the net, seeing what he could come up with.

"Remember those stories about heroin traffic and political connections when Mrs Tansu Çiller was Turkish Foreign Minister in the Islamist coalition?"

"Yes," I said, getting mildly pissed off with Chuck's desire to impart information which I already knew, "I know who Mrs Çiller is. It's all *vairy* interesting. Also recondite, remote, irrelevant and, in the circs, a bloody waste of time."

"Not so sure about that." Chuck reckons minds are for processing intuition while computers stick to facts, and logic of a kind. He awards himself high marks for intuition. "Get stuffed, anyway. Recondite! Where did hairy-arsed marines like you get hold of words like that?"

"Hey," I said, "something important. I've just realized a great gap. No one asked the young Palestinian terrorist in Cairo how old The Turk was."

While Chuck got us some beer out of the fridge, I phoned Jeremy Sims at home in Cairo. He was out. I left a message.

"Stupid of me not to have thought of it before," I said. "I fancy I must have drunk more of that disgusting water in the dock than I thought."

"You took quite a pasting this morning before we picked you up." He nodded. "I know. Vic told me. As they say these days, you're entitled. You're right, any road."

I smiled. Chuck had spent a long week-end in Durham with an actress three years earlier and had affected the northern, dialect variant, ever since.

"It's important," he went on, seizing the thread. "The Turk might be much older. Different generation altogether. Not just an older, older brother but a senior, organizing terrorist. Or gangster."

"But why should he want to get involved in this senseless massacre? It must have been planned as a terrorist act, a political gesture; a warning to tourists, to the Egyptian government, to Israel."

"To Armenians?" interposed Chuck.

"That was chance, a mistake. But why should anyone important risk a hands-on approach?"

"You know what it is, Ben? It's you. You've acquired a kind of negative serendipity. Instead of stumbling on happy discoveries when you're looking for something else, you come up with bloody disasters."

"I wasn't looking for anything else," I said. "I was just minding my own business, watching the world go by."

"Wrong world, wrong time, wrong place. Comes to the same thing."

"Thanks," I said, "thanks a lot. Negative serendipity: just what I needed."

Two beers later, we had completed the who-why-when circle yet again and achieved zero. Chuck returned to the Internet and I took Eloïse out to dinner.

The answer from Cairo didn't come until after I'd been to the airport and said goodbye to Eloïse and my mother in the VIP lounge. As it turned out, Superintendent Angeloglou was not there. It was his detective-inspector who had shepherded Eleni from the identity parade. She said it had been rather an ordeal, seeing them all, in the flesh, as it were, even though through a one-way mirror. She seemed a bit hot to the touch and her foot was paining her. I picked her up and put her on a settee, her legs outstretched. It seemed better than the wheel-chair. The nurse and Eloïse made her comfortable. Her damaged foot was loosely bandaged and then cocooned in polystyrene for protection. It must have been pretty hot although the VIP lounge veered towards refrigeration in its air-conditioning.

Doctor Pappaioannou came hurrying in, bouncing on the balls of his feet, followed by Cousin Sam. While the doctor examined Eleni, and told the nurse to take her temperature and check her blood pressure, which she had done ten minutes before, Sam walked over to talk to me.

"Is this going to work?" He gestured towards Eleni, doctor, nurse, Eloïse and then he saw my face. "What the hell happened to you, Sunny Jim? Fell among thistles?"

"You heard what happened?"

"Only that Angeloglou nabbed his man, the Croatian."

"That's right," I said.

"Good work," he said. "The police are not at all bad, whatever the journalists and do-gooding liberals say."

Eleni gestured to me to come over. By now she was rather enjoying her Madame Recamier scene with a cast of thousands dancing attendance.

"I saw your nice sergeant, Vic Malone, at the police station," she said, drawing me close and grasping my left hand tightly with her right. Her voice dropped. "He told me what you did. That was brave. Your father would have been proud of you; as I am. Very, very proud. I hope they put him away for a really long time. I'd honestly prefer them to kill him. Do you think that's an awful thing for a liberal-minded person to think?"

I shook my head but she didn't wait for a reply.

"I don't know why," she went on, still pressing my hand, "I was giving you such a hard time yesterday over my little cross. Suddenly it seemed terribly important. I kept thinking of that lovely priest, Father Dimitris. He was a saint, you know. He looked after me, protected me. His whole family could have been arrested by the Gestapo. They too would have been sent on the transports. To the camps."

She shivered, seeing a line of familiar ghosts I had never known, and she hardly.

"Never mind," I said. "It's the air-conditioning. They've got it turned up too high. How's the foot? Is it hurting horribly?"

"Not at the moment. It just throbs and aches. When I move—that's something different: white-hot needles. Doctor Pappaioannou explained there are so many nerve-ends in the feet in a very small space. Of course I wonder if I will ever walk properly again; feel the wet sand under my toes. Have I any toes? Dance? You know when I was with them and feeling unhappy, sometimes Father Dimitris would show me the steps of the dances he had learnt as a young boy in a village high up on Mount Pelion. And seeing him lift his skirts and tread those intricate steps would make me laugh for joy. And there wasn't much joy to be had in those days, I can tell you."

Her voice tapered off, into a long, long pause, and then returned.

"When will you come and see me?"

"As soon as I can. Next week, anyway."

"If I don't come out of the anaesthetic . . ."

"Come off it, Mum. It's a foot not a liver transplant."

"Anaesthetics are anaesthetics and old people react differently."

"You're not old. You're not yet 65. Come on, Mum."

"I know what I know. And anaesthetics are always dangerous. Particularly for the young and the over-sixties. And there you go again. I really thought you'd given up calling me Mum."

"I hoped he had," said Sam, joining in. "He's old enough."

"You get him to tell you what happened at the ship with those nice, competent policemen," said Eleni. "And then you'll see how old he is. And how brave."

"Shshsh," I said. "Mum's the word." She giggled. I kissed her and extricated myself. Sam looked puzzled.

An airport official came and spoke to the detective-inspector. I gathered the aircraft was ready and cleared for take-off. Eloïse and I made for each other and embraced half-way. She was looking even more fetching than when I woke up this morning and saw her brushing her long dark hair and gazing intently at me. She was wearing a very fine, blue-and-white patterned cotton shift and an absurdly large straw sun-hat that was pushed back onto her neck and tied with a satin bow. Her blue sapphire engagement ring, which I had bought months ago but had only got out of the safe yesterday, sparkled. So did her eyes. As we kissed goodbye, she patted my penis and whispered, "Keep it for me."

Sam, who seemed to be everywhere today, muttered, "That girl has no shame. Not much taste either if she's going to marry Benjy-boy here."

"Ring me," I shouted as the procession moved off, Eleni now on a stretcher. "See you in Athens. Good luck. *Perastiká.*" Eloïse looked back and waved. "I love you," I shouted. That would do for both of them.

A few minutes later, the doctor came back and said Eleni was very comfortable in the plane. His friend had arranged a good team to meet her in Athens. I need not worry. She would get the best attention possible.

"And," said Sam, "insurance, one way or another, is picking up the bill."

I walked out, in bright sunlight, with the two of them and separated as they went to the VIP car-park. I had put the hired Opel some way down an old, and now unused, approach road which was miles from any other car. I opened the door and immediately smelt a mixture of sweat, aftershave and cigarette breath. It lasted how long? Three seconds, perhaps, and then it was gone. I don't smoke. I don't use after-shave. I'd driven the car to the airport myself and there were no such smells. Of course, I could have dreamt it. Smells are both highly evocative and highly evanescent. Perhaps it was an illusion: imagination playing games.

103

I rolled out of the car instantaneously, deciding to take no chances. As I was running back to speak to airport security, I'd made perhaps 20–30 metres, a blast knocked me off my feet. It was the Opel. I waited, lying on the ground curled up in a ball, in case there was a secondary explosion, counted to two hundred and then got up, dusted myself off, turned back and was wondering about the insurance position and trying to remember if I'd left anything in the car, when a fire engine, sirens going, overtook me. My next thought, however irrational, was that I was glad the bomb had gone off so that no poor bomb disposal expert had to risk himself, like Dad, disarming it. Later, Chuck was to suggest, helpfully and reassuringly, that it might have been radio-controlled and they hadn't really meant to kill me. I reckoned it was more important that I hadn't got a cold at the time.

Chapter fifteen

Larnaca, Cyprus

The police had brought me back to Larnaca, after the airport contingent had questioned me. I turned down the offer of a lift to casualty to assess health and stress: I'd had enough of hospitals, one way or another, these last few weeks, to last an eternity. OK, they said, have it your own way and I landed up in CID headquarters. Not under restraint, they said, but under advisement, whatever that was supposed to mean in the circumstances.

I was reading the day before's *Cyprus Mail* and drinking some coffee when I heard the next tell-tale crump; a medium-sized bomb not very far away. The coffee spilled, the windows shook and rattled and the desk moved half-an-inch. And then another exploded a little further away. Both, according to the police loudspeakers, were in populous parts of Larnaca; one near the coach terminals on Finikoúdhes Parade, another ten metres away from Lefkara Buses, close to the Pavion Hotel. By a miracle, no one was seriously hurt. These were not large explosions but there were lots of glass splinters flying around, and some damage to cars and nearby windows. The television footage later showed quite a bit of blood too but it was from superficial cuts, said the hospital spokesman.

From my vantage point I saw policemen rushing in all directions; police cars, fire engines, ambulances zooming away towards the disaster areas, sirens wailing. Telephones were ringing in the office, so I left the window and went to answer one of them. I was lucky, very lucky. At the height of what turned out to be diversionary activity, the real targets were attacked. Two bigger bombs went off, at the same time. Two very loud explosions, with shock waves. The windows in the CID office shattered, raining splintered glass down on the floor and chairs and desks. One bomb had exploded right outside the police station, where I was, and the other, I heard over the communication system, had been at the prison where remand prisoners and those awaiting trial were kept.

In the chaos and confusion, emergency services stretched every which way, some police and civilians injured, plenty of noise and smoke and fires burning, both Croats and one of the Turks escaped. The other Turk fell over and knocked himself out and a policeman picked him up. No one noticed where the others went; whether there was a car or van waiting for them; or indeed saw them at all. They just vanished.

"That was well-planned," said Sam, giving the devil his due. Sam had arrived at the Alasia shortly after the police had let me go home, having pointed out that they had more urgent things to do than detain me.

"I suppose they figured they might as well take you out at the same time," he went on. "Two for the price of one. A diversion and a removal."

"Oh, I don't know," said Chuck, "this might have been a warning, If they'd really wanted to kill Ben, they'd have done so."

"Rub-bish," said Sam, dividing and eking the word out. "They may be good but they're not that good. Now come on boys, come clean. Just who are they?"

The fax machine was squeaking and pip-pipping away. It was Part II from Sims in Cairo. Part I had been in dialogue form. Compressed, it read: *Yes, he was older than the suspect's older brother; older, even, than his oldest (dead) brother.* Older than his father, perhaps? *No.* So how old was his father? *Old.* 50? 60? *Maybe.* 70? *Don't know.* How old was his oldest brother? *Don't know.* 30? 40? *Maybe.* Nearer to his father or his brother? *Not sure.* Think hard. *Perhaps father.*

So, as Chuck had scribbled on the fax, anywhere between 40 and 60+ seemed likely.

Part II, which I picked up while Chuck was explaining to Sam that we still had no idea, gave the name of a Special Forces staff officer, Colonel

Partridge, who was temporarily attached to Dhekelia. A signal was on its way to say that I would be in touch.

"And another thing," said Sam, "since you're both so busy playing games, way out of your depth, you realize you aren't safe here?"

He was right, of course. Chuck said it would take a few minutes because of changing fax numbers and transferring the e-mail address to a different line.

"Electronics," Sam spat the word out. "The end of rational discourse. Not to mention speedy action. When I said a place is not safe, I expected my boys to get out tidily, taking all they needed and leaving nothing incriminating behind, in ten minutes max."

"When was that, Sam? 1947?" asked Chuck, needling him, as he packed floppy discs, sent messages to CompuServe, unplugged modems and fax. I took a selection of useful clothes, some books, my service revolver and my private back-up Berretta with soft-nose bullets. We were out in a little under half-an-hour.

"We need to change cars," said Chuck.

"Where will you be?" asked Sam.

"Don't call us. We'll call you," I said. "Through your office?"

"OK. This time be sensible. Take care. I'll stick around, just in case. If you want help, you can always ask. I may be useful. Your old cousin Sam knows a thing or two. Has a contact or two."

He sounded uncharacteristically diffident, fragile, almost as though he thought himself past it. I gave him half a hug.

We drove round to Vic Malone's bungalow and found him in. The television was noisily covering the earlier mayhem caused by the bombs and the twins were crying in the background. I asked him to keep an eye on things and to explain to Frosso what was happening.

"Of course," he said. "I just wish I knew myself what the hell was happening."

"Likewise," I said.

"*Epeésis.* Me too," said Chuck completing the round.

We had decided that Chuck's mother's house was too obvious. His father, who worked and lived in Nicosia and had remarried after the divorce, had a flat in an anonymous block in downtown Larnaca and a hideaway cottage on the coast, near Vasilikós, west of Zíyi. Chuck reckoned we should set up base in the flat and then consider how to use the cottage. But first things first: cars. We both agreed my long-garaged red Triumph Stag was too much of a rarity, too noticeable. His mother's Peugeot had to be sold, hidden, rented out, something. I could hear the cogs whirring. Chuck was evolving some complex plan.

"With their Turkish connections," I said, "they'll have been in the north long since; a quick dart via Four Mile Crossing, over the Attila Line, and straight into Famagusta."

"Yeah," he said, "that goes for your Croatian chum and his mates but just think of the others; the ones who organized the break-out; who planted and primed the explosives. They'll still be around; and looking for you. Make no mistake, Ben, these guys are vocationally dangerous. Like the Royal Canadian Mounties they're used to getting their man. As to the escapees, they're out of anyone's reach here, except the Turkish Cypriot authorities and why should they worry?"

We live in an island that has been split since 1974, with the Turkish Cypriots, protected by a large contingent of Turkish military, and their population expanded by an intake of mainland Turkish emigrants, occupying the north; while the Greek Cypriot majority inhabit a heavily shrunk down version of the original island-wide Republic of Cyprus, the south. UNFICYP still guards the Green Line that runs through the capital, Nicosia, and separates the Turkish-Cypriot north, which no one except Turkey recognizes, from the south. Everything that happens, and doesn't happen, in the island, takes place against this intractable and tragic situation which has made thousands homeless and forcibly removed thousands of others, where mothers are still weeping for the undiscovered bodies of their sons and husbands. Four Mile Crossing is a narrow splinter of British Sovereign Base Dhekelia land which pierces the Turkish-Cypriot buffer line close to Famagusta. It is a quick and easy escape route if you have the right contacts and you don't happen to be Greek.

Chuck drove me to another of our old school friends, Joe Paramatta, who had a wholesale tea and coffee business. It was an old-fashioned, two-storey, rather spacious office-cum-warehouse with three new large, temperature and humidity controlled sheds at the back, in what used to be the garden. I explained to Joe, who had always been tubby and was now decidedly fat and bald, that I was temporarily un-housed and would be grateful for the loan of an office and a telephone.

"You're welcome to use Father's office; very welcome. Use it for as long as you like." His jowls quivered and the rolls of fat round his neck rippled up and down. "Sorry to hear about your mother." He had become almost obese, I decided, but underneath, without any struggling, lingered his usual charming, generous, sociable self.

Calliope, his stylish, rising-fifties secretary, about whom we had all had sexual fantasies in our adolescence, assuming her to be his father's mistress, showed me into "Mr Paramatta's room", patting the polished brass and leather desk-blotter, making sure the water jug was full and turning on the large wooden-bladed ceiling fan. The father had been dead ten years or more but he was still Mr Paramatta and Joe was Mr Joseph.

I sank into a marvellous large, swivelling leather chair with linen covers for the summer heat, surveyed the partner's desk, picked up the telephone and asked how I got an outside line. Calliope, who sounded even more seductive on the phone, said she'd get me whatever numbers I wanted. She too had been appalled to hear about Eleni.

Philip of Aphrodite Rent-a-Car was not best pleased to hear from me. "Who's going to pay?"

"The insurers?" I said tentatively.

"No way. If it's not an act of God, and it isn't, it's excluded under civil commotion, riots and explosions. No, my friend, I think it's you."

"I had nothing to do with it," I said. "I was just seeing my mother off to Athens."

"With half of Cyprus's finest protecting her from mayhem. Come on Ben, who do you think you're fooling? Of course, they were trying to get you. You and your mother. I don't know who they are. I don't care why they're after you. I don't want to know anything about it. I just want a replacement. Now. OK?"

"Don't be daft," I said, "how the hell . . ."

"I've located one in Limassol. Only 20,000 on the clock. A lighter blue. No dents or repairs. A1 condition. Top o'the range tyres. Decent radio. Knock down price. Seven K. Half now; half in three weeks time. Then I get the full log-book. OK?"

"Seven thousand what?"

"Pounds, Benjamin, Cyprus pounds. What d'you think I'm talking? Bloody roubles?

Cyprus pounds, for the unwary, are worth rather more than sterling. Often between fifteen and twenty per cent. So for 7,000£Cyp read 8,000++ GBP.

"No way," I said. "Bloody nonsense," with great restraint in deference to Calliope on the other extension. "I've got no liability. I've done nothing wrong. I don't feel any guilt. OK you were doing me a favour and, of course, I'm sorry that someone blew up your car; sorry for your business. So borrow one for the moment till your insurers have sorted it out and I'll help you out by halving any additional costs."

While he hit the hard curse button, I put the receiver down. He had no idea where I was calling from.

I tried using the remote accessing of my answerphone. It informed me primly that I had two calls.

The first was from Ginger in lovely, quiet, desirable, leafy, church-spired Norwich. "Where are you both? No word from you since Chuck left. Are you all right? They've doubled the ante on Karazdic and Mladic. It's seriously serious money now. You're sure you're still not interested?"

The second started with heavy breathing, and went on, gutturally, viciously, "You're dead. Dead. You and your bitch of a mother. You hear . . ." Calliope broke the connection. It must have been the Croat. I didn't like the sound of it: violent, intimate, shocking. He was at large, on the loose. He wanted to kill me, painfully. And Eleni. At that moment I had no doubt I wanted to kill him too.

I was still shivering when Calliope knocked, entered and poured me a cup of Lap Sang Souchong. "It was what Mr Paramatta always had at this time of day," she said. "I expect you need it." There was no milk which was fine because I don't take milk. How did she know? But of course; Mr P. never took milk either. Not with China, rarely with India or Ceylon.

I thanked her and said perhaps I would need something stronger, a bit later.

I phoned Eloïse in Athens. Her aunt answered. She was at the hospital. I tried the hospital and eventually spoke to a Greek nurse. No: I couldn't speak to my mother right now. The doctor was with her. Very brisk and pleased with herself, pleased with being discourteous too. When should I ring back? Dialling tone.

Calliope returned with whisky, ice and water and a large, heavy crystal tumbler. I wondered how much more of the Mr P. treatment I was going to be given. She quickly tracked William Mikoyan's flight. It was going to be twenty minutes late. She spent some time finding where he had booked in. It was a luxury hotel near Paphos; a suite for Mr and Mrs Mikoyan. Why Paphos, the other side of the island? Who was Mrs Mikoyan? His mother? I asked Calliope to send some flowers from me. I gave her a cheque made out to Henry Paramatta & Son.

By the time Joe came to say that he was packing up for the day, I had still failed to get through to either Eleni or Eloïse. I had however eventually spoken to Dr Haralambopoulos, who sounded kind, competent and resolutely patient. He explained it was a difficult and slow business. There was skeletal and neural damage, as well as the visible, near flaying of the sole of the foot. The putting together of the small bones of the foot was an intricate game, rather like a very fine jigsaw puzzle. It wasn't just a question of the bones but also of muscles and nerves; and of keeping them in place so that they could rejoin and heal. So what was his prognosis? He had good hopes but he could not, would not be precise. He would certainly venture no surgical intervention for several days. My mother would be in hospital for some weeks, as far as he could presently judge it. Of course, he would make sure she was comfortable and that she got enough proper exercise and physiotherapy and massage. He was looking forward to meeting me.

"I hope you don't mind if I start locking up now," Joe said. "It takes me about five minutes. Do come back tomorrow. Calliope and I have enjoyed having you here. It breaks our humdrum routine."

"What a sweet man he is," I said to Calliope as I gathered my attaché case, and she her various bags and parcels, and made for the front door.

"Just like his father," she said, "but he's putting on much too much weight. I told his wife but she said was it was nothing to do with me." She sniffed loudly, in disapproval. "I'd offer you a lift," she added, smiling fetchingly, "but it's such a little car and I know Mr Joseph would love to run you home." She paused and thought. "Or wherever you're going."

By the sound of it, Joe was arming the alarm and deadlocking the side door, the front door having been locked and bolted from inside. Calliope waved from her deux chevaux and drove off. Joe made for his BMW, held the passenger door open for me and asked where I wanted to go.

Chapter sixteen

I had looked around to see if there was anything, anybody untoward; but of course I should have carried out the whole drill, including examining underneath the cars. That's if Chuck and Sam were right and there were still people trying to kill me. I wasn't convinced. I knew the Croat would kill me if he found me but he, I was sure, was over the border, probably off the island by now. And I couldn't take the others seriously. Against that, there was the risk of innocent people getting hurt, like Joe and Calliope. I should, I knew, have been more careful for their sake. For now, it was sensible to take minimum precautions. Chuck hadn't phoned and I had no key to his father's flat. I asked Joe to take me to a comparatively quiet bar-café patronized by locals. I thought it would be easier to spot strangers there; an illogical argument because they would use locals if they had any sense.

I drank my beer slowly, skipped through the rest of the morning's newspaper that someone had left behind and watched the coming and going. The CBC television news which was on in one corner of the bar made no mention of my being the driver of the blown up airport car. It just said it was a rent-a-car. You might have got the impression it was waiting for an arriving passenger or had been left by a departing one.

Once the news was over, I phoned the Levendhis flat. Chuck picked up the phone on the second ring.

"Where the hell have you been? I've been doing my nut. I rang you at Joe's but it was closed. We-are-open between-eight-and-five-and-if-you-want-to-leave-an-order-do-so-after-the-beep. How do people decide between beeps and tones? Are you at a bar? It sounds like it. Is it safe? Sorry I'm a bit adrift, it took longer than I thought to get rid of the Peugeot . . ."

I told him where I was and he said he'd be around in quarter of an hour. Perhaps I could wait just inside the door until he drove up. He'd be in a black Lada.

"A Lada?" I said. "Why?"

"Just till tomorrow. Confound the enemy."

A black, not very new, Lada drew up and I got in. It had taken him twelve minutes.

"You see," he said. "Nobody's going to notice this."

He took off with a show of acceleration and aimed towards the plusher and more desirable residential areas and then drove down the ramp of the underground parking of the apartment block. The caretaker noticed our arrival and the slot we occupied.

"I quite like that," said Chuck. "Not easy to palm yourself off as a resident, if he doesn't recognize you. He watched me unpack earlier. After a while he came up and said you're Mr Levendhis' son. Not asking, telling me. I hope he's all right, he said. Nothing wrong, I said, reassuring him that the old man hadn't kicked the bucket. I gave him a couple of quid and he very nearly offered to helped me carry one of the suitcases to the lift."

We waved as we went past his cubby-hole of an office. The flat was spacious and air-conditioned with three decent sized bedrooms and a large living room, now littered with flashing electronic gear and partially unpacked suitcases. Mine, still pristine and closed, were in the nearest bedroom, dominated by a large, red Mark Rothko abstract.

Chuck took two beers from the fridge, flipped the crown corks into the sink and gave me a bottle. While tipping back his beer, he started playing with the Nokia.

"I thought you told me," I said, "that even GSM cellphones weren't totally secure."

"Never use a mobile," he said, "for anything you don't want overheard. That's the safe answer. That's why I was transferring the modem to the telephone line here. I'm disabling the Nokia in case it could be traced. Might be used as a bug to trace us."

He wandered into the kitchen and started opening cupboards and freezers.

"OK, Ben, what are the plans? Who do we contact? What's the agenda for tomorrow? Fill me in while I find us something to eat."

He settled on spaghetti, boiled some water, opened a tin of tomatoes, added garlic, salt, pepper, and some leaves of basil, and had them bubbling and reducing before the pasta was folded into the boiling water. I grated the only cheese I could find; an Irish, KerryGold, Regato.

"Since when was Regato an Irish cheese?" I said. Chuck said nothing. He probably hadn't heard me. He took his food seriously, and therefore his cooking. "First," I went on, "are you listening?" He nodded, as he was trying to drain the pasta. "I have to phone young Mikoyan. Any moment now he should be at his hotel in Ktimo Paphos. Don't ask me why there. Incidentally, I still haven't managed to speak either to Eleni or Eloïse; but I was given a perfectly sensible briefing by the doctor."

I was laying the table, trying to find where knives, forks, plates and glasses lived and avoiding Chuck and his boiling water.

"Are you still listening? I don't think I can take all this hide-and-seek nonsense seriously, Chuck."

"Why ever not? You were the one that was nearly blown to Valhalla. You'd have thought with your father's example before you . . . No: I'm sorry I said that. But, Ben, you know what I mean. You're the last person in the world to take this sort of threat lightly. Aren't you? Surely to God . . ."

He put the dishes on the kitchen table, went back into the living room and returned with a loaf of bread. We sat down and started to eat, both of us hungry as schoolboys.

"All right," I said, "I've been given a contact name at Episkopi. If you drive me there tomorrow, I'll try and get some advice and/or assistance. Professional, a staff officer. OK?"

"OK, provided you play fair and tell him everything we've got."

"What does that amount to? Not a hell of a lot," I said. "I promise I'll tell him everything we know." I crossed my fingers under the table not because I was telling a lie but because I knew, and I suspected Chuck might not, that the special forces liaison colonel couldn't be of much help, even if he wanted to be; and that was pretty unlikely. "Anyway, let's get it right," I went on, "it's not these psychopaths who are chasing me: I'm after them. I want the buggers caught and put away for several lifetimes. I'll hunt them down wherever they are."

"Right on," said Chuck. "Great sentiments. Marvellous motivation. Only trouble is, up to now, they've been doing all the hunting. And just tell me where we start looking. The Yellow Pages?"

"Not so much of the wit, Levendhis, and a lot less of the we," I said. "You're staying here, on base. I'll take friend Mikoyan with me; on the assumption that his and my affairs are linked."

"*Tha dhoúme.*" A Greek catch-all phrase, meaning "We'll see . . ." or "we'll see about that."

I put through a call to William's hotel. Yes: Mr and Mrs Mikoyan had arrived. Twenty minutes ago. Did I want to be put through to their suite? I did. William answered.

"Welcome back to Cyprus," I said.

"How did you know where I was? I was just going to try your number again, Ben. Your voice-machine was on."

"Yes; I'm moving around so don't bother trying to reach me at home. I'll ring you. Probably try and see you tomorrow. But why Paphos? It's a couple of hours away, depending on traffic."

"It's a surprise; explain when I see you."

"I know," I said. "You're not alone."

He laughed, almost a giggle.

"William," I said, "have you got anything more? Any clues, any leads? Any ideas."

"I saw the young Palestinian terrorist . . ."

"I know; but is that it?"

"Yeah. Kind of all. Maybe . . ."

His voice drifted into silence.

"OK, Mikoyan. Not to worry. See you tomorrow. I'll ring in the morning."

"Not too early," he said, recovering his earlier mood.

If it wasn't love, at least it was sex and with a bit of luck William might have found something better to do than chase international terrorists. I could then pick a trained team and go single-mindedly after the Croat instead of being quagmired with amateurs chasing an unknown target as an equal priority. After Chuck's paranoia, Mikoyan's assumed, new preoccupation seemed healthy and forward-looking. I felt quite cheerful.

Chuck dropped me off at the Episkopi base shortly after 11:30 next morning. We had made good time, the only delay being at the garage where he returned the Lada and waited for the two-year old Xantia he had bought, to be ready. They were fixing the air-conditioning. We strolled up and down looking at cars in various states of undress being worked over by mechanics.

"In the end," I said, "what did you do with your mother's Peugeot?"

"I felt a bit of a swine, trying to sell it. She was pretty fond of that car, you know, so rather than get rid of it, I got a bright idea and took it to a body shop for a respray. The foreman reckoned they couldn't start on it for a couple of weeks. I said that was fine. I'd pick it up in three or four weeks' time. They had plenty of space and didn't mind housing it. It was just their order book that was full. I gave them something on deposit."

"What colour?"

"Sunrise orange."

"Your mother will skin you."

"She'll get used to it. At least she'll have the same car. Incidentally, earlier, it must have been at some ungodly hour, didn't I hear you phoning Eloïse?"

"Yeah. At her aunt's flat. She was fine. The hospital was great, the doctor a genius, Eleni wonderful, comfortable, confident. She was less sure about some of the nurses but she'd be popping in for a couple of hours, keeping an eye on things. Good girl. She was hyped up. She'd made contact with her father and was going to see him in a couple of days' time."

"It must be weird," Chuck deliberated, "meeting your father for the first time for what? A quarter of a century? Not really knowing what he looks like even. Remembering very little about him."

"She has some memories of him," I said. "She was five when he left. But they'll be faded and imprecise. Her mother destroyed all photographs of him after he abandoned her."

"Didn't he go off with a Lebanese waiter?"

"So they say."

"Was he bisexual? A closet homosexual?"

"No idea," I said somewhat abruptly. I found I didn't want to discuss him. It made me feel uneasy. I had always known a father-less Eloïse. I didn't like to contemplate an Eloïse with a shady progenitor of unknown origin and mysterious sexual proclivities. I wished she wasn't going to meet him.

Chapter seventeen

The Xantia turned out to be a good buy, a nice, comfortable car with good acceleration and road holding.

"Of course, my dear fellow," said Chuck when I congratulated him. "I not only know my cars, I know my dealers and *garagistes*."

He was being insufferably pleased with himself. I had arranged with William that Chuck would go ahead and brief him. They had never met and William wanted to know who and what he was. I told him Chuck was my partner. I would get a taxi and join them later, after I'd finished my business at the base.

Unfortunately I had been unable to raise Colonel Partridge. No one denied his existence but he wasn't answering. Was he in today? They couldn't say. Had he perhaps an assistant, someone who took messages for him? They weren't answering either. Should I try again later? Had they any idea when he might be in? Try at 11:30.

I thought I might as well turn up then and chance my arm, in person.

I walked in to the main building. A civilian, a Cypriot girl, asked if she could help me. I said I wanted to see Colonel Partridge. She handed me over to a male sergeant who gave me a form, a temporary pass. I wrote down Ben Bolton to see Colonel Partridge.

"Is he expecting you, sir?"

"Yes," I said. "He's had a signal telling him I was coming."

Of course the trouble with having more than one identity is the doubt as to whether you're wearing the right one. I had debated for some time whether to go in uniform and use my military pass but then I had assumed that Sims would have used my civilian name, Ben Bolton, the name he knew me by. I had compromised by wearing a pair of uniform trousers, but they might have been from an ex-service junk-sale surplus store, and an open-necked white shirt. I had my uniform tunic in a black plastic bag inside the attaché case, which I was interested to see no one searched. I had, of course, removed the hand-guns and Chuck had put them in a safe in the flat. It's true there was some kind of x-ray/magnetometer arrangement as you came through the door. Perhaps that was enough of a security check. Perhaps they had all sorts of fancy, invisible detection equipment.

The sergeant turned away and made a telephone call. It seemed to go on for some minutes. Then he came back, looked at his watch and filled out the time on the form, initialled it, gave it to me and said if I went up to the third floor, I'd find room 311 on the left. He gathered I'd have to fill out some more documents there.

Room 311 was singularly unwelcoming. The door was locked and there was a pad with numbers on the lintel where you tapped in the pass-code. A large flashing light said WAIT. I waited. A new message came up. TAP IN YOUR ID AND CODE.

I waited. IF YOU HAVE NO ID USE THE NUMBER ON YOUR TEMPORARY PASS. I tapped it in. There was a further delay and then a green light came on, the door opened and the message light said ENTER.

The office was minuscule, perhaps a third the size of a normal secretarial office. Opposite you, as you came in, was a partition wall, up to the ceiling, painted white with a computer monitor set into it and a ledge coming out into the room, carrying a keyboard. The monitor had a green screen background and not very legible messages in white.

THIS IS AN UNMANNED OFFICE. PLEASE READ THE INSTRUCTIONS CAREFULLY. TYPE THE ANSWERS ACCURATELY AND THEN PRESS RETURN. DO YOU UNDERSTAND? PRESS Y FOR YES, N FOR NO.

I pressed Y. The screen said WELCOME and then YOUR NAME?

I typed in BOLTON, BENJAMIN JAMES and added, in brackets, aka DITCHLING, DAVID, RM. Then it asked for date of birth, address, who I wanted to see and why. I left that at "Confidential". Then it told me to wait and two minutes and 40 seconds later, I timed it, it came up with, PERMISSION REFUSED. RESUBMIT REQUEST IN 48 HOURS. Three coloured buttons showed on the screen. You pressed the green button to open the door and let you out, the yellow if you wanted further information on the British Sovereign Base Areas (SBAs) and the red if you were unsure what to do next. You're damn right, I said to the screen, and pushed the red button. There were sounds of a telephone ringing and then a rather supercilious voice said: "There is no one here to answer your enquiry right now. The office is closed until 2 pm. Try again later." It didn't sound like a prerecorded message: it sounded like a live telephone call trying to sound like a recording. I touched the green button, a buzzer sounded, the door sprang open and with a bound Jack was free.

I took myself and my attaché case to a men's lavatory I'd marked out on the way and locked myself in the shower room which was somewhat more spacious than the loos. I put on my uniform tie and jacket and was preparing to tuck the cap under my arm when I heard the outer door open and shut. Two people had come in and, by the sound, were pissing companionably together.

The one was saying, "I don't know what you do about some of these bloody civilians but they've no idea the trouble they cause, the money they cost." It was the same voice that had been pretending to be a prerecorded message. "They expect us to be at their beck and call, like servants. Take this chap just now. Got hold of the colonel's name somehow, probably wants to sell him something. Has the impertinence to say his business is confidential. I asked the colonel if he knew him and he said he'd never heard of him. I sent the usual message back, saying not today, José, try again some other week and the bugger has the nerve to push the red button and sound the alert. I put on my telephone voice and told him we're shut for lunch. Talking about which, old chap, come and have a drink."

I opened the door gently and just caught the back view of an infantry captain with sandy hair going out of the door. I went to the wash-basins took out my SBA pass and ID, pinned it under my left breast pocket and returned to room 311. This time I entered my ID and gave Ditchling, David, Major, RM as my name, with Ben Bolton as the aka. When it came to purpose of visit, I typed in "To visit Colonel Partridge, see signal from Sims, British Embassy, Cairo."

The reply was: PLEASE RETURN AT 2 PM ... REPEAT ...

118

RETURN AT 14:00 HOURS . . . 2 PM=14:00 HOURS . . . PLEASE
RETURN AT 2 PM . . . REPEAT . . .

I pressed the green button and was sprung.

The bar was beginning to fill up in the officers' mess but there was still
plenty of room, and it was easy to find the sandy-haired captain. He was
talking to a much larger Sapper. I came up on his blind side, ordered a beer
and, addressing the bar steward and anyone who cared to listen, asked if
Colonel Partridge was in the mess. It was the RE major who answered.
pointing down at his companion.

"Don't think so," he said, glancing around quickly. "I've been out all
morning and haven't run into him. This is the chap you want, young Fuller
here. He works closely with Partridge."

Fuller failed to acknowledge. Without turning round, he said in a
loud voice, either to his companion or to the barman, "Is this man a member
of the mess?" and stalked off, taking his glass with him, to sit down for
lunch.

I showed the bar steward my card and said to the sapper, "Dhekelia.
David Ditchling."

He shook my hand and said, "Jack Leonard. Sorry about that. Happy
to have you as a guest; would be even if we didn't have an arrangement with
your lot. Don't know what's got into Richard, been biting everybody's head
off today. Maybe he's had a hard morning."

I raised my eyebrows.

He laughed. "Perhaps not. Have a refill?"

"Thanks," I said. "I've had a frustrating half-hour with a computer.
It's nice to know there are humans still around."

"You've been trying to contact Partridge through that computer
set-up?"

I nodded.

"Silly bloody nonsense."

Fuller strode up to the bar not, it would seem, because he had thought
better of his intemperate behaviour but more likely because no one had come
to serve him and he wanted another drink.

Leonard called over to him; "Richard, you owe this gentleman an
apology."

"Why?" For the first time he turned to look at me. He was in his
early thirties, compact, not very tall, with a fair, almost ginger moustache,

a paratrooper, with wings, and, he would let you know, the balls to prove it.

"Because," Leonard drawled, "he's your superior officer, belongs to our brother-sorry-sister mess at Dhekelia and you behaved like a silly, bad-tempered little shit. And because he's spent half the morning on your ill thought out computer programme."

Fuller moved along the bar towards us. I saw the change in his face as he hoisted in the major's crown and the SBS insignia and I watched him checking the DSC+ and the South Georgia, Falklands, Oman and Desert Storm ribbons. The latter he wore himself.

"Richard Fuller," he said, putting out his hand, which I shook reluctantly. "Sorry if I seemed rude. Just in a filthy temper. Need to mind my manners."

I nodded. He'd need to mend rather more than that. He was a right little tick.

"The unmanned office," Major Leonard intervened, "it's a new gimmick. Fuller says he had to do something. Every young squaddie, and half the male Cypriot population of Limassol, was trying to see the colonel and join the SAS."

"Unfortunately his name," Fuller piped up, "and Special Forces linked to it, somehow got into what they call the public domain. Hence the nonsense with the computer. You should have rung."

He couldn't keep a querulous tone out of his voice. I stared at him, more of a glare than a stare. He looked away.

"Of course, I phoned," I said. "Several times. They said no one was taking his calls." I paused to give him the chance to say something. Nothing. "Perhaps you'd be good enough to tell me whether Colonel Partridge will be in this afternoon."

"He'd bloody better be," said Fuller. "There's a mass of incoming signals waiting for him."

I said I had to make a telephone call. As I went off, at a slow, dignified pace, Jack Leonard said to Fuller: "You did yourself a large bit of no good there. What's wrong with you?"

"The man's a phoney," said Fuller.

I had been thinking along the same lines. I didn't suppose I would pass my medical and even if, by some unaccountable miracle, I did, I doubted that I would be properly fit enough to do the annual Arctic, Jungle and Desert trials, let alone the underwater swims and dives. I'd really have to face up to giving the SBS up before it gave me up—even as a mere officer on the reserve. I was going over the hill, I supposed; autumnal thoughts, decline, decay, ageing, enfeeblement. Then I thought: rubbish! It wasn't the end of the world. I would still be a major on the reserve list of the Royal Corps of Marines and what's wrong with that? And for the moment I was still part of the SBS, still on the strength, as I had been for the last seventeen years.

I finally raised Chuck on his mobile. He was in Paphos and had spoken to William but had yet to meet him. They were due to have lunch together in half-an-hour. I said I'd try and get a taxi to William's hotel when I'd seen the colonel. And no, I had no idea when that was likely to be.

Back in the mess, I was thinking of sitting down to lunch on my own when Jack Leonard came and took my arm and led me to a table.

"Fuller's a fool," he said. "I think he must have heard he's not being promoted, been passed over again. But no excuse for that sort of behaviour. No excuse at all."

"Have you known him long?"

"We served in the SAS together, a few years back. Only reason, I suppose, I put up with him."

We had an agreeable enough lunch—no shop in the mess—and Leonard took me back to his office. 312 was on the other side of the corridor and it led into 314 where there was a secretary and 316 which was the colonel's so far empty room. Apart from a few, carefully framed, recruiting posters from the 1930s extolling the rural and overseas delights of being a member of His (King George V's) Majesty's Armed Forces, his office contained two computers, four telephones, a printer, several army and MoD manuals, instructions, standing orders and regulations, and two exquisite miniature steam engines, working models of gleaming, brass and copper and steel. Fuller's room, he had shown me, was across the way, 313, next to the unmanned office.

Shortly after two there was a commotion, a spurt of activity with doors opening and closing. Leonard got up, went through the communicating door to 314, and closed it behind him. Five minutes later he returned and said the colonel would see me now. He ushered me through as the colonel came out of his room, hand outstretched.

"Partridge," he said. "Gather you've been waiting hours. You met my assistant, Captain Fuller. Just had a word with him; told him to find another job. Absolutely useless. I inherited him and after a fortnight, I looked forward with dread to coming into the office. It's like going to a class on Wednesday afternoons when you hated and despised the schoolmaster who always took it. Why Wednesday? Halfway through the week and cricket in summer, rugger in winter, to follow. Except he'd keep you in, if he could. He blighted the day. At least it was only one day a week. With Fuller it's a daily torment.

"I read your file after I heard from Cairo. Impressive." He was tall, lanky but filled out, muscular, with deep-set, dark brown eyes, thin, aquiline nose, large hands, long, fine fingers, thinning brown hair. "Sims explained your predicament and brought it up to date with the capture and escape of . . ." he looked at the notes on his desk, ". . . Stjepan Zkrakovic. I gather you were responsible for the first and not for the second." He looked sternly at me. I nodded. "What did you think we could do for you?"

"Thank you for seeing me, sir." I said. "I was wondering if there were any plans for using Special Forces for seizing more war criminals. If so, I'd be quite useful with this one. Failing that, is there any way I could borrow two or three men for a detached, an unofficial, hunting party for, say, a week? They'd be on leave and I'd fund them."

"To plans, probably. To your official/unofficial involvement, no. You're on the reserve anyway, and signed off sick, wounded, whatever. And no to detaching troops. We're far too short-handed and frankly I don't think Joint Command would approve the scheme. Also your Croat is not on the list—which you know, of course, doesn't exist. And as far as anyone is aware, he's not making for former Jug-land, which is the only region where our rules of engagement &c. &c."

"I suspect," I said, tentatively, focusing on his OBE and DSO, "you know a hell of a lot more than I do. Perhaps, Colonel, you could give me a steer or two. I'm not asking for top cosmic intelligence, just any crumbs that might help."

"Three things." He counted them, tapping with his left forefinger on the knuckles of his right hand. "Your Croat went not to Istanbul or Ankara or Izmir but to Bodrum. Private jet. He joined the ordinary ferry to Kos and made for the airport soon after. I expect he's in Athens by now and we'll have lost him.

"Two. An American, Mike Cable, Rear-Admiral USN, NATO, Naples and further East, has been asking after you." He shuffled some papers on his desk and came up with an envelope and half a sheet of notes. "Here's his contact number. Says he knew you in Washington on account of the

Falklands. Halfway through, he said. Spoke warmly of you. May have information, blah blah, of use to you. Whatever the hell that's about.

"Finally, get in touch with the Naval and Air Attaché in Athens. I'll route any information through him."

I thanked him and got up to leave. He saw me to the inner office door.

"We never met. Jack Leonard tried to answer your queries, unspecified. He told you you're not cleared by the medics, you're still on sick leave and, for the moment, you may be reserved but you're not on the active list. Whatever your official status, you're to be considered retired until you're called back. Is that clear?" He paused: I nodded. He smiled sympathetically, a charming smile, highlighting the developing, already deep-etched lines around his mouth. I reckoned he was ten years my senior; maybe more. "You're on your own," he said. "Watch your back. It's not like being part of a beautifully trained and select company, properly equipped, resourced and backed up."

"Don't I know it," I said, but with a valedictory wave of the hand he had disappeared into his office.

Major Leonard signed my original day pass, made out in the name of Ben Bolton. I changed, in his office, back to modified civilian rig, and he walked me downstairs, saying that he didn't know anything about my business but if there was any way he could help, give him a buzz. He made sure I handed in the pass, avoiding later security panics of the-one-that-came-in-and-didn't-go-out variety. I waited twenty minutes in the entrance hall for my taxi to appear. It seemed a long day.

123

Chapter eighteen

S omewhere I remember reading, Paphos now claims to have taken over from Limassol as the most populous resort. That means it has more tourist beds available. It also means a rush of not very edifying buildings, often put up with little thought either for the environment or the aesthetic. Oh hell, I'm just getting old; once you're past 35, you've as many memories as expectations and, whatever your politics, you're going to start bemoaning the past. Paphos is all right: it's just that it was better before all the developments, the explosion in tourism, took place. A lot better. William Mikoyan had sensibly booked into an agreeable, old but renovated hotel, with spacious rooms and a traditional atmosphere, a sense of having been around for a century or two and not one of your re-enforced concrete and cement Johnny-come-latelies. It was in Ktima which is the upper town of Paphos and it had a decent view of, but was not on, or for that matter, very near to, the sea.

Paphos, Cyprus

I met William at the bar. He looked bronzed and well, a little less rounded in the face and waist, but, as always, elegantly clothed. His mother sent her regards. He had been horrified to hear from Chuck about what had happened to my mother. He had had no idea. Was this connected in any way to the Cairo killings?

I made one of those Greek facial gestures that means: maybe, perhaps, probably, but who knows? and, on the other hand, six of one and half-a-dozen of the other.

"Could be," I said, in case he hadn't picked up the right signal. After all, the Armenians probably had a different system of gestures, tics, eyebrow movements, twistings of mouth and fluttering of hands. Not everyone was lucky enough to be brought up on the expressive cartoon illustrations of "Pappas".

"Chuck told us about your Croatian terrorist. That was courageous, Ben. I admire you enormously. That was very good."

He looked at me, his large brown eyes lambent with hero-worship. I made a depreciatory shrug. "It would have been a damn sight better," I said, "if he hadn't escaped."

"What now, Ben? What do we do?"

"We go to Athens. But first we sit down and have a drink."

He ordered some kind of mixed liqueur cocktail, all colours, crushed ice and glacé cherries and I had a horse's neck, Cyprus brandy, ice, lemon and ginger ale, a restorative, a reviver.

"When?"

"As soon as we can book a flight. Realistically," I said, "tomorrow."

"I'm not quite sure about tomorrow." He sounded dismayed.

"But William," I said, "where's the hot, familial piety, traditional revenge; the vengeance of the godly. I thought this was your version of the vendetta. You wanted, you told me, to catch the bastards—and then consign them to the everlasting flames of hell. Or something along those lines."

"Oh, I do. I do. But what's the point in going to Athens? We have no lead."

"We have my Croat," I said.

"But he's got nothing to do with Cairo and my family."

"How can you be sure? Anyway I get the message. You're not showing quite the same eagerness. So perhaps tomorrow. Maybe the day after. Or the day after that?"

"Yes," he said, with some alacrity. "You go ahead. I'll catch you up. A day or two later. You'll want to see your mother of course. And Eloïse."

"OK. Fine by me. But remember I have a target, a name, a face: you haven't. If I run across The Turk, I'll give him your regards."

"Don't be angry," he said, a plaintive small boy.

"I'm not angry," I said, "just tired. And maybe a mite bewildered."

"I think," I said, after a pause, "I'd better get back to Larnaca. I've a lot to do. Where's Chuck?"

He looked at his watch. "He'll be down in a minute. With my Surprise." He smiled to himself, pleased. "Have another drink?"

"As long as Chuck's fit to drive."

The second horse's neck seemed weaker, without fizz and zing; stale, flat and unprofitable, like the day itself. Why was I bothering to keep this show on the road?

"Oh, I nearly forgot," William said, hand in breast pocket, "a letter for you from my mother."

"What's in it this time?" Having been bitten twice and feeling decidedly shy of wily Armenians bearing gifts, I wanted to be forewarned . . .

"I don't know. Truly. She didn't tell me."

I opened it quickly; a short note wishing me luck, thanking me for all I was doing to help William (probably better directed at his new girl friend, I thought, whoever she was) and enclosing a credit card, in my name, to be filled out at once, debited to her account, a Gold American Express Card. Wow!

126

"You better sign it at once."

"I'm going to," I said, through gritted teeth, and had just finished doing so and putting it in my wallet, when Chuck materialized and said, all bouncing with joy, "I've discovered a place for *meze* round the corner; quite stunning."

I looked up. It wasn't all he'd discovered. The adjective, it was clear, had nothing to do with the food: it was transferred from Katie, Sims's absconding Australian wife, William's Surprise and, by the look of it, Chuck's newest downfall.

"Long time no see, Ben," she said, bending down to kiss both my cheeks before I could get to my feet. I had forgotten the sheer, uncontrolled volume of her voice. "Surprise, surprise."

I had been going to treat myself to a business class ticket, I was getting the taste for more spacious travel, partly to test the Gold AMEX, but as it turned out I had no choice. The flight was full: it was business class or nothing. The beneficial effects of the additional comfort and, marginally, of space had dissipated themselves by the time I joined the usual, long, disorganized, taxi queue, abetted by a weary policeman, in the afternoon heat at Athens airport. You had no option, took whichever vehicle presented itself as you came to the seething head of the column. My taxi was small, middle-aged and, of course, without air conditioning. It smelt of sweat and stale, stubbed out cigarettes; the air outside of pollution, the Athenian *néphos*. As we set off I saw the clock wasn't running. I pointed to it.

"Your meter," I said in English "isn't on." He looked bewildered. Perhaps he was. I pointed again.

"*Ti thélete?*" he said. What do you want?

I told him in a burst of Cypriot Greek which I knew he would find difficult to understand but might get the drift. After a second or two he recognized it as some form of probably Ancient Greek and nodded acknowledgement of the odd, recognized word or two with a nod. He turned the meter on with an "*O'ti thélete, kyrie*", having the sense of "Whatever Sir desires".

"*Apó pou eísaste?*" A good question: where did I come from? I hastily said, "*Apó ton Kypro*" before I got bogged down in any further soul-searching. "Oh, Cyprus. Really?" I think he was saying in Greek which I barely hoisted in. "What's it like, these days? You can't believe everything you read in the papers." Something along those lines. But I nodded off.

I had asked to be taken to the Grande Bretagne, no longer perhaps the most fashionable or the most comfortable but still the grandest as well as the most historic hotel in Athens. I suggested the taxi-driver wait while I booked in and handed over my bags but the doorman, tall, commanding and rigged like a full dress admiral, took one look at him and told him to move on. I paid him off and petitioned for another taxi, in ten minutes' time, to go to the hospital.

It wasn't altogether what I had expected; more reminiscent of some medieval lazar-house than a contemporary hospital in a European Union capital city. The corridors were jammed with the sick, ailing and supplicant. Doctors moved through them like gods from another planet, ignoring the pleas, the grasping hands, the proffered suppurating limbs, the failing hearts. Nurses, supercilious, brutal in their disregard for the congregating, would-be patients, saw themselves as cloaked in some slightly dimmer celestial light, lesser demi-gods maybe, but still universes above the surrounding, beseeching, all too evidently mortal, ruck.

Once I fought my way through to Eleni's ward, it was a transformation. She had a room to herself with air conditioning and if it wasn't exactly *Home and Gardens*, it was pleasant enough apart from the noxious bright blue-green paint on the walls. She was looking rather well and beautiful, though her face seemed to have lengthened, to have become like one of those Byzantine icons of St Helena. An icon with lines and wrinkles added. Was the suffering continuous? I watched her for some while before she noticed me. She had her ear-phones on and was listening to a CD. I walked round the bed till she saw me. Her face lit up and she took off the cans and held out her arms.

"How lovely. I thought I couldn't possibly expect you until the day after tomorrow. A splendid amazement for a Tuesday."

Constantinople fell to the Osmanli Turks on a Tuesday, the 20th May 1453 to be precise, and, ever since, Tuesday has been a day of ill omen, not the day to have an operation or make up your mind to do anything important. Mum, in her Greek Orthodox mode, could be as superstitious as any black-garbed village *yiayiá*.

I bent down and kissed her.

"Come and sit down Benjy and let's look at you."

I sat down on the end of the bed and subjected myself to the same maternal inspection, it seemed to me, that I had undergone since first going to school, with an equal measure of well-worn comfort and resentment. Dammit. I was grown up. I'd washed, shaved, polished my shoes and even had a clean handkerchief in my trouser pocket.

"Well, *you* don't look too bad," I said, getting in first. "What have they been doing to you?"

"You're looking tired," she said accusingly. "And you've lost some weight; not that that will do you any harm."

"Where's Eloïse? Has she been visiting you?"

"The dear girl's been popping in every day, sometimes twice a day. She's very good at dealing with the nurses and" – her voice dropped and she looked carefully to make sure none were within earshot – "between you and me they're not up to much; need a good shake, bone idle and truculent with it. Except today, that is, she's not been in. She said something about meeting her father and going to get some new clothes. The other way round, more like. But I wasn't listening too carefully. The foot was hurting away as though it was being gnawed by a rat. Doctor Haralambopoulos says that's because it's healing. Sounds a bit glib, that little explanation. Just a little? *Lígo, lígo?* Don't you think? But it lets up after a while." She paused, contemplated her pain and added. "Usually."

Another pause to shift gear, change subject. Enough about her. She looked tired, almost sleepy, her eyes getting smaller by the minute.

"Do you always have to carry that confounded attaché case around with you?"

"Yup, I surely do, ma'am," I said. "Clean pants, socks, the odd sexual aid and my mobile phone. Couldn't do without it."

"Go on with you, soppy date." She laughed, her eyelids fluttered and stilled and she slid gently into sleep.

I thought I'd phone Eloïse but I couldn't get any sort of signal inside the ward. I left the room and tried to find a public telephone. They were all in use. Back at the GB, I got through to the apartment. Her aunt said she was out but expected back for dinner. I could try again, after 9 p.m. Aunt Aspasia didn't sound wildly enthusiastic, not overflowing with friendship, offers of hospitality and affection. Why? She'd never met me, as far as I could remember.

I went out for a stroll round the block. Summer was over and Athens was back to normal. There was always the hiatus, the blissful few weeks when the traffic halves and all Athens—bar tourists and the few misguided foreigners who pretend to continue working—leave the city. Then, after August 15th, the feast day for the birth of the Virgin Mary, the city starts to fill up again, the traffic revives, as does the pollution, and at the first hint of autumn, the temperature still up in the 30s, inhabitants start wishing each other a happy winter. It might have been September but it was a decidedly hot day. Now with the days drawing in, the evenings were a bit cooler and I had been thinking of sauntering across to the national gardens but Syndagma, Constitution Square, was made hideous, as was many another traffic roundabout, by the still continuing construction work on the metro. So I just circled the rectangle, refusing to get led astray into crossing any roads. Police whistles were being blown aggressively to encourage the traffic to move faster. Tempers were getting frayed. Taxis were hooting, buses were edging cars out of their lane. Dust was everywhere and if I'd been wearing a face mask it would have been clogged. I darted into the air-conditioned and filtered comfort of the GB corner bar.

It was going through one of its recurrent changes in atmosphere. This time the excellent barman, Tassos, the pianist with his slightly intellectual, slightly jokey, versions of jazz and night club classics, were unchanged, as of course was the décor: it was the clientele that had metamorphosed from didactic, witty, cultural, political observers of the daily scene, to what looked like small town mafiosi and their mistresses, with flashy gold on the men and flashy jewels on the women. They were also loud-voiced and spoke, almost exclusively, about money and deals. Not, to be honest, that I understood their jargon or their accents all that well.

I was finishing my first draught beer when Tassos passed me the telephone. It was Eloïse.

"Darlink," she said. "How lovely to know you're here. I'm so sorry I missed you when you called earlier. I've got so much to talk about. Discovering a parent, a father. Darling Ben, it's been so exciting, I cannot tell you. He's very attractive, not so much physically, but in personality. He's magnetic and fascinating. I've missed you too, of course. Often; especially at night. When did you arrive? When can I see you?"

"How about now? Why don't you get a cab and come down to the GB? I don't think your aunt would want me there. I get the impression she's not very keen on me. I'll be in the corner bar, the small one."

"Anastasia is a bit of a b—," she changed her mind, "witch. She's rather anti-Semitic, you know. She speaks about Those People; meaning Jews. I think when she was in Alexandria she sold some of the family rings to a Jewish merchant. Afterwards she was sure he'd done her down. Perhaps the rest of the family blamed her and she needed a scapesheep."

"Goat," I said, "scapegoat. Well that's all right then; I'm glad to know it's nothing personal."

"How could it be, darling? She's never met you; has she?"

"And your Egyptian father," I said, "how did Aunt Anastasia feel about her sister marrying a Muslim?"

"Badly, I think. Anyway, it turns out he's not an Egyptian; he's some kind of Turk, a Kurdish Turk or a Turkish Kurd. Imagine how my Greek family felt: a Turk! He's very strange, that man: mysterious, fascinating. You feel that things happen around him. I find myself drawn to him. Funny? But then half of me comes from him. He keeps on saying he wants me to come to Turkey with him."

"What does he do?" I said.

"I don't know. Something shady, I think, not quite honest. But I don't really know. He wants me to see his home, it's my family home too, he says, and see how nice young Muslim women behave. Sometimes he makes me shiver."

"Perhaps I should come and stand by you, meet him, face him down."

"No, that would not be a good idea." She laughed. "He's—what's your phrase?—got it out for you."

"Got it in for me," I said. "Why? He doesn't know me, never met me."

"You're Jewish, darling, and sleeping with his daughter. He doesn't say that. He says dating me. No: it would not work. I have to see this through on my own. My father, my problem. It's no big deal. And anyway, it would be fun, seeing where I come from with him, my just restored Papa."

"So what about your newly arrived fiancé? How about grabbing a taxi and coming down to the Grande Bretagne now?" I said. "Or, if you'd rather walk, I'll set off and meet you halfway up Voukarestiou. It's still early. I want to see you so much, Eloïse, my love."

"That's sweet of you Benjy dearest but I'm really horribly tired and, if truth were told, headachy. We're just going to eat and I did promise to be in tonight, have dinner with my aunt and uncle. You do understand, don't you, sweetest? I've been out every other night."

"Not with me, you haven't."

"You were in Cyprus, silly. How could I have? Of course, I'd rather be with you. We'll meet to morrow. If that's all right. Is it? Please."

I paid for the beer, went out, walked round the corner to Zonar's and had an undistinguished but perfectly comforting meal on my own. I'd see Eloïse tomorrow evening. I too was tired. An early night was a good idea. The father sounded pretty dire. Could she, should she, cope on her own? Was she right to try?

I was put through to Cy Drucker at half-past eight in the morning, as soon as I phoned the US Embassy. He was, he said, very pleased that I had rung. Couldn't rearrange anything this morning. He had a heavy schedule. But how about lunch? What was the name of that semi-Turkish, Istanbul, restaurant?

"Yerafínika," I said. "Spelt with a Gamma. pronounced with a Y."

"Yeah; that's it. Gerafinika. See you there. Two-thirty? OK? I'll get one of the girls to book. Watson."

"Watson?"

"Nom de guerre. For table bookings. That type thing. Like in, elementary my dear Watson. Who was that actor? Nigel Bruce, wasn't it? Basil Rathbone was Sheerluck Jones."

He sounded different, more confident, less gushing.

I rang the British Embassy and, remembering I was in Ditchling mode, spoke to the Naval Attaché. Yes, he'd heard from Partridge. Yes, he'd be happy to see me. 12:30. Couldn't give me lunch. Not today. Apologies.

Completing my diplomatic round, I phoned an acquaintance at the Embassy of Cyprus and told him where I was staying, in case Detective Superintendent Angeloglou or either of the men from the ministries wanted to get in touch with me.

I also phoned Eloïse. Her aunt said she was still asleep. She would tell her I rang when she woke up. I decided to walk through Kolonaki to the hospital and see Eleni. It would be a reasonably decent hour by then for visiting patients and it was a short stroll to the British Embassy, so I would be well set up for my next appointment.

Chapter nineteen

By the time I arrived at Gerafinika, pronounced Yerafínika, to find that Mr Watson had not yet put in an appearance, I was ready for a drink. I ordered a raki, putting my case on one of the empty chairs. I had refused the offer to have it taken to the cloakroom. The restaurant was crowded and mostly, it seemed at first sight, with Japanese businessmen. Perhaps a convention, a trade mission, was in town. But there were isolated pockets of Greeks, Brits, French, Germans and even a pair of Turkish dips and one table of Americans, combining business and pleasure by the look of the wives.

I rang Eloïse again. Her aunt said wearily that she was out but if I was Ben, she had said she was meeting me later, this evening. Thank you; funnily enough, I knew that. And if I weren't Ben? Would she be asking why I wasn't wherever Eloïse was waiting for me? Was there someone else waiting for her at another restaurant? The tennis partner from Cyprus? Paranoid jealous nonsense; she was probably on her way to the hospital to visit Eleni. Still she was acting a bit strangely. Probably the effect of the father. I'd hear all about it when we met. I didn't like the sound of him.

Drucker arrived, sweaty and contrite. He was twenty minutes late. "Couldn't get away sooner," he said, accompanying the explanation with a limp, moist handshake. "Large regional meeting chaired by host Head of Mission, five ambos present. Hey" – this to a waiter – "how long does a man have to wait for a drink here? You could die of dehydration. Two beers. How about you, Ben?"

I said a beer would be fine.

"OK, three beers then. What beer do you keep? Got any of that new local brew, Mythos? Good. And when you have the time we'd like a menu. OK? But be sure and bring the beers first. Soon. Like now. OK?

"That's better." He opened his jacket and eased his belt. "I was right: there's always so much noise here no one can overhear anything. Not that we're going to discuss anything too confidential, are we? So how's the mysterious Mr Bolton? Caught any more Croat racial cleansers lately? What's your buddy Mikoyan up to this time round? They tell me he's back in the area. And your partners at SATIS? Any good scams? Christ, what's taking him so long, if you'll pardon the French? All he's goddamned got to do is take the beers out of the fridge, put two glasses on a tray, bring them here and pop the caps.

"Can we start all square, Ben? Forget the Cairo hotel scene. I was told, *told*, to baby-nurse him. Find him a nice hotel. I fixed him up in what had been the best bordello room in the city. I hope you enjoyed the little joke with the two-way mirror; that's if you were there in time and I think you were. I thought you ought to know what he was up to. Yeah, well I'd heard your name around town. Anyway I can't abide that crap. I hate being tugged at a distance by people I don't know. Getting on to Foggy Bottom. Strings being pulled from State for Christ's sake, by these unknown Armenians."

"Anything wrong with Armenians? You not happy with them, Cy?"

"Where's that turd of a waiter? Of course, I get on with Armenians. I'm tolerant as all get-out; have to be since I'm half-Egyptian. What did your Tommies call them; Gyppos? Half-Gyppo that's me; my mother. Father was solid, all-American, WASP, class act. Groton and Princeton. He's coming, that apology for a waiter. At last. You took your time, friend, but don't get me wrong, grateful for small mercies. The beer looks good, Ben. Tastes good."

He paused, long enough to finish one bottle and start on the next.

"As I say I don't like being jerked about. Makes me bombastic, disagreeable, falsely humble, Uriah Heep and didactic. OK? You know I've got good Arabic, good contacts. You guess I'm not CIA." His voice dropped.

"You bet I'm not a regular, career dip, State Department bright boy. So what am I?

"Where's that waiter? He's disappeared again. Didn't I ask for a menu some hours ago?" He waved his napkin, snapped his fingers, hit the table with the flat of his hand. He'd have made a marvellous undercover agent. Every table looked at us. So eventually did a senior waiter who came over and asked if everything was all right. Drucker told him. Then ordered for both of us. Hot *karavéedes* and sirloin steaks, all from the grill.

"Let's just say I'm a kind of Fed. All sorts of agencies, not just Langley, need to know, want to know, find it useful to know, about the Arab world. I'm their man on the spot, their hound dog, their eyes and ears at the embassies of the near east, in the souks and bourses of the Levant."

The food arrived; a salad and the delicious small crayfish. He ate delicately, silently and reverently.

"All right," I said, "so crime and counter-terrorism in FBI terms; firearms; drugs; money-laundering; treasury matters; presidential security."

"Shshsh!" He looked round warily. "Someone will hear you. Walls have ears."

"You should have thought of that before you started thumping the table."

"I don't reckon any of these guys," he examined a table or two, "constitutes much of a threat."

How the hell did he know? Bloody amateur.

The steaks came and while we ate them, he made light conversation. Did I know that Katie had left Jeremy Sims? He'd never thought it would last. Sad for Jeremy though. He wasn't likely to marry again in a hurry. Personally, he confided, he was not much of a marrying man. I might wonder what sort of a man was he then. That was a good question but he wasn't sure quite how to answer it. Maybe when he knew me a bit better, he would find the right way of doing so. Maybe.

We had coffee and fruit and, for him, an ice cream. Would I mind coming back to the embassy with him? He looked at his watch, paid the bill and we left. Outside there was an embassy car. I told him I wanted to go back to the hotel first. The truth was I didn't want my attaché case searched, x-rayed or opened; and if I had to risk tampering, the concierge at the GB seemed a safer bet. I gave it to him with a 5,000 drachma note, told him not to let anyone else touch it and to keep it in his sight. I'd be back within the hour.

135

At the US Embassy I went through the full security drill with a marine sergeant and then the various checks as we proceeded through the building, passing more sensitive areas. Drucker was using a middle-sized office with no name on the door but a title; Counsellor, Cultural Affairs.

"Coffee? Juice? Iced water? Cognac?"

I shook my head.

"I'd like you to look at some of these photos, see if you recognize anyone." They were spread over his desk. There must have been a dozen. He collected them, shuffled them in some sort of order and handed them over to me, watching my face intently. Some of them were police mug shots, properly and unflatteringly lit, full face and side face. Others were grainy, as though shot at extreme range with a telephoto lens. Others looked like blown up snapshots from a family album. The penultimate was my Croat.

"That's Stjepan Zkrakovic." I said.

"Certain?"

"Swearable. On oath. Bankable."

"Look at the rest."

"There's only one pic left," I said and looked more closely. It was of a heavy man in his early fifties, perhaps, with a large, strong face, staring, protuberant, dark eyes, what looked like black, curly hair, worn long, a wide mouth with thin lips and no neck to speak of. It seemed as though he was hunching his shoulders up, and the one was appreciably higher than the other, not to the extent that he was deformed but so that there was a suggestion of permanent imbalance. There was something about the man that I felt was almost familiar; but I didn't know him, I didn't recognize him.

"No," I said. "Just the Croat."

"Now, listen up, young Ben Bolton. There are, as the Hollywood scriptwriters used to say, wheels within wheels within wheels. Perhaps your Croat is employed by one of the gangs who run drugs and arms and anything else that pays. I'm putting my money on a family in Turkey with fingers in most pies. They're fiercely Islamist, anti-western, anti-Atatürk reforms. They're big in hard drugs and arms of all sizes but not averse to a bit of useful terrorism, like shaking up the Egyptian government, killing a few Jews or Armenians on the side, preparing the basis for a properly Islamic Egypt and an Islamic Near East, tolerant to wholesale drug trading. A weird morality, that. Same thing with the Taliban in Afghanistan. Death if you touch alcohol. Smiles if you sell opium to the kids of the rest of the world. You can see why Mother, returning to her homeland, after Father died, rejected any idea of coming home to Islam and opted for the Copts as a suitable compromise, Egyptian of its essence but also Christian to its backbone and very ancient. It suited her well. I know you met Father Elias. He told me. He took to you, thought you spiritual, gentle."

He snorted with more of a grimace than a smile, looked at me intently.

"Somewhere along the line, among the informants I've been cultivating, there was a whisper, a name; a Britisher, it was said, from Cyprus: Bolton. Bad news to the faithful, this guy. Heap big trouble. Knows too much. Kill."

I shivered, geese walking over my grave.

"I wish to hell I had some kind of inkling what the too much was that I'm supposed to know. It might help to chop short this farrago of nonsense. Not to mention prolong my life."

"Yup," he said, judiciously. "It might do just that."

"The Turk the young Palestinian terrorist was talking about, is he your drug-dealing Turk?"

"Possibly. Except my guy's a Kurd, but no matter, a Turkish Kurd from a powerful Kurdish family who threw their lot in with the previous Islamist government of Turkey and are still banking on an Islamicization of Turkish politics and institutions. And keeping a large whack of their drug-and-crime empire. And so far there's no identification to put him, or any other, member of the family at the slaying of the Armenian bus load."

"Why would he want to take part?"

"Who knows? Blood lust; Islamic fervour; exercise of direct power? Dare the Egyptian government to catch you? Prove yourself? Win friends; influence; admiration? Who the hell knows? He's probably a psycho. Perhaps it amuses him, killing little old ladies."

I got up to go. "But we don't know it's him. We don't know he was there and we don't know where he is now?"

"Yeah, that's about it. And I've got so much invested in this thing I'm not even going to murmur another word. OK?"

"Sure," I said, "I've only got a life to lose. Not like a job or a mission or a crusade. Ciao."

"I'll get a car to take you back. It'll be waiting for you outside. Shalom, Benjamin son of Rachel/Eleni."

"Oh, shit," I said. "Not another anti-Semite."

"In no way. You do me wrong, friend."

137

"OK." I shook his hand but I wasn't convinced; not one hundred per cent.

The concierge at the GB handed me back my case of tricks and no, there were no messages. It was just gone 5 p.m. and I wasn't due to meet Eloïse till quarter past eight. Plenty of time for shower, siesta and getting dressed. First things first, unpack the goodies from Partridge.

I had got the packet from Captain Gooding RN, the British Naval Attaché. It had come through in the bag from Nicosia. I hadn't liked to open it at the time—it seemed impolite—so I had put it in my case.

Gooding was an ascetic-looking four-ringer with very pale blue, hooded eyes and thinning blond hair with silver glints. He called me Major Ditchling throughout. I got the feeling he didn't much like Special Forces. He apologised for wearing uniform but said he was going to a NATO lunch. The only other thing he had to proffer was that he had been asked to tell me that the Croat had arrived in Athens and gone to ground. The watchers had lost him. Sorry about that. Nothing to do with him. I asked if it were possible to use a reasonably secure telephone to try and contact Rear-Admiral Mike Cable USN. He buzzed and a slight, young, smiling two-and-a half took me to his somewhat smaller office and raised a circuit. The admiral was visiting Turkey, we were told. His staff would ring us back with a contact number, good for 24 hours. Lieutenant-Commander Ray Parker, the Assistant to the Naval Attaché, said he'd get the message to me at the GB but if I wanted a secure line I'd better come back and let him fix one up at the embassy.

Here in the hotel room, several hours later, was the first time I had been alone and in comparative privacy and able to examine the packet. It was carefully sealed and Sellotaped, and took me a minute or so to undo. Inside was a note and two quite heavy small parcels wrapped in what felt like an industrial grade version of carbon paper. The note said: *This gizmo might help. It's supposed not to show up on scans, x-rays &c. Read the instructions carefully before assembling, let alone using!*

It was a hand-gun, barrel and stock separate, but neither were made of steel or any other metal; plastic perhaps or carbon fibre. In the other parcel were the bullets and they again were non-metallic. I took my clothes off, lay on the bed and read the instructions, which were unbelievably complicated, slowly and diligently. It was an hour, at least, before I had the thing properly assembled and ready for use. It felt comfortable in the hand, even my poorly right hand. Loading and unloading were simple enough exercises but short of going on a range there was no way of testing how it shot. It had an electronic firing system and was said to be "quiet". The final piece of advice was: "*ONLY USE IN AN EMERGENCY.*"

Also in the packet was a very neat little underarm holster. I experimented with this and with drawing and aiming the gun. Fitted to my satisfaction, I fell asleep with it making a ridge in the bed cover.

I was woken up by the telephone. It was Chuck in Larnaca.

"I've been thinking," he said. "You shouldn't go around believing that you're chasing them. They, most decidedly, are after you. And they know more about you. They know where you are, who you are and they know why you're a danger to them—and you don't. Nor do you really know who they are. So be careful, Ben, very careful."

It was half past six. I got up and had a shower. Chuck was right, of course. This was no time for arrogance or make-believe. They held most of the cards. I would take care.

The phone rang again. It was an encore from Chuck.

"Sam's trying to get hold of you," he said. "Some Israeli mates of his have interesting information; interesting to you, that is. He seemed to think it urgent."

"OK," I said. "Sam always thinks his messages are urgent. I'll wait and see. I'm going off to meet Eloïse at 8.15. I'll give her your love. Have a nice evening."

At ten to eight the telephone rang again. Guess who?

"I was thinking over what you said," Chuck said, "about having a nice evening and I thought you ought to know I'm having a lousy evening. I've fallen madly in love with that Australian Katie and I'm corrugated with jealousy. Damn William Mikoyan. Enjoy yourself with Eloïse."

He rang off before I could say anything minatory. I left the room five minutes later and just as I started walking to the lift I heard the phone ringing. To hell with it, I said, I can't face yet another of Chuck's *arrières pensées*. If he has anything more important to say the message will keep till I get back.

Chapter twenty

Voukarestíou, the Greek translation of Bucharest, is a not very long but quite steep street, running from Stádiou, one of the main traffic routes into Constitution Square, up to the prominence of Lycavitós, the charming wooded hill, with its chapel of St George on top, that rises virtually in the centre of the city. From Akadimías to Skoufá much of it is a comparatively narrow pedestrian precinct, although some vans and cars still make deliveries. It has jewellers and clothes boutiques and furniture shops and antique dealers and restaurants and cafés. I was walking up from the bottom end and Eloïse, or so I imagined, would be walking down from Skoufá where her aunt's flat was. She had said let's meet at the upper of the two cafés that take up much of the middle of the street. I timed it exactly and arrived at twelve minutes past eight. I sat down at a table for three and looked at the *vólta*, the passing show, mostly couples, moving up and down Bucharest Street, dawdling at the shops, window shopping, talking, holding hands and, so many of them, smoking. Greece has never got to the point of thinking smoking is anti-social or even, if the numbers smoking is anything to go by, that it might be bad for your health.

I looked at my watch: 8.25. Eloïse was reasonably punctual but not excessively so. I should have expected her to be here by now but I wasn't willing to go to the stake on it. I ordered a coffee. I wouldn't look at my watch until it came. The coffee arrived. It was 8.32. So? She's only a bit over a quarter of an hour adrift. OK that's not like her but things can go wrong. She may have been held up somewhere, and couldn't get a taxi, or decided to catch a bus and the bus broke down. Although many of them are new, Athens buses always have the air of being about to break down. She might have set out and then realized she'd left her bag behind and gone back to the flat to fetch it. All sorts of things could have happened and none of them dire. So all right, for once the girl was a bit late. So what? No reason for panic or anger or jealousy.

What was the time anyway? It was 8.45. I ordered a beer and said I'd be back in a minute. I suddenly thought perhaps she had said, or meant, the lower of the two cafés. I ran down the two blocks. She wasn't anywhere there either. I was sure, on reflection, she had said (and why not meant?) the upper café. I walked back, sat down at the table, sipped my beer. At nine o'clock, I asked the waitress if I could use their telephone. Someone else was talking volubly and likely to continue. She pointed to a telecard box further up the hill. By the time I got there the queue had reduced to five.

I went back to the café. Three empty tables now and no Eloïse. I thought I'd better get myself back to the GB in case some emergency had come up and she'd left a message for me. Later I would try the hospitals and police stations. It was while waiting for a traffic light to change and allow pedestrians to cross I saw a man, at the other side of Venizelou (otherwise known as Panepistimíou, University St), get into the front of a taxi. It looked much like the Croat. Climbing into the back was a thickset, large man, with little or no neck and one shoulder higher than the other. As he got into the cab he shrugged the lower shoulder, it was almost a convulsion, and he turned and looked straight at me. It reminded me of something quite else, menacing, disagreeable. He couldn't have seen me, I was a good 30 metres, six traffic lanes away and in a bustling, elbowing crowd but I could recognize that he was close to being the twin of the original of the last of the photographs Drucker had shown me.

Where the hell was Mikoyan? Where was Eloïse? Could there possibly be a threat to her, as disastrously there had been for Eleni, for having a connection to me? Were the Croat and the hunched shoulder man, Mr X, involved in her disappearance? What could I do? Where had Eloïse gone, my darling, my love?

And then, unworthily, I heard underneath, a steady, sullen drumbeat: she's left you; she doesn't want you; she's found somebody else.

141

Chapter twenty-one

William Mikoyan, it turned out, was in the air, flying to Athens. He had booked himself into the Hilton; hadn't liked the sound of the GB. I found this out from Chuck who'd left a message for me to phone him. Commander Parker had passed on the number for contacting Mike Cable and renewed his offer of assistance. There was a fax from Freddie in Cairo asking if it would be a good time to come and visit Eleni. And there was, it must have been the first of the messages, the call I had heard as I walked down the corridor, an apology and a cancellation from Eloïse.

"Sorry darlink," she had said. "I'm going to have to cancel our supper this evening. I hope you aren't already on your way but I expect you are. Something has come up. Or someone. It's my father. He wants to drive me to Kámena Voúrla. It's a kind of resort, where my aunt, his sister, has just come in on her yacht. He won't take no for an answer. I know it sounds silly but I'd quite like to meet my aunt. I went to Kámena Voúrla once, a few years ago, with Maman. There's a very nice hotel there, the Hotel Thermopylae. I'll meet you tomorrow evening. Say eight o'clock? I remember it well. It's where we stayed. I'll book us a room. Sorry about tonight. Make up for it tomorrow. Love you darling."

I smiled. It was authentic, vintage Eloïse. I even phoned her aunt to tell her that Eloïse had gone off for the night with her father. She didn't sound best pleased but that may have been because Eloïse had told her already, It was only when I was trying to ring Chuck, that I began to consider the message more closely. I suppose the relief at having some sort of semi-rational explanation had momentarily clouded my judgement.

Chuck came on the line at last. I put Eloïse's mystery aside for the time being and listened to his cheerful voice telling me that William was on his way to join me in Athens, albeit putting up at the Hilton; that Katie was staying behind with him in Larnaca for the moment (he sounded very happy about the arrangement); that of course he'd come over if I thought he could be of any conceivable use in the field, as it were; and asking what should he do next. I gave him a quick rundown of events as I saw them and asked him to stay where he was and be prepared for a call from me between 1900 and 2100 tomorrow. If I hadn't rung by then, he had better pull out all the emergency stops and try and find out what had happened to me.

"Don't be such a gloom-hound, Ben. You and William will make a great team. You and half the spooks of the western world." What did he think was happening? Who did he think was helping?

"Just stick close to the phone and fax," I said. "Eloïse might try you if she can't reach me. Have you seen Angeloglou? You might tell him that his ex-prisoner is thought to be in Athens. Address unknown."

"Your cousin Sam phoned again and said the same thing about the Croat. He wants you to get in touch with him. Soonest, I think he said. He's at his Paphos number. How's Eleni? The sawbones doing her some good?"

"Looks like it but it's a very slow business. I should think she'll be here for weeks, finding it more and more tedious. How's Katie doing?"

His voice changed. "Fine, just fine."

"Is she there?"

"Certainly is."

"In the room with you?"

"Yes, indeed."

"Well watch it, Charlie boy. Long red hair and darling little retroussé nose, not to mention the freckles."

"Yes, yes," he said throatily, enthusiastically.

"Take it very slow and gentle. No rash decisions. No repenting at leisure."

"Talking about which," he said, returning to normal, "get Eloïse back from her father and don't let her out of your sight. You hear me?"

"Just so," I said. "Thank you, pal. Adio."

Sam, when I finally was patched through to wherever he was, said some of his Israeli *confrères* were anxious to interview me. About the Armenian slaughter. They'd fly me to Israel.

"Not right now," I said. "I'm very involved."

"Look, Ben, it's important—perhaps for you too—so don't take too long before getting in touch."

"As soon as I see clear water, Sam."

"I mean hours, days—not weeks. OK?"

I wrote a brief fax to Freddie, saying Eleni would love to see him and so should I, were I still in Athens when he arrived.

I tried the number for Mike Cable in Izmir. He was out to dinner. I left my name and hotel.

And all the time I was worrying about Eloïse. It wasn't the message that was mysterious: it was the behaviour underlying it. What had really happened? Why had she decided to go off, just like that, with her father? And, along the way, stand me up. Was it really her father or was it another man she was having an affair with and couldn't bring herself to tell me?

I was lying in the bath, thinking troubled thoughts, when the phone rang. There was a bathroom extension. I reached for it and sank back into the water.

"David?" I switched hastily to David Ditchling mode. "It's Mike, Mike Cable."

"Hello, Mike," I said.

"We have things to talk about, young David. But not now and not on this line. I need to see you pretty damned soon. How're you fixed? I'll be in Turkey five more days. Can you get yourself here? Don't answer. Signal me tomorrow. If not, we'll set something up. First priority, clean communications. Second, an early meeting. OK? See ya."

I had room service bring me a chicken sandwich which I gobbled with an unseemly and unexpected spurt of hunger and then went to bed and an uneasy sleep peopled with shapeless terrors.

William had got to bed late, he said. He was looking thoroughly uneasy. We were sitting at the Hilton bar. I was drinking beer and he had ordered a Manhattan.

"The plane was only ten minutes behind schedule," he said, eyeing everyone at or near the bar with overt suspicion. "But they'd lost my bags.

By the time they'd found them—they were still in the aircraft, would you believe—and I'd grabbed a cab and got here it was one thirty. Then I tried to phone Katie. I know it was late. So maybe she was sleeping. But I tried again this morning and they said she'd checked out."

"Don't worry," I said, "Chuck will know where she's gone."

"And that's something else I'm worried about."

I was not feeling particularly sympathetic. He could deal with his love-life himself. I had worries enough of my own, mostly, admittedly, to do with Eloïse, who in a manner of speaking was my love life.

"Look," I said. "I have no choice. I've got to go to this Kámena Voúrla RV. Something feels funny but in case it really is just what Eloïse's message suggests, a delayed romantic tryst, I've got to behave as though it's a slightly abnormal get-together. And you'll have to play gooseberry."

"Stop," he raised his hand, the barman came over solicitously, he waved him away, "you've lost me. What's this RV stuff? Gooseberry?"

"RV: Rendezvous. Playing gooseberry means being a third, a non-observing, pseudo-chaperon to a pair of lovers. If the set-up isn't what it pretends to be, then you're going to be watching my back, protecting me. OK?"

He looked bemused.

"Look William," I said. "You haven't got to come in on this. Maybe it's got nothing to do with Cairo, although I feel in my bones it has. Somewhere there's a connection. But you don't have to join in. As I said, I do. It's up to you. Whatever you decide, I'll still try and help you, if we get any leads."

I called the barman over and ordered refills. William played with an olive and looked pensive.

"I think I'd like to try and speak to Katie," he said. "Have you got Chuck Levendhis's number on you?"

I wrote out the mobile's number and he went out to find a more private 'phone; from the one on the bar everybody could overhear your conversation.

It had not been a productive morning. I thought I'd ring Cy Drucker to thank him for lunch, to ask what he knew about the hunch-shouldered man in his rogues' gallery and to say that I thought I might have seen him in company with the Croat in Athens last night. The embassy switchboard said they had no one of that name. But I saw him at the embassy yesterday I remonstrated. "I was not here yesterday, sir," she replied, "but there's no

Mr Drucker on today's list. Is there anyone else who might assist you, sir?"

"How about the Counsellor, Cultural Affairs?"

"I'm sorry, sir. Mr Walton is not in today. He's on leave."

I had waited half-an-hour at the British Embassy for Lieutenant-Commander Parker to come and pick me up and take me through into the secure Chancery area. He had been summoned to his master, he said, apologising. Mike Cable was also in a meeting and wouldn't be free for several hours, so his staff in Turkey said. I left a message saying I was tied up for a day or two at least. The Croat I was interested in was still at large, last seen in Athens. Was he interested in him too? If so, we might exchange information. I'd get in touch when I had a spare moment.

Parker was fascinated. "Tied up?" he said raising his eyebrows. "Spare moment?"

"You thought I was being cheeky to an admiral?"

"Well," he said, "I thought, for a major of marines, you were coming on pretty strong to a flag officer, even though he was United States and not Royal Navy."

"Ah," I said, "it's the SBS coming out in me. We're a stroppy lot."

"So I've heard," he said. "So they say."

"No," I said, "it's none of those things. I've known Mike a long while. We met in '82, in Washington."

It was a long time ago. I had been a young subaltern when we embarked on Operation Paraquat and the evicting of the Argentinian scrap merchants from South Georgia. We had gone on to the Falklands to prepare the way, reconnoitre, and observe, for the main assaults when the troops arrived a couple of weeks later. After the landings had been made, I'd been told to take some confidential documents to Washington by way of Ascension. I'd spent a few hours on the island waiting for the large American transport Galaxy on its regular run to Antigua and Miami, much of it with the US Air Force major in command of Ascension's airfield.

Wideawake was normally the sleepiest airport around. Apart from being a regular bus-stop on the US provisioning route for satellite tracking stations and a variety of intelligence outposts, it had the occasional and routine visitor from RAF Brize Norton. Suddenly, one day, with an RAF armada refuelling and taking off, it became the busiest airport in the world, overtaking Fort Hare, Chicago, in numbers of aircraft movements. It was difficult to judge who had been more surprised, the adrenaline-charged RAF pilots when they saw with their own eyes, whatever their briefing might have said, an American uniformed CO or the USAF major and his staff of mostly civilian, Pan-Am, traffic controllers, when they contemplated the actuality of the Falklands campaign.

On the long flight to the States, I decided that someone in the US military should be told of the sterling work their solitary field officer had done. So after I had reported to the then Commander Mike Cable and been taken by him to his admiral, where I delivered the despatch case which had been chained to my left wrist, and got myself thoroughly de-briefed, I asked if I could see the Secretary for Defence, or one of his deputies. Mike was so taken by my chutzpah, that he invited me out to an enormous lobster dinner and we became friends. In the end I did have a brief interview with the Secretary, Caspar Weinberger, who had taken, one might say, a particular interest in the campaign. I thanked him for all the help the US was giving Britain—I was very good at doing that sort of thing off-the-cuff, unauthorised and spontaneous, when I was a subaltern. And the US major was promoted.

I never did find out what was in the despatch case.

William returned with a determined face. It would seem the telephone call had not been a success.

"Everything all right?" I asked with what I hoped was the right degree of insensitivity.

He gritted his teeth and said, "Yes. Fine."

"Good," I said. "So what have you decided?"

"I'll come along with you."

He didn't sound very enthusiastic but at least it was a start.

"Excellent," I said."Good man, William." I clasped him round the shoulder and we clinked glasses and emptied them. "This is what we're going to do. We'll keep our rooms in Athens but take overnight bags. I've a couple more things to see to but I'll be back here with my traps by half-past two. Meanwhile you're going to rent a comfortable but unremarkable car. Then we'll go and visit my mother. She very much wants to meet you. After that we'll set off for the resort, giving ourselves plenty of time for a recce. We'll also have to sort out what to do with things like guns."

"Guns," he said, in shock, "I haven't got a gun. I'm against firearms."

I wasn't sure that I didn't prefer him in his bloodthirsty, vengeful mood, before love, sex and Katie corrupted him.

*   *   *

Kámena Voúrla is a seaside spa with hot mineral springs, a traditional resort, catering for Greeks more than foreign tourists, a few miles down the road from Thermopylae—so named after its thermal sulphur springs—where in 480 BC Leonidas and his gallant 300 Spartans died, defending the pass against Xerxes's 30,000 Persians; another of history's glorious defeats. They held the narrow pass for two days until a Greek traitor, Ephialtes of Malis, showed the Persian royal guard the secret path that outflanked the pass. Xerxes had his come-uppance at the Battle of Salamis, later the same year, when the Athenian fleet, fortified with hoplites acting as marines, lay alongside the Persian ships, who had no sea-room to manoeuvre in, and knocked the stuffing out of them.

There had been a fair amount of traffic out of Athens and it was a not particularly fast highway, so I had plenty of time to look at the map and muse on the Persian Wars while William drove; a trifle sullenly, I thought. He had been very polite and charming and solicitous with my mother but relapsed into a morose silence as soon as we got into the VW Golf.

"Would you say Chuck Levendhis was reliable?"

It was the first thing he'd said for an hour or more.

"What do you mean by reliable?"

"Is he safe, then, with another man's girlfriend?"

"Safe?" I said. "That's a funny concept in the circumstances. Katie's an adult, probably older than you . . ."

"She's only three years older."

". . . and Chuck is a bit older still, my age. It's up to them what they do."

He looked at me, furious. "She's my girlfriend. I want to marry her. I love her. It's not just up to them. I'm part of the equation."

"That's for Katie to decide," I said. "After all, she's still married to Jeremy Sims and I dare say he thought he loved her and she loved him, too."

"Well he didn't and she didn't love him. They lived a cat and dog life. That's why she left him. And that's how we got together. She's a marvellous girl. Brave, and beautiful too."

"Yes," I said, "and very determined. So, bully for you and may the best man win, and all that rot, but the light will be going soon and the turn-off should be close so let's keep our eyes glued to the road and peeled for signposts. OK?"

It was more of a slip road than a crossroad and we nearly missed it, turning off at the last moment and negotiating a steeper bend than either of us were prepared for. The little town was curved round a gentle but elongated bay. The sun had gone down behind the mountains. Lights were beginning to come on and there were clusters of shops, little blazes of fervent light between the more shadowy glow of the hotels. We found the Thermopylae Hotel easily enough about halfway down the main street. It faced the sea, looked a nice, comfortable, traditional, slightly old-fashioned hotel, the kind that patrons would return to for the same fortnight year after year. It was painted a pale terra cotta and had two Corinthian columns framing the entrance. It advertised rooms, restaurant, thermal spa treatment and "*Thálassa Therapeía*".

We had agreed that William would drop me a few metres further on, in the next pool of shadows, and would give me twenty minutes before trying to book into the hotel himself. If Eloïse was there, which I half-doubted, I didn't want William busting in on her before I had time to explain. So he would complete the circuit and come back and park.

I took my bag and walked up to the hotel and went in. A quite imposing entrance hall, marble floors and pillars and chestnut brown walls, not perhaps overly welcoming, but nicely proportioned. I took myself and bag over to the reception desk where the lights were brighter, elsewhere they relied on two chandeliers with half the bulbs lit and three wall-bracket half-globes. At the far end of the room, there was an old gentleman, under the glow of a reading-lamp, looking at a book. He was the only visible representative of the residents. I pinged the bell and before the echo had died away, I was being greeted, my hand shaken, by Kyrios Aristotélis, the owner.

149

"You must be Mr Bolton," he said in flawlessly unaccented English, "I'm the hotelier. Been in the family for three generations. Please call me Aris: Aristotélis is a bit of a mouthful, particularly when you're used to saying Aristotle. Same chap, different stress and final syllable. Oh yes, I meant to say, your young lady has called several times." He looked at his watch. "She was here just three-quarters of an hour ago and she said she'd ring again at eight o'clock. I fear she is not able to join you this evening. But we'll do everything we can to make your stay enjoyable nonetheless. Mind you with the quality of the help available these days it's an uphill struggle trying to maintain a first class service."

He shook his head and a rich crop of silver curls kept time. He was probably in his late seventies, early eighties, not very tall, round-faced, with cherubic smile and pink cheeks, wearing a cream seersucker jacket, dark trousers, white shirt and plain silk grey tie which almost matched his eyes.

"I'm very sorry about Eloïse," I said, largely to myself. "I wonder what can have happened to her? Incidentally, Kýrie Aris, I have another friend coming to join me."

He looked at me, both eyebrows raised interrogatively.

"A man," I said, hastily. "He'll be checking in shortly. That is, if you have any rooms free. I'm sure you'll make us very comfortable." I handed over my passport, first making sure it was the Bolton one. I had left the other one in my attaché case, together with the gun, in the safe at the GB. I had decided that the gun was likely to be more of an embarrassment than an advantage. But however sure I was about the passport, I always liked to check, to make absolutely sure.

After I'd signed in and got my key, he summoned a porter to carry my bag and show me the way and the amenities offered. "Dinner," he said, "if you wish to avail yourself, is served up till 10.30. We're country bumpkins here and used to early nights, not like your Athenian midnight's-the-time-for-mezes crowd."

The porter was a young lad full of energy and enthusiasm. He took me into every public room, opened up the sea-therapy rooms, showed me the equipment; baths with fearsome hoses, steam cabinets with showers overhead, a strange looking sarcophagus, which he opened up to reveal warm sea-water. It was called, according to the brass plate outside it, a "Relax'n Float Chamber". It had been manufactured in Soviet Eastern Europe and was guaranteed to reduce tension and float away the cares of stressful, everyday life. There was a large Jacuzzi and a half-size sea-water swimming pool. Then we went into the hot springs room, reeking of sulphur but I looked at my watch and cut the tour short. Eloïse would be ringing in a couple of minutes.

We hurried to my room. First-floor front with a nice balcony and a large double bed. It seemed that when she booked Eloïse had anticipated joining me. I could smell her scent: it was everywhere. There was some faded but pretty grey-backed wallpaper with a pattern of large tea-roses on it, an outsize marble hand-basin, gray curtains sweeping the floor. I pulled them back and looked out at the almost traffic-less road beneath and a tranquil sea beyond. The porter opened the bathroom door and turned the lights on to show me the period but very adequate plumbing. I tipped him and he disappeared. I turned the bathroom lights out and was staring, in the gloaming, out to sea where a light was flashing, presumably from some buoy, to mark a rock or wreck, when the telephone rang. It startled me.

I turned round in the semi-dark and groped for the 1950s hand-set, finding it after the fourth ring. I stood up seeing how far the cord would run and made for the balcony window.

"Ben? Ben darling?"

"Yes," I said, "it's me."

"I'm phoning from the yacht. I'm sorry I couldn't wait for you but they had to sail, something about tide, I didn't think there was very much in the Aegean, and time of arrival. And you all on your own with that great bed. What a waste! But I couldn't do anything else."

"Where are you going? And what are you talking about, love?"

"We're speeding to Turkey. I'm not sure where. The idea is I should meet the family, visit the family homes. Plural. Get to know my father properly."

At that point I heard a click, as of a lock, a cupboard door, something, opening. I half turned but the room was in darkness.

"He really is a fascinating man," Eloïse was saying. "Weird, funny peculiar. I don't understand him. But strong, decisive, wilful. Knows what he wants and for the moment that's me. He's charming; no, that's wrong. He's not charming: he's attractive and determined. He's devoting himself to me and that's flattering. For the first time in my life, I've got a proper, adoring father."

"I'll drive back to Athens now," I said.

"Don't be silly," she said, "we're not going to Piraeus. He's my father and I have nothing to fear. *Honestly* darling, I can handle this." She was beginning to sound almost irritable. "Anyway, I want to. Don't interfere, Ben. I'll ring you as soon as I know where we're going."

"I don't like the sound of this at all," I said but she had put the phone down.

I heard a whoosh and then a deafening crack as something hit my head. Pain. Searing flashes of lightning and deeper darkness. I struggled up from some dark red depth, only to feel a blow, perhaps a kick, and sickening pain, around my kidneys. I vomited, choked and passed out.

I hurled my arms out and hit metal and howled. I opened my eyes. It hurt like hell. Darkness, absolute, black, impenetrable darkness. Where was I? I ached all over. I smelt vomit, and tasted blood. I was blind. I felt round me.

151

I was floating but there was a roof close to my face, almost an arm's length above me. It was salt water. I tasted it. No, I wasn't blind. There was a small, an infinitely fine thread of light, outlining an elongated oval overhead. How long? Perhaps a metre, a metre and a half, with a maximum width of around a metre. I tried to push it up. My head seemed to be splitting with stabs of pain coming from fore and aft, port and starboard. I felt dizzy. Was I short of oxygen? Couldn't be; plenty of space for air and anyway the seal wasn't absolute; otherwise no light. Wouldn't do for a submarine. I pushed again, it was almost at the extremity of my arms and I had no strength. One more try. I must not pass out. If you lose consciousness you drown. There was plenty of water to drown.

I realized I was feeling a bit cold. Was this because I'd been out for the count before I'd been put in the water? Or was it merely that there was no heating and the water was leaching the heat out of my body minute by minute? *Think!* What was I in? I'd seen something like this recently. What was it? Where was I? I shouted. My voice came back to me. I doubt if it was audible at any distance. I tried to thump on the metal. Little impact. I paused and contemplated. *Don't get discouraged!*

EUREKA! What's the depth? I pushed my feet down, my trousers felt as though they were billowing out, filled with balloons of air. I hadn't noticed till then that I was fully clothed. And I suddenly felt bottom. I could stand up. As I did so, I banged my bruised and bleeding head and screamed at myself for being such an incompetent idiot. I felt very woozy again. *Don't fall into the water head first! That way you drown.* I tried to keep standing but in a crouched position. The giddiness cleared. I gently unwound myself, uncoiled and slowly moved head and shoulders towards the filament of light. I stretched out my hands, waited until I was breathing normally and then pushed. Nothing moved, nothing gave. I was cast into despondency, disconsolate. I felt my head. It was mushy, sore to the touch, the hair matted with still seeping blood. I couldn't use that as a battering ram. However hard they tell you the skull is, there must be a limit to the punishment it can take and mine would seem to have got close to it. All of which illogically reminded me that I hadn't done my exercises with the little yellow ball today. Was it still today? What was the time? I couldn't read my watch. Insufficient light. Can you lift with your shoulders and not hurt the head? But my shoulders, even on tiptoe, were a centimetre or so short of the top. It also hurt my neck and I fell over, dizzy again, my face went under and I came up spluttering and exhausted.

I waited for my pulse to slow down and examined the bottom with my feet. They found nothing; no useful iron bars or pick-axes. Therapeutic flotation chambers weren't likely to come so equipped. That's what it was; part of the seawater therapy. Great therapy; particularly for me. Another eureka! There would have to be some way a patient who got the willies, could summon help, or get out, before being driven mad by claustrophobia. I could imagine how terrifying that would be. I was getting a touch desperate myself. I felt round the lid, painstakingly pressing and probing each bit of it. Nothing. It didn't seem to yield anywhere. And there were no buttons to press, no different textures or materials, no happy little in-an-emergency-break-the-glass safety features.

OK. No panic. There must be a logical solution. Pause, take thought, take a deep breath, let it out slowly, controlled from the lower abdomen. And then in again, expanding the sides of the chest, as though pushing out against the world. Another white hot stab of pain in the kidneys. I gagged, brought up a gobbet or two and emptied my bladder simultaneously. And that hurt like hell, too. My salt water sarcophagus was becoming a not very nice place to be. What next? Loss of sphincter control? *Please not that!*

There must be a way out. Perhaps it wasn't made of metal. I couldn't remember clearly what it looked like from the outside. If it was a heavy plastic, like one of those water tanks, maybe I could rock it from side to side and get the water to help me throw it on its side. I rocked. It shifted a millimetre and returned to the absolutely vertical. It felt far too stable. I tried again, and again, and again. Something happened, something fell off. I heard it. It was the first sound except my own breathing and shouting that I seemed to have heard in a week or two. The water really was getting appreciably colder. I was beginning to shiver. One more shove and rock, shuck and jive. I hurled myself into it, hitting first one side, then the other. Something else fell off and hit the deck. I suddenly thought maybe some thug had put bars on top of the escape hatch. I pushed upwards again with my outstretched arms. There was some give but my damaged right wrist was still too weak to play its proper part. I remembered the little yellow ball. It was in my left trouser pocket. I gave one almighty thrust with my left arm and saw the area of light enlarge, I slipped the yellow ball into the new opening with my right hand, and felt as though I'd solved the riddle of the Sphinx.

All I needed to do now, was enlarge the gap, slip the ball round, breaking the seal until I could clear the whole hatch. I relaxed and drew

153

breath and then had another heave, moved the ball a few centimetres, and felt another something fall off and hit the deck. And then, as I shouted for joy, I heard a voice, coming nearer, perhaps running.

"What's that? Is it you, Ben?" Brighter lights came on, the hatch was removed. William and the porter helped me out, looked horrified too when they saw what condition I was in. Out of the water, I couldn't stand. I slumped to the floor and my wits swam away.

I came to, lying on the carved wooden double bed. William was saying to Mr Aris something about taking me to hospital. Mr Aris was sensibly saying he would send for a friend of his who was a doctor. Good old Aristotle; he could be relied on to think straight.

"Who on earth could have done this to your friend?" Aris said, in a half-whisper. "Why?"

William said nothing and Aris said he'd be off and get the doctor.

"What time is it?"

William looked at me, astonished.

"I thought you were out; asleep or in a coma."

"What time?" I croaked again.

"Ten after ten," he said.

"P.m?"

"Yes, night-time."

At most, I could have been in the torture chamber two hours. At the time, it felt like two days. I knew it couldn't be but I feared it might and there was more to come. I remembered why I wanted to know the time.

"William, phone Eloïse please. See if she's all right. On her mobile." I managed to recall and mumble the number.

I heard him dial but I couldn't hear him speak. He might have been in another room.

A little while later, he came over and said, "She's not answering. Maybe it's turned off."

Chapter twenty-two

I

Athens—Izmir, Turkey

took the bandage off my head before I got dressed to go to the airport. The effect was more dismaying than startling, odd parts, where the sawbones had put the stitches in, had been scythed to a stubble, rather as though he'd been clearing the undergrowth in certain areas to preserve some rare, earth-hugging plants. No attempt had been made to even the thicket out. And to think that surgeons used to be barbers.

On second thoughts, surveying the face with its heavy bruising under the eyes, the swollen nose, it was not a sight for the weak-hearted. I couldn't work out quite how I'd got all the bruises and swellings, mostly, I think, in the first fall after being hit on the back of the head. The dark blues of my irises were nicely set off by the fading red of the conjunctiva, what were laughingly known as the whites of the eye. Stick to the shades, boyo. I quickly put my sunglasses on and sheltered behind them religiously for the next several days. Mind you the face might have been, was, a fright but the shoes were gleaming, the uniform pressed and near-pristine. I would pass muster. Just.

Military aircraft may not be the most comfortable transport for passengers but the arrangements beat the hell out of Athens Ellinikon Airport. You slip in and out almost unnoticed. No queuing, no nonsense with airport staff, a quick check of ID and passport, a short wait, a jeep ride and whoosh and away. The arrival in Izmir was just as smooth and even less trouble. Mike had sent a Lieutenant (JG) USN to greet me and take care of my bags and transport. Within minutes, it seemed, I was being taken to a very decent room in the American Officers' Mess and being shown how the ice-maker in the corridor worked. There was an unopened bottle of bourbon on the table with four glasses on a tray, a bowl of peanuts and a fridge full of beer. With the admiral's compliments. The lieutenant would be back in half an hour to take me over to meet Admiral Cable.

Precisely 25 minutes later there was a knock at the door and Mike himself walked in, a touch older, a slight thickening of the abdomen, a slightly weightier jowl, a full head of short-cut silver-grey hair. He would always be a tall, slim, handsome, athletic-looking man for whatever age he was; with a pair of laughing blue eyes and a wry sense of self-depreciation.

"Hell's bells, Davey-boy," he said, feinting with his left for my stomach and thankfully not hitting it, "must be seven, eight years. London. Right? You took me to a memorable Kashmiri meal and on to a ratty night-club with a superior jazz quartet, which just about redeemed it. Remember the slinky red-head that wouldn't leave me alone? I never told Marie, you can bet your life. It looks as though she'll ship out to Naples soon. Well maybe she will, maybe she won't. If you're still around these parts, and she does fly out, I know she'd love to see you. Come and spend some time with us, eh? And if she decides not to leave the family—hell they're all graduating from high school or being sophomores at college, ready to leave the nest— there's always me and I'd be glad to have you stay whenever you feel like it, partner. So what's all this tale about leaving the Corps? I heard you'd put yourself on the retired list. Think you wouldn't make colonel? Then I hear reports of travel agents. Of a specialized end of the market. Right?"

"Forwarding agents," I said, pouring out a bourbon on the rocks apiece, "as much as travel arrangers. Do most things. Go not quite anywhere."

"OK. Pays well? Decent life? Satisfying career? Good pension? Thought you'd never open the bottle." As we drank to each other, he examined me more closely. "Plenty of action?"

"Enough," I said, rubbing my head.

"Pray tell."

He sat on the bed as I started.

*　　*　　*

Back in Greece, as William had taken my bags to the car and prepared to leave Kámena Voúrla, Kyrios Aris ran out and opened the passenger door.

"A keepsake," he said, pressing on me one of the smaller weights that had almost prevented my escape, and it being my right hand I very nearly dropped it. "A reminder that the gods can be kind; intervene to save the brave and the strong of heart, Mr Bolton. You have my deepest apologies. Our hotel has not treated you so well.

"I'd been thinking of getting rid of it, I want you to know. I'd never liked it and in my mind it had become a cenotaph. Also it needed a service and probably some sort of renovation. I seem to remember it had this webbing or canvas support—like a small hammock—but it rotted away. The man who sold me it was a rogue, promised me it was unique, only one in the area, would do wonders for my guests and my reputation. And guaranteed for five years, free service on the spot annually. Later I found out he'd sold it to two other hotels here and three establishments fifteen kilometres away in Thermopylae. He came and gave it one service and that was that." He wiped one palm against the other, dismissively. "Finish."

"But, you know," he went on, almost swinging on the car door, "all you had to do was push in the middle of the lid and it would have lifted. Except of course that someone had put all those training and lifting weights and bar-bells on top. Making it, I should suppose, not just difficult but well nigh impossible. Except perhaps for an Irakles or a Samson."

He grasped my hand and put in it an envelope which he took from his breast pocket. We waved goodbye and sped off. When I opened the envelope it was the credit card slip for the bill, across which he had written "Cancelled" in large red letters.

Mike was attending a dinner given by the Vali. He had arranged for his deputy, Jim Cordier, to give me a meal at 19:30. He would see me at his office the next morning at ten o'clock. Captain Cordier, originally a naval aviator, was better than average company and seriously interested in the classic Turkish cuisine. He spent much of the evening subtly and courteously exploring the connection between his admiral and this lowly, louche, limey marine major: but it was a game at which I was both more experienced and more skilled. We called quits at half past nine, having eaten richly, and I was lying in bed by ten, wide awake, thinking, wondering, worrying about Eloïse. What had happened to her? What was happening to us? Again, there was no answer from her phone. At least, I was in Turkey and that's where the yacht was heading. But where in Turkey?

Another Tuesday, another bad day for decisions. Uniform or plain clothes? There was a printed notice under the shaving mirror. All officers on base, it said, must wear uniform at all times except when participating in approved leisure pursuits. Underneath, someone had added, neatly typed; "e.g. masturbation, fornication, baseball, tennis, handball, squash, swimming, weights, sauna, troillism . . ." I put on my uniform.

First off, after breakfast, the full cholesterol house, I decided to try the club barber. After I explained the problem, not that it wasn't highly visible, he gave me a modified brush cut which did nothing for my face but at least made the head tidier. The same Lieutenant (JG) who had picked me up from the plane, took me off to NATO HQ.

It was a very different Admiral Cable, this morning, in uniform, with tie and jacket, and medal ribbons galore. We were in a large, impersonal office, with desk and high-backed executive chair in one corner and panoramic views out of the adjacent window and a panelled larger area with slatted

jalousies shading the glare and a large conference table and chairs. A few of these were already occupied. No one smoked and there were no ash trays. A large water cooler stood in the far corner with plastic cups and a tray of glasses and next to it a refrigerator and ice-maker.

Mike greeted me and took me across to the table, placing me on his right hand.

"You know Jim Cordier," he said. "Next to him, Captain Webster, Jane Webster, USAF." Late twenties, early thirties, round, pasty face, little sharp currant eyes. "Colonel Lester, Doug Lester. Pentagon: on loan." Medium height, inclined towards the tubby, smiling, West Point signet ring. "Bob Pearson." Unexplained civilian, tall, gangling, all wrists and large hands, large glasses, prominent Adam's apple. "Lieutenant Jill Cushing," USN, mid-twenties, lively, pretty. "And Andy Ross, your conducting officer who'll take notes."

We were all seated around the head of the table. "You start, Jane."

The lights were dimmed, the shades, which I now saw were not true jalousies but wooden-slatted blinds inside the room, were closed and a screen came down on the wall facing us. A still, a large photo; seen first at a distance and frozen.

"Odessa," said Jane. "March 12 this year."

We zoomed in and froze again.

"The Odessa Steps," said Colonel Lester.

"Eisenstein," said Jill Cushing.

"No pram," said I.

"The Battleship Potemkin," said Jim Pearson, the civilian.

"Pot*yom*kin," I said, quick, automatic response, correction. "Like Khrushch*yov*, written Khrushchev."

"The mutiny nearly succeeded. 1905 or was it 1907?"

"Stop showing off, you bunch of pseudo-intellectuals." This was Mike. "Here's my 5c worth. Serge Mikhailovich Eisenstein. Latvian. 98–44. Made *Potemkin*—pronounced Potyomkin – 1925. Also made unfinished *Ivan the Terrible*—Stalin banned part 2—*Strike, October, Alexander Nevsky*. He was a great image-maker, a re-writer of history."

We all clapped. "OK team back to business."

Jane zoomed in further and showed, at the first platform from the top, coming down, a crowd of people, further zooming brought us as far in as was possible. She then, using a small laser pointer which doubled as a ball-pen at the other end, illuminated the face of a man in profile, shaking hands with another. It was, as I might have guessed from the beginning, the Croat, Stjepan Zkrakovic.

"Doug?"

"To the best of our belief this is a meet between the representative-stroke-organizer of an Islamist Turkish-Lebanese-Palestinian-possibly-Egyptian group with a Russian mafioso who is selling arms. Missiles."

"Source?" I asked.

"Russian. Protected. Reliable. Not revealable."

"As you probably know," I went on, "the man in the spotlight, your alleged purchasing agent, is a Croat wanted by the International War Crimes Commission at The Hague for Crimes Against Humanity. He is said to have tortured and killed Serbs, ethnically cleansing part of Bosnia, on behalf of the Muslims. Well attested, plenty of witnesses. But you must be aware of all this."

"To hell with that," said Mike. "How about some positive identification?"

I opened my attaché case, for once not setting off the alarm, and produced the set of pix.

"This is your man," I said. "Stjepan Zkrakovic. Jane, can you project these on your screen?"

She produced another piece of equipment, an epidiascope, and ran the enlarged face and shoulders alongside the Odessa photo. Full and side face.

"Good enough," said Mike. "Everyone agree?"

There were nods all round.

I told them what I knew about the Croat, said I thought it unlikely he was a principal or organizer, and suggested it was more likely he was being used as negotiator because he spoke Russian. I then asked for the laser pointer and moved it around, illuminating those closest to the two men shaking hands. One of them, seen mostly from the back, face turned away from the camera, could have been the high-shouldered Mr X. But then again he might not.

"Any of you recognize anyone here?"

Shaking, negative heads.

"Probably Russian mafiosi," said Doug Lester. "We know none of them."

"Jim, anything to add?" said Mike.

"The arms, we are told and seems likely, came from the Soviet Black Sea Fleet, locked into Sevastopol by the Russia-Ukraine dispute about who owned the fleet. We don't know whether they were sold by Russians or Ukrainians to the Mafia. We were given a rough indication of what was on offer . . ."

Mike had been looking pointedly at his watch.

"Well that's got us a bit forrarder, as you Britishers like to say. Coming up to eleven. Jim, Doug, Bob. 11.30 here. David, you stay with me."

He stood up, opened the outer door and they all filed out. He went over to his desk, picked up a phone and asked for some coffees to be sent up. Andy Ross came back in and said there were two urgent messages for Major Ditchling.

One was from Chuck who had booked in at the Büyük Efes in Izmir and would stay there till I got through to him. The second was from Cousin Sam in Istanbul.

"Use my desk," said Mike. "I've got to go along the corridor."

I sat down and phoned them both. A long, and not very encouraging, talk with Chuck; a brief, business-like one with Sam. No news of Eloïse.

Mike came back and I returned his chair and desk to him. I moved over and reclined in an armchair as a young servicewoman came in carrying a tray with two coffees, cream and sugar.

Mike said, "I was mentioning that Chris, our oldest, was in his sophomore year. He's at Rutgers. What I didn't say," he was staring at a family group in a silver frame, "was that he is 28, that he dropped out of Harvard at twenty, took to heavy drugs, heroin, and agonizingly, and heroically, kicked the habit three years ago. He has just told us (a) that he is bi-sexual and (b) that he's been diagnosed HIV positive. I'm not clear whether from dirty shared needles or anal intercourse. I don't think I want to know. That's the real reason why Marie doesn't want to come to Europe."

"Oh hell," I said. "I'm sorry."

"OK friend. Now your turn. Tell me the other half; about you and the Croat."

When the six of us got together again, Mike stayed at his desk and the rest of us sat in easy chairs facing him in a semi-circle.

"David," he said, "says that ex-comrade Zkrakovic, son of an Ustashe enthusiast and ardent Nazi-supporter, killer and torturer of Serbs, is a psychopathic torturer and killer himself. He is convinced he is an employee not a strategist."

"All we know is that we were fed this information by a very reliable source. Repeat very reliable," said Doug Lester. "Someone was buying missiles from this particular Russian gangster—sorry he may have been Georgian, Uzbek, Chechen, for all we know. Someone with a Turkish-Arab-Palestinian connection. This photograph came our way—from a similar source. OK? We learnt a deal had been done but no details. We set about locating the guy you call Zkrakovic, finally picking him up in northern, Turkish, Cyprus. We lost him in Athens, after a few days, but picked him up again, briefly, in Turkey. We've got him, we think, within our sights. That's about it, I reckon, Admiral."

"David of course wants him handed over to the War Crimes judges at The Hague. Admirable intention but not on our agenda. Our priority is identify his collaborators, find the weapons and destroy them, confiscate them, whatever."

"Has this," I asked, "got anything to do with the Turkish-Israeli military pact? More particularly with the tripartite fleet exercise in the eastern Mediterranean?"

"Told you he was a bright boy," said Mike. "Give him the story, Jim."

"We picked up a rumour that some unidentified group wants to wreck the Turkish-Israeli connection, hit some US naval target during manoeuvres, embarrass the hell out of the Turkish military and get a pro-Islamist government back into power in Turkey."

"That's about it, David. All we know."

"You haven't told me whether we're talking nuclear warheads, or what?"
"Bob?"

Pearson, the civilian, said, tersely, "Don't know for sure. Haven't seen the invoice, or the goods. But I'd bet on it. Have to assume it."

"Any more clues," I asked, "what was on offer?"

"We were told three small surface-to-air or surface-to-surface and two larger missiles. Whatever that might mean. Not much help. They couldn't be state of the art. Much of that, perhaps all that, Black Sea Fleet outfit armament is junk. Rusting, out of date, unserviced, unreliable and probably as dangerous to the Russkis or Ukrainians as to their targets. Doesn't mean we can rate them as other than a serious hazard."

"All right, Mike," I said, "I understand. Not my game plan but I understand. How big would the missiles be? And the warheads?"

"The littlest are quite portable," said Pearson, "say, three-four feet long maximum, probably less. Depends which model and mark. The longer-range, conceivably nuclear warhead carriers might be seven or eight feet. Could be larger. The warheads are usually .75 metres long and .35 diameter."

162

"This is our brand of high stake poker; speculation abetted by supposition," said Colonel Doug Lester. "Ball park figures; rough guesstimates. Truth is we just don't have any hard information."

"OK guys. Thank you. I've got to go see the Turkish Admiral and I want to give David a farewell drink first. Thank you David."

We all shook hands and the others left.

"You know, Mike, my Favourite American Admiral," I said, "if I get to him first, it'll go rather differently. I'll certainly watch out for your missiles. And maybe even your interests. One thing more, Rear Admiral Cable: surely you've got him tracked? With all your satellite systems able to photograph the boil scars on his neck; with commercial firms now selling GPS and GMS private automobile tracking worldwide; you must have him, as Jim Cordier said, within your sights. Provided you managed to plant a bug, I suppose. So where is he?"

He looked at me, chucked me a small packet and said, "Going home present. Don't worry, not an expensive bribe you'll feel you'll have to refuse, just a key-ring. OK; so maybe we have him tagged, maybe we haven't, but we know he's here, in Izmir, I'll tell you that, buddy boy. Right out there." He pointed out of the window and described a wide arc, before pouring us each a scotch on the rocks.

"Confound their politics, Frustrate their knavish tricks." He sank half his whisky. "A good toast that. I've always admired those lines from your limey version of what every right-minded person knows is really God Bless America."

He sipped a little whisky and regarded me over the top of his glass.

"If you phone Jim every so often, he'll give you a movement update in the form of a weather report, like depression moving into central Anatolia. Don't eat your heart out, Major D. We'll get to him and his missiles first. You can have him later. What's left of him."

We drank up and parted. "Think about a visit, David. It's been good seeing you; be better still without the hassle, you prematurely superannuated leatherneck. Hell, you're not even going bald yet."

It was just not possible for Mike to understand anyone leaving the service before he or she had to. He kept on trying to get out of me the real script, the double bluff or whatever, and every time I told him the truth, he veered away like a swallow in flight. Briefly, I wondered if he were right. What had I gained by getting out early? A fair amount of grief for me and my mother and, the drumbeat marking the passing of time, the bolting of my wife-to-be; the loss of love.

Shortly after midnight, I heard my mobile canary-ing away and groped for it in the dark.

"Yes," I said.

"It's me. Eloïse."

"Where are you?"

"At sea. This is the ship-to-shore. Are you hearing me all right? You sound a bit faint."

"It's fine. How are you?"

"Wonderful. This is the best, zooming along at 25 knots, an empty sea, a starry night. And Father sits for hours at the wheel, conning the ship, singing old songs and I squat beside him and he ruffles my hair. He doesn't talk much. He doesn't criticize. He accepts me. It's magic: I can do no wrong. I've come home to the other part of me."

"Oh good," I said. "Well, that must make up for all the years of deprivation."

"Don't be like that, Benjy. It's been a healing experience for me and I want to share it with you."

I thought she sounded drunk, a touch defensive too.

The line began to break up.

"Can you hear me?" I asked. "Where are you going to be? When can we meet? I'll get to Turkey to pick you up. I'll be at the Büyük Efess in Izmir."

But the line had gone.

Chapter twenty-three

Izmir—Tel Aviv, Israel 165

The getting to and preparing for the next magic lantern show was more stressful. It started the same way, swift military airport departure, fast, exciting operational aircraft, quick, rather uncomfortable, flight. Then Tel Aviv and into the hands of Mossad, Shin Beth or whoever. I was back to civilian life with a vengeance, no salutes, no courtesies, Ben Bolton himself, plain and unadorned. My passport got a gruelling examination even though my minders were standing beside me and were there to speak for me. Or were they? One was a little older than me, thickset, medium height with a lined, anxious face, protuberant eyes and reddish hair, thick on top and running down to his fingers from his arms, coming out of his ears and nostrils. The other was lithe, olive skinned with dark, sunken eyes, a good ten years younger, taller, an athlete. Both of them wore white open-necked shirts and light-coloured sports jackets. Outside of asking my name, they had said nothing.

Cheesed me off, that. I was doing them a favour. Perhaps they didn't know it, hadn't been told. It was only because Sam kept pressing me, insisting on their eagerness to see me that I'd agreed to come to Israel. I couldn't see any profit for us.

"Where are we going?" I asked.

"Ashkelon Hotel," said the ginger, older man. He turned round, they were both sitting in the front of the small, rather battered Renault, and looked at me with something of a glare that turned slowly into an expression halfway between amusement and disdain.

"You Jewish?" he said. It was an American accent. Bronx?

"Not very," I said, sounding to myself like a Hollywood Englishman. "I'm not really religious at all. But yes, I suppose I'm a Jew. Like my mother."

He made some remark in Hebrew and his partner chuckled.

"So what d'ya put on immigration forms?"

The driver put in his twopenny worth. "Reluctant Jew?" He sounded more home-grown, a Sabra accented English.

"Say, that's not bad. Well how about it, Mr Reluctant Jew?"

"If there are Nazis, fascists, racists around, I put JEW. In capitals. If there are orthodox Jews around, I write Atheist. Anywhere else, I leave the question blank, unanswered, none of their damned business."

That got a muted, half-laugh.

The younger one said, "So you speak a little Hebrew then?"

"Not so as you'd notice."

But after that, they switched to Arabic when they spoke to each other, which suited me fine. I had been taught classical Arabic in Oman and made to listen to and speak enough vernacular variants, such as Egyptian, Gulf, Syrian, Iraqi and Palestinian, to allow me to understand most of what they were saying, once my ears became accustomed to regional variations and accents.

They were discussing me; wondering who and what I was and why I'd been flown in on an Israeli Air Force plane. They were not very complimentary. They left me at the hotel and said they'd pick me up at eight o'clock for a meal. I'd have preferred to have been on my own but it was a gesture of hospitality that I felt I shouldn't turn down.

The Ashkelon was a decent enough 1960s hotel, with what sounded like a Jumbo-load of American Jews in principal occupation. It was, I assumed, designed with package tours in mind. They'd given me a twin-bedded room with a view of the sea. The plumbing worked, the bed seemed comfortable enough, and my mood chimed with the anonymous décor.

I turned on the TV. There had been a suicide-bomb attack in Jerusalem on Saturday and the last of the eight funerals had taken place today. There had also been a disaster with an Israeli naval raiding party landing in Lebanon and being ambushed by a joint Hezbollah, Jihad, Amal and regular Lebanese Army force, with considerable loss of Israeli life. It sounded like almost 100% of the landing party.

At that moment the right and wrongs were irrelevant. I felt a sort of professional empathy, in my guts. I was immediately back in that exalted, pent-up anticipation, with its twin poles of determination and fear; waiting for the off; waiting to be lowered at cruising speed by surface ship, or launched by submarine, or dropped by aircraft; sensing that in minutes we'd know whether it was going to work or not, and, along the way, whether we'd survive or not. A moon with clouds scudding across it, a dark, seething sea and a hostile shore, more than likely dense with men and guns and, somehow worst of all, powerful lights. I shuddered and got into a warm bath.

It had, so far, not been a good week for the Israeli special forces and their intelligence and counter-intelligence communities. They weren't often shown to be so wrong-footed. Was it bad luck, bad planning, or the cumulative effect of what a good many saw as Mr Netanyahu's misconceived policies? Whichever, there'd be plenty of glumness, anger, sadness, disappointment and guilt going the rounds. My visit wasn't exactly opportune.

167

And what in heaven's name did Eloïse think she was really doing? I kept on going back to the hotel in Kámena Voúrla and the nightmare flotation tank. How could it have happened? I couldn't believe she had set me up. But what about the mysterious, non-talking father? Had she been under some constraint? It hadn't sounded like that. She'd been saying something about how weird her father was but also magnetic when I got taken out of play; how he wanted her to come to Turkey with him; but she could handle him. In fact she'd been getting impatient, almost angry with me. Well, she was grown-up and he was her father. Then there wasn't another man? No: there was no elaborate deceit to write me out of her life. She was my girl; we were happy together.

The telephone rang and I jumped rather too eagerly out of the bath, emptying a good third of the water on to the floor. It was Chuck. He had tracked me down via Cousin Sam and was excited to the point of breathlessness.

"Eloïse is definitely in Turkey," he said. "She phoned your Mum in Athens and Freddie was there. He spoke to her. It was, I quote, a very short conversation. Clearly someone interrupted her and she started singing a Greek song. *I Smyrni . . .* And you know what Freddie's like, he half-hummed and half-sang as many words as he could remember. That's where the Turks got the name Izmir from—from *I Smyrni*, he said, what we used to call Smyrna. Did you know? So to cut the story short, he reckoned this was a message to say she was somewhere in or around Izmir. A bit fanciful perhaps but we have nothing else to work on."

"Marvellous," I said. "I'll try her mobile again."

I tried at least a dozen times at five-minute intervals and at last she answered. She must have had it turned off before.

"Oh Ben, I haven't got the charger with me and the battery is running down. I'm staying with my aunt and a female cousin. It's weird. They're both very tall and rather grim. They keep a sort of purdah and wear covering-up head-cloths and loose all-embracing down-to-the-feet robes whenever they go out, chadors or whatever they call them here. We're somewhere close to Izmir."

"When you feel like it," I said, "go to the hotel, the Büyük Efess in Izmir. I'll be there tomorrow evening. So will Chuck, probably earlier."

"Don't fuss, Ben. I'm fine. It's just that *mon père* suddenly changed his spots; switched moods and plans and rushed off south. I don't know what he's playing at. He shouted at me when I asked him what he was doing. Told me to shut up, pushed me into the arms of his sister. Don't worry about me. I'll get to the hotel somehow. Probably tomorrow. Ciao."

I phoned Chuck and told him the good news.

"We're in tenuous contact," I said, "and she's alive and well."

"The main thing," he said, "the main thing." Then, going all Greek on me, added, "*Dhoxázo to Theó.*"

"I take it that means thanks be to God. Or thereabouts. Will you make sure you're in the hotel in Izmir tomorrow and you stay there?"

"I'll try to."

"What's William up to?"

"Not a lot. Mostly trying to play house with Katie in the Hilton. And, my fervent hope, not succeeding."

"Thank you, Chuck. Bless you."

I phoned Eleni at the hospital in Athens, spoke briefly to her and even more briefly to Freddie, who seemed to have taken up residence there. All was going well but *sigá, sigá*; slowly, slowly. But it didn't matter. Eleni was on the mend. And my world had changed: Eloïse was safe and on side. And even, perhaps, a bit disenchanted with her father.

*   *   *

Life in Izmir, traffic apart, had seemed relatively quiet. There was very little shouting except by tradesmen plying their wares or crafts. By contrast all Israeli street conversation seemed to be conducted at high volume, as though every exchange was an argument. It was warm, sultry, lively and noisy. Dizengoff Street gave off enough decibels to drown a pop group.

I was in the bar when the minders returned, in coloured shirts and dark jackets. They joined me in a good, long, iced beer and, for the first time, gave me their names, or at least their names for tonight; the younger one was Rafi and the older, David—and I nearly said Snap, almost forgetting I had reverted to Ben Bolton. One of these days I must get rid of my alter ego, it's becoming more of a trap than a liberty. We walked a couple of blocks away from the sea and settled in an agreeably no-nonsense restaurant with rather garish lighting, heaped plates and no music. The roar of conversation was enough, most of it in Hebrew. The beer came in pitchers.

"It has not been a good time for us," said Rafi, "we have lost some good friends." And then in case I had missed the point, he added. "Dead, all of them I think. Not in prison, thank God. That would be worse, much worse."

"Yeah, you're goddamned right, it'd be worse if they'd taken them alive, tortured them, held'em to ransom, all that shit. As for those terrorist bastards, those suicide-bombers," said David, "who's got an answer? Not us, for sure. Catch them and kill them is all. Psychos who blow up babies. Deranged animals. What can you do with them? Soon as you catch one, another five spring up."

"Would it have been different if Rabin hadn't been assassinated?"

"No way," said David. "no way."

"Yes," said Rafi, "maybe there would be talking instead of bombing."

"Bullshit," said David. "once a killer always a killer. Once a terrorist always a terrorist, once a Palestinian terrorist . . ."

"If you'd been a Palestinian," I said, "I expect you would have been a terrorist too . . ."

"Maybe . . ." said Rafi, perhaps to protect me, and then let fly with a burst of Hebrew. The argument screamed into top gear.

I let it rage. Apart from having started it, there was little I could do except putting up a hand every so often and saying "Sorry, chaps. I didn't mean to . . ." From time to time, recognizable words like "nudnik" and "shlemiel" erupted from the flow. And then David switched to Arabic and I started listening, hearing no good of myself.

169

"Why did you start this row in front of him, this ignorant idiot of an Englishman who like all Brits understands nothing about Arabs?"

"Listening to you, he would be convinced that he was right to be a reluctant Jew."

The waiter came with the main dishes. We had been eating avocado pears with a variety of yogurt, aubergine, hummus, garlic and tahina dips, and as he cleared the table and put the new dishes in front of us, the argument wound down, the shouting stopped. Nobody else seemed to have noticed. The other tables all sounded as though they were arguing too. We settled down to eat our rather heavy beef and paprika stews. David ordered another pitcher of beer.

"They want a meet at 8.30 tomorrow, so we'd best have an early night. OK?"

"Fine," I said. "Suits me."

He was obviously trying to restore the hospitable mood.

"I forget," he said, "you've been to Israel before?"

"Twice, I think. I've also travelled a fair bit round the region; Egypt, Jordan, the Gulf, Lebanon."

170 "Iraq?" asked Rafi.

"A little."

So what have we got here, David was saying in Arabic, MI 5, MI 6, MI 99? I decided I couldn't play this game any more, so I launched into my fairly fluent Arabic.

"How did you think, you pair of braying donkeys, we were going to stop the Scuds hitting Jerusalem if we weren't operating far back behind the lines in Iraq?"

Whether it was the fact that I spoke Arabic or what I was actually saying, they were shocked into momentary silence and then into roars of appreciative laughter. Several beers and back-slappings later, they left me at the hotel bar, where I had persuaded them to have one for the road, to return to their wives.

There was an American in olive green chinos, a multi-coloured Hawaiian long-sleeved shirt draped over his belly, standing next to me, talking apparently to the barman.

"A terrible thing to happen to our boys," he was saying, his European origins audible, "an ambush. What went wrong? Our intelligence is always so reliable. A SNAFU. It's not like us. And it would happen to some of our finest and best."

An Israeli on his other side, slammed his glass down on the counter. It cracked and Coca-Cola started to run stickily down the bar.

"Tell me, sir," he said aggressively to the American who was old enough to be his grandfather, "what do you mean by 'our'? Are you a parent or grandparent of one of the dead? An uncle or great-uncle? A relative of some kind?"

"No," said the American placatorily.

"Perhaps you just meant in general terms, our Israeli boys, heroes, patriots."

The American started to nod his head in agreement.

"But are you an Israeli?"

"Well, no," said the American.

"Perhaps you're a citizen of the USA."

"Why yes," said the American.

"So what gives you the right to call our Israeli boys yours?"

"Well," said the American, firmly putting on his dignity as armour, "First, I'm a Jew. Second, I'm on your side, I'm cheering you on. Third, I've always contributed to Israeli funds and charities, as well as Jewish ones . . ."

"Just shut the fuck up," said the Israeli and walked out of the bar.

Shocked and bewildered, the American turned to the barman and said, "What did I say? What was all that about?"

The barman gave him a look. "That guy," he said, "was saying what he feels, what some of us . . . Look, Mister, he's a combat pilot and his little brother, a para, got killed a couple of months ago."

"I'm sorry," said the American.

"Yeah," said the barman. "I'm sure you are. You want another drink?"

The American put some money on the bar and as he stretched out his left arm I saw the tell-tale tattooed numbers. He walked out, bent but unbowed.

"You noticed?" I said. The barman nodded his head. "Tell your hotshot pilot friend, next time he comes in. I expect the American had lost more than his little brother in the camps."

I went up to my room and shot into the bathroom where I emptied some of the beer I'd drunk, then took off my clothes and had a long shower. One of the beds had been turned down with a good-night bon-bon placed on the pillow and I was making my way to it, damp towel around my waist, when I smelt a strong whiff of perfume and a voice from the other bed said, "My name's Pnina."

She was raven-haired, nubile, naked, as far as I could see, and barely too old to be my daughter. With my towel slipping, I felt at some disadvantage.

"Did someone say I asked for you?"

"No," she said, "we just get told to go to certain rooms. "Your name's Benjamin, isn't it? I've always liked Benjamins. You know the Benjamites were the smallest tribe of Israel. Or was it Judah?"

"Who told you to come to my room?"

"Oo, I can't tell you that."

"Fine. Just get out of that bed, get dressed and go; or I'll phone the desk and ask them to send someone up to remove you."

"You wouldn't do that, would you? What would the other people think? You wouldn't want to have a noisy row, would you? Just let's have a little cuddle and then I'll go quietly."

"Anyway," she said, I thought a touch smugly, "the hotel security people know I'm here. What's wrong with you? You don't like girls? You're a gay? You want me to find a young boy for you?"

I walked over to the bed, pulled down the cover sheet, picked her up and set her on her feet. She was tall and attractive, with a lithe, rather beautiful young body and smelt very sexy. My towel started to slip down; my loins, as they say, to stir, and I reckoned I was on a hiding to nothing.

"Look lady," I said, "you're lovely and sexy, and in the right circumstances I'd adore to spend the night with you. But not now. I need to sleep."

She kissed me on the mouth, pulled away my towel, looked down and laughed.

"Pity," she said. "It would have been fun." With a quick tweak of my penis, she went over to the wardrobe, got out her dress, knickers and high heel shoes and started to put them on.

I made a bee-line for the other bed and got in and lay down and watched her. She was good to look at, slim but nicely rounded, and she moved with the elegant precision of a dancer. It would have been fun.

"What were you going to ask me? What do your employers want you to find out?"

"Would you really answer some questions?"

"Depends what they are."

"Well I know you're probably Jewish. The little tell-tale when you're naked."

She came over and sat on my bed and started patting and stroking my body through the sheets. Perhaps she thought that didn't count. I took her hands away and put them in her lap, where they reposed demurely for the next few minutes.

"What do you do? What's your work?"

"Pass."

"What are you doing in Israel?"

"I'm not sure. Meeting some people."

"What people?"

"Don't know."

"You must have some idea. Business people?"

"No. Government, I suppose."

"What part of Government?"

"Let's say if you don't know, then I'm not going to tell you. And I'm not sure that I know."

"You a journalist?"

"No."

"I'm not going to get much out of you, am I? In any sense."

She lent over and kissed me gently on the mouth and walked over to the door, picking up her small bag from the back of a chair where it had been hanging.

"You're one of those my grandmother used to warn me against, the kind that you can't tell whether they're wise fools or foolish wisemen. Either way, good night, fool."

Fool, I said to myself, fool indeed. "I'll regret this," I said out loud, "But spare me the home-spun philosophy of harlots with hearts of gold."

"I'm not a harlot," she said indignantly, "I work for my country. I'm a patriot."

And she closed the door behind her with a small slam, not enough to raise the neighbourhood.

When I awoke from an unquiet sleep at six a.m., I thought of going for a proper run but I retreated after a couple of kilometres of mugginess and the already heavy traffic fumes. I returned in a muck sweat and showered and went down for breakfast. I was still laughing at myself and the Pnina episode and wondering what the hell they thought they were up to; whoever they might be. The right hand again not knowing what the left hand was doing, I supposed. It was a massive breakfast buffet with barrow-loads of tropical fruit, eggs, breads, cheeses, and smoked and soused fish, if you felt strong enough at that hour of the morning.

At eight o'clock, having packed, I phoned Chuck. Eloïse had made contact. She had arranged to come into Izmir to go to a western style pharmacy. She would dish her duenna and come to the hotel. She sounded confident. Bravo, I said; the day is starting well.

Rafi came up to my room and said I'd better check out but not to worry about the bill, it was being taken care of. The meeting had been moved to nine o'clock but with the traffic the way it was, we'd better be on our way.

It was an anonymous, unmemorable building in the midst of a complex of equally undistinguished but larger buildings. A military compound, plenty of soldiers around, of both sexes. What would Pnina look like in uniform? Pretty fetching. So would Eloïse for that matter. But in head-scarf and chador? A knock-out.

Another conference room with a rectangular table taking up most of the room. This time there were no windows and plenty of ash-trays. Almost everyone was smoking. A noisy air conditioner was clunking away. On the table were clusters of bottles of water and ice buckets and glasses and several cartons of orange juice. Slumped at the end of the table was a middle-aged man with a large head, half-moon glasses, short grizzled hair and a comparatively small body. He was rolling a toothpick around his mouth and occasionally pausing to chew it. When he got up, he was as tall as I was, with disproportionately long legs and arms. He smiled, removed the toothpick and came over to greet me. No one else seemed to pay any attention. They were reading newspapers, files, documents and chatting amongst themselves.

"Hello," he said, "Ben Bolton? It's very good of you to come. I'm Hannan. I'm a long-time friend of your cousin, Sam. How is the old devil?"

There was an Irish lilt to his voice.

"Sam's fine. Getting on a bit but still the same difficult old cuss. People like him don't change with age, they just get more like themselves. Forgive me," I said, "but were you by any chance brought up in Ireland?"

"No, I'm a Sabra, born and bred here. My grandfather and father came from Dublin. And to play out the family nostalgia, after I'd done my military service I went to Trinity College. And TCD is what you're hearing." He laughed and put his arm round my shoulders. "Before we start, Ben, and I hope it won't take too long, because I know you want to get back as soon as possible—don't worry I've got transport laid on—if there's anything you don't want to share with us, just say so. We, you can take it as read, know quite a bit about you, young Bolton . . ."

"Not through Mistress Pnina you don't," I said but the arrow missed the target. He didn't know what I was talking about, looked bewildered, but decided to go on, all the same.

"Yes," he said as though the meaningless interruption had not taken place, "we know a fair bit about your activities and those of your 'friend'," the emphasis was clear, "'Major Ditchling of the SBS'."

I gave nothing away but I was severely rattled. This was the first time anyone, as far as I knew, any outside agency had made the identification.

"And your very neat SATIS operation. Is it a side-line, I was wondering, or is it by now your main business? Anyway, you shouldn't be letting me interrogate you like this. I'm becoming a discourteous old bore. Shall we return to our muttons and get on with the agenda?"

He walked me to the head of the table, sat me down beside him, and called the meeting to order.

"Well now," he said, "we won't want to make this a long, drawn-out affair. So I won't bother introducing all my folk here. You wouldn't remember their heathen names anyhow. This, friends, is Ben Bolton from Britain and Cyprus. He may be able to help us. Screen, lights, let's be having it then."

It was another magic lantern show. A screen had come down, been pulled down, at the other end of the room. The lights went out, except for a blue emergency exit night-glow, and there was a whirring as the projector was turned on. It looked like an 8mm home movies Bell & Howell. No sound. There were the usual trailer blips and stars, a random slither of numbers, upside down and in reverse order. And then we were into it. I nearly fell out of my seat.

It was Cairo and there was the tourist bus with most of the Armenians already inside and a few stragglers still pulling themselves up and into the coach. The camera had obviously been some way to the right of my position outside the hotel, but it was recognizably the same scene. I was dreading the next few seconds. I found myself breaking out in beads of sweat on my scalp and forehead. I was beginning to feel faint, dizzy and nauseous. I must not keel over. I MUST NOT FAINT. I felt a tap on my left arm. It was Hannan handing me a glass of iced water. I drank it down as the camera panned to the right and showed two motor-cycles, low horse-power, old and covered in dried mud and dust, coming to a stop. Three men in burnous and with chequered Bedouin type, or Arafat style, scarves over the heads and across their lower faces, parked their bikes and walked slowly and deliberately up a small mound. The camera panned back to the bus, there was still one elderly man having difficulty getting in. The camera wobbled and, for a flash, I saw myself helping William's mother. The camera wobbled again, more violently, and this time the shooting had started.

It was eerie the silence, the lack of sound, because in my memory the automatic gunfire had the impact, the noise, the loudness of a major explosion, infinitely repeated. There they were, the three of them, firing away and there were the poor Armenians dying in their seats. Of course, we couldn't see much of the inside of the bus, only the windows shattering and the dolls inside jumping and slumping as they were shot. The cameraman held his nerve and panned so that the killers were in centre frame. They were not identifiable. The camera was fixed focus, no telephoto lens. Another man had come up and was doing something to the bikes. Probably starting the engines. Two seconds later, the killers were running for the bikes and getting on them and driving away. Now there were two men on each bike. The fourth man had got on behind the larger, taller of the three with guns. The bikes and the men disappeared, kicking up spurts of dust behind them.

"Cut," shouted Hannan. "Lights. Rewind." And we were suddenly back in ordinary artificial light in a humdrum, workaday conference room, wreathed with cigarette smoke. "Sorry," he said to me quietly, "that must have been a bit of a shock."

Conversations had been resumed, cigarettes taken out and lit. One of the men went out and returned with a tray of disposable cups filled with instant coffee and one of the girls went round distributing packets of sugar substitute and pouring from a carton of milk.

"Don't touch it," said Hannan. "It's not only lethal; it doesn't taste of anything you'd want to have passing your lips."

"How did you get it," I said, pulling myself together, "how long have you had it? Did anyone else know it existed? Amazing."

They were all staring at me.

"Ruthi," Hannan said looking at a round-faced young woman, with round blue eyes, round spectacles and a rose-bud mouth, "you explain."

"It was a fluke," she said, speaking a southern counties standard received English. "A man called Eli, his parents were from Aden, was an ardent amateur ciné photographer. I don't think there can be many of them left. Most of them have moved over to video." She paused, looked inquiringly at me. I nodded. "He'd saved up to go on this trip to Egypt and he took cameras and film with him, hoping that no one would start thinking he was a spy or anything. Because he wasn't; just a simple tourist. It was his group that should have been in the bus that was shot up. There was a late change in arrangements and the Armenians were slotted in to what had been allocated as the Israeli sightseeing tour. For some reason or other, no one had told him of the change. So he'd gone to the bus, carrying his camera, all ready for the Pyramids and the Sphinx, only to find out that it wasn't for his tour. Not knowing what else to do, he decided to use the bus and the Armenian group for what he called an establishing sequence. He told his friends it didn't matter that they were Armenians and anyway it was interesting: he'd never seen a group of Armenians before, not that he knew of. He went to a suitable vantage point and started taking general shots of the bus and the surrounds."

"Yes," I said, "and then?"

"After the massacre, he thought he could maybe sell his film to a television company. It might help to get him a job as a TV cameraman. He was ambitious. In the mêlée, the police fighting back the crowds, ambulances arriving, people trying to get the bodies, and the wounded but not yet dead, out of the bus, he pocketed his camera, these 8mm jobs are very compact, and got the hell out. He knew TV teams would soon be parachuting in from all over the world, so he waited, round the corner."

Hannan was stirring, restlessly beside me. "Look," he said, "he's an ordinary, simple, ignorant guy. He thinks he's sitting on a crock of gold. He doesn't know what to do about it. The cameras and reporters and microphones and lights arrive and he hangs round trying to talk to someone. Nobody wants to know. He keeps on saying I've got it on film, I've got it on film but everyone's too busy setting up circuits. Eventually, the police move him on."

Ruthi took the story up again. "For some reason, probably because the film needed to be developed and because it was Double 8mm which nobody uses any more, and it had to be split down the middle and no one had a suitable projector or the right processing equipment, he took it back to Israel with him and Eli began to have second thoughts. He discussed it with his mates at work and decided to present it to the Israeli authorities. Meanwhile he deposited it for safekeeping in his bank."

"OK. Enough of that," said Hannan. "Second showing. Slow motion. I want you all, and especially you, Ben, to concentrate on the gunmen. Frame by gory frame."

177

The lights went out, the projector whirred and flickered and the bus came up on the screen and the last few passengers jerkily pulled themselves up the steps. I concentrated till my eyes blurred and a pain drilled through my forehead.

"Break. Lights. Rewind," said Hannan. "Everyone out into the air. Walk around for ten minutes. Commune with Nature."

He shepherded me out, told me to put on my sunglasses, took from his back-pocket a battered silver hip flask and poured me a slug of Jamieson's and one for himself in silver thimble glasses.

"Anything coming back?" he asked gently, tentatively. "No. Don't tell me. We'll have one last slow run through. And then we'll be sharing any notions you have or, indeed, we may have. Will you be up to all that jerky filming again?"

We walked round the block, watched casually by a variety of young service men and women, sitting or strolling, some in sun, others, carefully, in the shade, and returned to work.

"All present? OK. Here we go. Last time." However noisy the air conditioner, it was certainly effective. The room had cooled down, the air been cleared of cigarette fumes—that didn't last long—and it felt fresh. I persuaded myself I was alert. The bus came back into view.

"Stop!" I suddenly shouted out. "Go back about twenty frames."

I hadn't been watching the gunmen this time, I'd been looking out for the fourth man, the one that goes to the motorbikes and gets them started and then jumps on to The Turk's, bike and drives off with them. And there, for an instant, his face was visible; not very clearly but enough. It was the Croat. He stood out from the other passers-by, frozen by the gunfire, almost all of them Egyptian.

"Again please," I said. No real doubt in my mind: it was Zkrakovic. I asked for that sequence once more and this time, I noticed something else. The Turk gave a funny, compulsive shrug to his shoulder, like Mr X in Athens. Could it be? They were together in Greece: they could have been together in Cairo. Perhaps. Maybe. Imaginings: if you try hard enough you see likenesses everywhere. It ain't evidence.

The lights went on. Orange juice was passed round. A few people got up and stretched.

"You've recognized something, someone, Ben. Let's be sharing it."

So I told Hannan and his team what I knew about the Croat's Ustashi background, his infamous career in Bosnia; about his questioning Eleni, being captured and escaping; about seeing him in Athens; about the rumour of his buying weapons from the Russian Mafia. I assumed they knew what the Egyptian police had on The Turk but I rehearsed that and added in the possibility that he was an ethnic Kurd. I left out the details of Eleni's being tortured. It seemed too personal, smacking too much of my own involvement. I didn't want to make a special case out of it.

The Croat was new to them. Or rather, one of them, a bright, dark handsome lad, called Nissim, immediately brought him to mind, once I put him in the frame, saying he was wanted by The Hague War Crimes Commission and had a known record of anti-Semitism. But, surprisingly, they had quite a lot on The Turk, including some smudgy, long-range photographs.

As the meeting broke up, Hannan took me aside.

"I didn't want to tell you earlier but this was the first time any of us had seen the film. It's not a pretty story." He looked at me and lowered his heavy eyebrows. "Eli's apartment had been ransacked and he'd been tortured. But he hadn't told them anything. He'd just died. It seemed he had a heart defect. They must have fled at once, got out of the country. They didn't find what they were looking for; the film. We did, eventually. It was in the safe of the local branch of the Bank Leumi. The torture? Bastinadoed feet, flayed with electric cord, and cigarette burns round his nipples. Resonant? Sounds like your Croat."

I shuddered. He took my arm.

"I'll take you to your plane."

Chapter twenty-four

Izmir, Turkey

Unexpectedly, Sam was waiting for me at the airport, looking anxious and ill at ease. Eleni, I thought: something's happened; she's dead. But it was nothing like that. He had messages for me and thanks from the Israelis, phoned through when they told him what time I was due to arrive back in Izmir.

Eloïse had turned up at the hotel and Chuck, he said, had taken her to the Greek island of Kos, because she wanted to catch a flight via Athens to Larnaca. There was some stuff for me in a safe deposit box at the Büyük Efes. William had gone to Ankara to consult with the US Embassy. A fat lot of good that was going to do.

Embracing and patting me on the back and shoulders with obvious affection, Sam looked bothered, a touch shifty, sweating. It was a fine, warm, autumnal day easing towards sunset with clear blue skies, streaking red and orange and purple, and a late shimmer over the sea. No cause for sweating though. Maybe he'd had a hard night, too much raki with old Turkish friends. Maybe he was just getting old, or was suffering a bout of fever, a recurrence of malaria, somesuch. Not like Cousin Sam at all. Mind you, I wasn't feeling all that bright-eyed and bushy-tailed myself.

We walked, his arm round my shoulder, towards the outside world of cars, taxis and buses. There was a sudden press of people engulfing us. Sam looked anxiously at all the faces, swivelling round as though he expected to meet someone who was already late.

"When I say go, run like hell," he said conversationally. "The car's a grey Rover. Don't wait for me."

"What?" I said.

"Go." He cannoned into me, pushing me aside. "Go!"

The Rover was slowly coming up to the entrance. When he saw me running, the driver accelerated and opened the passenger door. I hurled myself inside.

"Sam's nephew?"

I nodded. He shot off, tyres squealing.

"Cousin really," I said. "Not nephew."

"Password," he said. "Recognition. Couldn't care a fart who you *really* are." He accelerated round a bend and straightened out still increasing speed.

"What's happening? Do we go back and pick up Sam?"

A voice came over the loudspeaker. "Sam hit in left shoulder. Some blood. Bit of pain. Passed out temporarily, like maybe a minute; two at most."

181

I felt a wave of panic. Sam was invulnerable. Sam couldn't get shot; couldn't get shot particularly protecting me. For a moment nausea engulfed me. In the distance I could hear the conversation still going on.

"The airport people have sent for an ambulance. A doctor was handy, says the old sod's not in danger. I'll stand by."

"Any sign of the gunman?"

"Lost in the crowd. Probably joined his car and now on your tail. Out."

"Self-explanatory," said the driver, much my own age with short blond hair, sun-glasses and a soft leather jacket. "I'm Haggai, one of Sam's boys. Irvin on the other end of the blower. He's a brave old guy, your cousin."

"Why was he there?" I said. "What did he expect? Did he guess?"

"He thought there'd be an attack on you and he wasn't, he said, going to take any chances. I volunteered but he said he'd be better at getting you to run. Also he reckoned he might identify the terrorists. Wonder if he did?"

"Shouldn't we go back to see if we can help?"

"You heard what the medicine man said. And my life's just not worth disobeying Sam's orders. He told me to keep you out of it."

"Will Irvin be able to protect him, on his own."

"Sure: they're not after him. It's you they want."

He had slowed down but was driving as fast as the traffic allowed. We were coming towards the centre of the city.

"We'll go to the hotel first. Peter's waiting for you there. He'll keep an eye on you while you get your safe deposit box. Is there anything else you need from your room."

"Only my bag," I said. "Courtesy of the US Navy. I haven't checked in."

"We'll get someone to pick them up later and settle the bill."

He pressed the transmit button and told Peter we were within a few minutes of the Büyük Efes. Peter said OK.

"You want to take your case in with you?"

"Yes," I said. "I'll put the stuff in it."

"Don't take too long."

I walked swiftly, attaché case in hand, through the vestibule towards the desk. A lanky stage Australian in khaki bush shirt with koala patch on the top pocket and camouflage trousers bumped into me, muttered what I thought was going to be an apology but turned out to be "Sam's nephew I'm Pete" and bellowed, "Fancy finding you here, me old mate." He came with me to the assistant manager who looked after the safe deposits, passed me the key to match the one the manager took with him into the little room which housed all the boxes. Once the manager had opened his half of the lock and seen that my key opened the other half, he tactfully left the room. Pete and I shoved everything into my case, when I'd got it open, and we made for the exit. Pete put himself ahead of me, motioning me to stay where I was until he'd checked the outside.

He was gone some time. When he came back, he looked grim.

"Come on," he said. "Into the taxi."

We got into a local taxi and he gave some instructions in Turkish. He was turning round and watching to see if anyone followed us.

"What happened to Haggai?"

"I don't suppose he'll understand," he said, gesturing at the driver, "but play it cool. I knew something was wrong, like, when the Rover didn't zoom up as soon as I showed. I walked over to the car and then round and behind it. There was only one guy in the car and it wasn't Haggai. He didn't know me from Adam. He was, like, sitting in the driver's seat. I gave him a surprise, OK? Opened the door from behind, yanked him out onto the deck, put a knife at his throat. He hadn't much English but he managed to show me, smartly enough, where they'd, like, bundled Haggai. A schmuck like that couldn't have taken Haggai on his own. He'd have been knocked out. Wouldya-believe-it? Haggai? The unarmed combat champion of the free Semitic world? Anyway not dead; I listened, normal breathing, like. Might be concussed, I s'pose. Bloody hell, hope not. I folded his jacket under his head, made him comfy, called Irvin and told him to pick him up. I knocked the wanker out and nicked his nose, as a warning, like, and pocketed his gun. What he was going to do with you, boss's nephew, I dunno. Expect there's another of them around. A clever bugger. Not trench-fodder like this one."

We were in the moneyed suburbs now; large villas, gardens, water-sprinklers, high walls, trees. Pete looked round, getting his bearings, checking to see if any numbers were visible. He told the taxi to stop. We got out, he paid and we waited for the taxi to turn round and disappear.

"Should be third or fourth house from here," he said. He'd taken out a revolver and was rotating the chamber. "Always make sure you've got one in the spout," he said. "Play safe and find yourself dead. That's my motto. They tell ya keep an empty one opposite the hammer. That way no accidents. Right? I tell ya that's a way to intentional death, like. Your own."

It was getting dark suddenly. There were no street lights, just the occasional scatter of light coming from one of the substantial houses, set back some way from the road. There was a loom of light and the sound of a car approaching fast. Pete threw himself, and dragged me, down into a shallow ditch. The car swished past and accelerated into the distance. We dusted ourselves down. The ditch was dry and full of old, desiccated leaves, skeletal and fragile as cobwebs.

"I think it's the next one," he said. "Dunno what we'll find there. Take it quiet and slow, like."

What we found was a locked gate and an entryphone, There didn't seem much choice. Pete pressed the buzzer, said "Sam's nephew" and whoever was inside opened the remotely-controlled gate. It swung open with a groan and a rasp and a long creak and as soon as we were in, it swung back and clanged shut with a noisy finality.

"Christ knows whether we've given the game away like to our enemies or we've won the jackpot." His gun was still in his hand. "Here you'd better take our Turkish chummy's neat little automatic. Ever used one?"

"Yes," I said but didn't tell him about the state of my hand. It felt quite light. I put it in my pocket for the moment.

It took three or four minutes to approach the house. When we were within hailing distance, an outside spotlight lit up the porch and us. Pete muttered an "Oh hell" or two and I noticed he'd pocketed his gun, keeping his hand on it, ready to fire.

The door swung open and Pete put himself in front of me. A servant in white jacket beckoned us in. He said something which I supposed was a welcome in Turkish. Pete made a clearly suitable response. The man smiled and led us through an ill-lit, rather cavernous hall into a very brightly illuminated reception room with a great chandelier blazing away amongst its crystals. It was a large, much-furnished drawing-room with acres of fine antique rugs scattered over the polished wood floor, sofas and Ottomans lining the walls, long, low tables in front of them, and large framed ornamental Tuğras, monograms, imperial signatures, of long-dead Sultans. In front of a wood-burning fire stood a white-haired septuagenarian in velvet smoking jacket, with what looked like a long-barrelled Smith and Wesson ·45 in his right hand which was pointing unwaveringly at me.

By now the servant was bringing up the rear, shepherding us towards our host. I looked round and saw he too had a revolver in his hand.

"As you can see," he spoke in clear, fluent English, "you are covered. So don't make any sudden moves. Mehmet, search them. Which of you wishes to speak? To establish your bona fides?"

"I'm Ben Bolton," I said, as Mehmet removed the gun in my pocket and moved on to Pete. "I'm Sam's nephew, and I assume you know him. My passport, if you want to check my identity, is in my attaché case."

"I dare say, I dare say." Mehmet had by now discovered and handed over to his boss the pair of revolvers found on Pete. "And so are many other things. More guns perhaps, explosives enough to blow us to perdition, who knows what. Tell me more. Convince me."

"What can I say? My father's dead. My mother's name is Eleni. She lives in Cyprus and has a hotel in Larnaca. I've just been off on a short trip and Sam, really my cousin not my uncle, met me at the airport."

"And why, may I ask," he turned to Pete, "did you come by taxi and then walk suspiciously along from house to house, instead of coming in the car I was expecting?"

Pete explained succinctly. Our host's gun disappeared into his pocket, ours were put into a drawer in an escritoire and trays of drinks and small meze were brought in by two smiling and deferential maid-servants.

Adnan Bey was now playing the courteous, affable, old world host. He was probably nearer 80 than 70, with a handsome, foxy face. There were rows of books in ornately tooled leather-bindings, in a variety of languages, and objets d'art not so much dotted as lavishly scattered round the room. There was hardly a surface that wasn't supporting some elegant collection of porcelain or jade or amber. Marvellously coloured, giant worry beads, looped out of hollowed out lapis lazuli and black and green porphyry and pink-veined marble bowls.

He smiled. "I'm glad you approve of my little assortment of trifles. I saw you examining some of the books. Do you read Arabic?"

"A bit," I said, "enough to see you had some splendidly bound Korans."

"Some time you must examine them but now I think you would like a wash, perhaps, and somewhere to put your clearly very important attaché case."

Mehmet, the steward, took me to a first floor bedroom with a large bathroom off it, put my case on the bed and disappeared. I ran a bath, washed the dust and ancient sweat off, and was soaking the stiffness out of muscles and joints, when I heard the phone ring, inside my case. By the time I got it unlocked, wet footprints all over the rugs, and drip marks across the bathroom floor, whoever it was had rung off. I tried the Reply List but the local network didn't support that service. It was probably Chuck. I rang him while I towelled myself dry before putting on again the clothes I'd been wearing all day, it felt more like a week, since I'd got up that morning in Tel Aviv.

Eventually I got through and Chuck answered.

"Where were you?" he shouted, accusingly. "I've rung and rung and rung."

"I was having a bath," I said. "Felt a bit grubby."

"Are you back at the hotel?"

"No," I said. "At a friend of Sam's."

"And you're having a bath there?" He sounded both incredulous and maddened.

"I came here straight from the airport. More to the point, where are you?"

"We're still in Kos. No ferry till tomorrow morning."

"Who's we?"

"I've got William with me. He arrived this evening but missed the girls who are now in Athens. Katie phoned to say they were all right."

He couldn't keep the admiration out of his voice. "She's a good reliable girl that."

"Unless you're married to her or, like William, think you're engaged to her."

"How could he be? She hasn't divorced Sims yet."

"Don't be silly, Chuck. She's a right little tart."

"No, she's not. That's very un-un-un-fair . . ."

"Take a deep breath."

"B-b-b-bugger you," he said but he took a deep breath, paused and spoke very slowly and deliberately. "It's just that she gets easily b-b-bored."

"OK," I said, "she's your girl not mine."

"I wish she was. Hasn't made her mind up yet."

"Forgive my interrupting your love-musings, *paidí mou*, but I'd be grateful for news of Eloïse, my friend, if you remember."

"And f-f-fiancée," he said eagerly. "Sorry, sorry; of course. There's not much to say. She's a bit shell-shocked, if you know what I mean; very quiet, rather remote, a look of mystification on her face. Physically she seems f-f-fine; maybe a bit thin. Says she wants to see you but when I suggested ph-ph-phoning you, she said something about not having anything to say. What can I say, she asked over and over again: what can I say?"

"Thanks," I said. "That's very reassuring. Call me tomorrow when you've got to Bodrum."

I wanted to think about Eloïse, why she couldn't talk to me, why she had nothing to say, but I looked at my watch; I'd been upstairs for half-an-hour.

When I returned to the salon, hot börek and köfte were being served. I asked Pete where our host had got to. Telephone, he thought. He went back to playing with some outsize worry beads cut from rose quartz. Adnan Bey came back to the room looking happier. He had just spoken to Sam, he said, who was on his way over, would be with us shortly.

"You must be as relieved as I am."

I said I was; deeply relieved.

"Before he arrives," Adnan Bey went on. "We should have a quick *tour d'horizon* of Turkish political affairs, at least as they affect your quest. All right?"

I agreed, without much enthusiasm, and he led me over to a well-stuffed ottoman where he poured us both some neat raki. He stared at me. It was almost a glare. He broke off in order to pass me a bowl of olives, another of pistachio nuts and an ashtray to put the stones and the shells in.

"Well," he said, in a bright, patronising, tutorial voice, "what do you know?" He paused and stared at me again. "Or what do you think you know?"

An accumulation of fury welled up like bile. I swallowed it back. There was no point in taking it out on Adnan Bey. He was Sam's friend, my host. He, at least, wasn't about to try to kill me. But, like the rest of them, he seemed to think that because I wasn't an intellectual, a spy-master, a diplomat or even a journalist but had been a front-line soldier, I must be pig-stupid. On reflection he probably didn't know that I was a marine. *Rein yourself in! Marshal your thoughts!* I could hear Colour-Sergeant Malone: *Don't let the buggers get you down, Major!*

"I'm not up to date," I said. He smiled tolerantly at me, forgiving me in advance. ". . . but OK. First, Economics: the enormous success of the Özal revolution. Second, Politics: the coming of the first anti-Atatürk, Islamist-led government, with the Army continuing its role as protector of the Atatürk anti-clerical constitution. More dangers and difficulties ahead there. Foreign Affairs: a) the 24-year old occupation of Northern Cyprus as a sub-state recognized only by Turkey; b) the anti-terrorist military campaign against the PKK Kurds and its spreading, cross-border into Iraq, which internationalized the Kurdish issue; c) the effect of all this on European Union-Turkish relations, Turkey's human rights' record contributing to the EU rebuffs, almost as much as Greek-led opposition over Cyprus. Lastly, the somewhat quirky relationship with Israel . . ."

I put down a slug of raki.

Adnan Bey grinned broadly, gave a soundless clap or two and said, "Not bad. Not bad at all. I liked the quirky bit. But to be serious . . ." Bolton put back in his box. ". . . let's look at what's happening now. Yes, Turkey is fed up with the way she's been treated by the EU. Our economy is strong. We ought to qualify for Monetary Union. As for human rights, we don't take kindly to being lectured by countries like Germany who some would argue brought about the bloody dismemberment of Yugoslavia; or Britain who failed to protect the Muslims in Bosnia against some of the most savage atrocities this century. We resent the ability of Greece, to veto our entry into the EU. Yes? And, as far as we are concerned, we're staying in Cyprus. And that's that."

I took a handful of nuts and inclined my head, neutrally. No point in arguing. He hadn't mentioned the threat of integrating northern Cyprus with Turkey, or the increasing number of incidents, at sea and in the air, of Turkish and Greek military confrontation in the Aegean . . .

"Look, we've a population of 60 million plus," he said. "We've a GNP of over $3,000 per capita in absolute terms, without the black economy. We've a large army and a vital, strategic position between East and West, North and South, Islam and Christianity. You think we should just stand there and allow ourselves to be rebuked like naughty schoolchildren?"

He shook his head, dolefully. I ate some olives and put the stones in the ashtray.

"And then Bosnia. Suddenly we saw Western hypocrisy for what it was, with Britain well to the fore. And the USA not far behind. But it was your Mr Major and your Mr Hurd who led the ranks of the . . . What is the word? Mr Neville Chamberlain in 1938–9 . . . Traitors?"

"No," I said, "appeasers."

"That's it. The English appeased the Serbs while pretending there had been an equality of suffering, a balance of cruelty. Of course there were Muslim atrocities as awful as those engineered by the Serbs. But they were infinitesimal in scale and scope compared with the ethnic cleansing carried out, with barbaric cruelty, on the Bosnian Muslims. There were no level playing fields and no even-handedness. The British, and others, appeased the Serbs who killed, raped, tortured, tens of thousands. The Germans backed the Croats even after the appalling bloodbath at Visegrad on the Drina. You remember Nobel prize-winner, Ivo Andric's *Bridge Over the Drina?* Do you realize that now there are *no* Muslims in Visegrad. *None.* And before? 15,000. So where are they? Dispersed elsewhere? No; most of them are dead, buried locally or flung into the river.

"To start with we looked on. We expected the Greeks to side with the Serbs; because they're fellow Eastern Orthodox Christians. But we thought better of the British and the Americans. We believed what they said about Serb withdrawals; about what Karadzic, Mladic, Milosevic promised; about what would happen if the Serbs didn't carry out their obligations. And what happened? Srebinicza and Gorazde happened.

"The chief perpetrators are still there today, still not brought to book despite one or two brave attempts—to give Satan his due—by you British, or rather by your brave SAS lads, to stop the rot."

He paused for a swig of raki.

"I digress. I have lost my thread," he said. "I know. Turkey and all the Muslim states eventually realized that ways had to be found to arm the almost weaponless Muslims who were dying in the Serbian-controlled torture camps and killing fields.

I nodded. I was remembering the reports from Bosnia; BBC, ITN, Ed Vulliamy in the *Guardian*; the frightening feeling of impotence in the face of ever more horrifying atrocities while Western politicians were posturing and wittering. We all knew that a decent show of force on the ground, a handful of American, British and French, infantry brigades; detachments of US Marines, Royal Marine Commandos, French Foreign Legion, assorted paratroops, with SAS, SBS, US Rangers for special duties, supported by artillery and air cover, would have faced down the Serbs. The Bosnian Serbs admitted as much, later, on television.

"Ah yes," he resumed, "the Kurds."

My eyebrows shot up. As a non sequitur, this was well up in the competition stakes.

"Amongst the people who were smuggling arms into Bosnia," he went relentlessly on, "were mafiosi chieftains. Some of them were also smuggling heroin. Some of them were Kurds. There are, you know, Kurdish deputies in parliament and some Kurds are pro-government; or more precisely on the side of some Turkish governments. You may remember reading about one well-known family, allegedly Kurdish drug-dealers from Lice in south-eastern Turkey."

In fact, I had drifted off into my own preoccupations. Perhaps I should have taken up the challenge to capture Radovan Karadzic, Ratko Mladic, "Arkan" and others. But realistically how could I have done it, even with a team, against NATO's considered positive inaction? I sprang back to attention in time to hear him say something about Interpol.

"Huseyin," he was saying, "one of the family, was arrested by Interpol in 1995 in the Netherlands. He was charged with trafficking in heroin. The following year, he was released and the Dutch government gave him refugee status. They also refused a request by Turkey for extradition. Huseyin meanwhile started giving interviews to the press, particularly the Turkish press. His gang, he said, operated within the government. They used army vehicles. It was sensational stuff. He accused a former Minister of the Interior of dealing in heroin. He alleged Özer Çiller, the husband of the then Foreign Minister, was laundering drug money. Later I heard he was being investigated

189

by the Dutch authorities themselves—serves them right—for allegedly being the head of a drugs cartel."

He mused for a moment or two, got up, refilled our glasses, emptied the ashtray of olive stones and pistachio husks before telling me about another Kurdish gang leader who had drug and terrorist connections in Egypt; who was gun-running in quite a big way. I began to sit up and take notice. Perhaps Adnan Bey worked on the Eurovision Song Contest procedure: Third, Second, Wow! First. This could be Mr X, The Turk, he was talking about, the one he had saved till last, the most likely candidate.

"This crime czar," he said, pursing his mouth at the cliché, "offered the Bosnian Muslims, missiles, chemical weapons, notably Sarin nerve gas, and a catalogue of biological bombs, Anthrax and the like, and nuclear warheads. He was also an ardent Islamist with political connections; a close relative was said to be a deputy in Necbettin Erbakan's pro-Muslim, Welfare Party."

I excused myself and ran upstairs to get the pictures the Israelis had given me.

Chapter twenty-five

Pete was lying on the bed, his feet, now that I noticed them, in rather fancy trainers, carefully protruding beyond the coverlet. Balanced on his chest was my attaché case.

"Tell me, sport," he said, "got any idea what you're doing?"

"Not much," I said, taking the case from him and slowly and deliberately unlocking it. "Have you?"

"I'm not meant to. I'm just a squaddie doing what he's told, like. I'm PBI with revolver. Sam'd sack me if I knew why I was doing anything. Well almost. That mobile phone of yours has been squawking away on and off. Thought I'd better not set off the alarms. Wouldn't it be better if you either carried it around, like, or switched the little bugger off?"

"Probably," I said. I dialled Chuck's number. "Don't tell me you've been ringing me for hours."

"I've been ringing you for hours. Phone your meteorologist chum." He clicked off.

I dialled the number for Jim Cordier. A younger voice answered. It sounded like Andy Ross, the lieutenant (J.G.).

"Andy," I said. "It's David. How's the weather?"

"Hi, David," I heard some paper being shuffled. "Storm warnings south and east Aegean. Weather system centred round Bodrum peninsula. Gales imminent repeat imminent. Next update 0600 local."

"Thanks," I said. "Sounds grisly."

"Sounds good to me," he said. "But I'm not at sea. Good sailing!"

I got the photos out, pocketed the phone, relocked the case and pulled Pete off the bed.

"Sam'll be here in a minute. The truth is I think I'm beginning to know more than I want to."

I showed the Israeli blow-ups to Adnan Bey. He put on his glasses and peered at the smudged images.

"They don't ring any bells with me but then my eyesight's going to pot and they're not very sharp pictures, are they. I just make out a blur sitting at a table, at least I suppose it's a table. Who it is, where it is, I have no idea. I'm not even sure it's the same blur. You'll have to wait for my son. He should be coming with Sam."

I had somehow not associated Adnan Bey with a son or indeed a wife: he had the air of an habitual bachelor. Peter loped over and joined us.

"What's your son do, Mr Adnan?"

192

Adnan Bey looked at him, over his glasses. "You might say he's in the family business." He laughed till he spluttered and had to go off and get himself a glass of water.

"What was all that about then, Ben or David or Sam's nephew or cousin or whoever the hell you are?"

"I imagine," I said, "he's alluding to his own, and for all I know his father's, trade."

"And that is, like what, when it's at home?"

"What do you think? Intelligence. Counter-espionage. Spymaster-in-chief. Who knows?"

"Yeah, that figures. Spooks Incorporated. Hey, that's pretty good; spooks in-corp-orated. Get it? Do Muslims have ghosts?"

There were noises off. Sam and supporters had arrived. It was the signal for dinner.

"About bloody time, too," said Pete. "I thought I was going to fade, spectral like."

Sam's left arm was in a high sling, his fingers touching his right shoulder. There were layers of bandage underneath. It was all right, he said, quite comfortable. They had immobilised the shoulder. The bullet had passed through doing no lasting damage. The doctors had done a good job of patching and sewing him up. They'd also looked after Haggai, who had come with him, looking pale and bruised.

Sam was sitting on my left, allowing me to cut his meat up for him, Adnan Bey on his left and Izmet, the son, on my right. Sam had launched into one of his tales. It was how he had come to meet Adnan, back in the dawn of history, the mid-sixties, early seventies.

Izmet was thin, gangling, dome-headed, balding and bespectacled. He was taller than his father by half a head. I wasn't sure about his age, anywhere between 45 and 55, I reckoned. His English was as sophisticated as Adnan Bey's but more transatlantic. He had, he explained, spent three years freezing at Cornell. He thought Ithaca, NY, very romantic; very romantic and very cold; happiest days of his life. I handed him one of the prints.

Sam was saying, "I found myself at the Officers' Club in Ankara. It was one of those occasions when the generals had taken over. On my right sat an American colonel, on my left a Turkish major-general, in front of each of us, a row of raki bottles." He pronounced it properly: rák*u*, the *u* unstressed as in "*u*pon".

"There were," he went on, "stewards behind each of us. I was having a battle to get some wine and when I next looked round, my neighbouring general had downed his first third of a litre and had opened the second bottle of raki. I introduced myself, He mumbled a name which I didn't catch. I asked him what he did. 'Je suis,' he said, 'chef de Deuxième Bureau.' I was suitably impressed but we had no further chat. He finished his second third and kept a glassy silence, till later, after the third third, he fell gently and quietly asleep."

Izmet recognized the background to the photograph at once. It was a café in Frankfurt, he said, frequented by foreign students, amongst them Turks and, perhaps, some Kurds.

"My other neighbour," said Sam, "was a US 'adviser' attached to the first army in Thrace. I learnt no more. I asked him if he attended parades. What did he do when there were disciplinary punishments, public floggings? He looked at me carefully, his moustache quivering with sincerity and said, as any southern gentleman might when his slaves were being disciplined, 'I turn my back, Sir; I turn my back.'"

Izmet, who may have heard Sam's story before, produced a magnifying glass, and said it really wasn't a very clear shot, was it.

"I looked round," said Sam, "to see if the *chef de Deuxième Bureau* had woken up. He'd gone. I decided then to seek out a civilian who knew something about counter-terrorism and discovered my good friend, Adnan Bey, here."

"Tell you what," said Izmet, "I think I know who it may be but I'd like to check. How soon do you want to know? How urgent is it? I can get some people in Ankara to fax through possible matches. Would tomorrow do?"

"Better today," I said. "It is rather urgent."

"OK," he said, pushing his chair back, getting ready to rise. "Come on, we'll go to a local office."

"Not that urgent," I mumbled. "Not split second urgent. I'd like to finish my Adana kebab, first. It seems a long time since I had a proper meal. And make one phone call?"

I tried Eloïse's mobile. There was no answer. I raised Chuck in Kos, apparently waking him up. She was safe in Athens, he said grumpily. He'd told me already and it was too late to phone her aunt, if she were there and he didn't know that she was.

194   Five minutes later Izmet was driving us down into the centre of Izmir.

The road to Bodrum is reasonably fast and reasonably safe but it does wind from time to time. It's 250 kilometres from Izmir and, apart from the first section to Aydin, it's not a motorway, an autobahn, an autoroute or an autostrada. The buses take four hours. Izmet was brought up in a different school, the school of Ayrton Sena. His Mercedes was new and powerful and we took not much over two hours. I thought it a bit on the risky side but I wasn't going to complain: we got there in one piece and I was undeniably in a hurry.

I had phoned the US navy exchange and got through to Jim Cordier shortly before seven o'clock. He sounded wide awake and chipper, "Captain Cordier. Is that you, David?"

I said it was.

"Right. Now listen up. No repeats. Storm over. All ships safe. One man overboard secured and now in treatment."

He was speaking fast but a measure of triumphalism showed through.

"Any lifesaving or other gear with him?" I asked.

"Not so much as a Very light with or without pistol." Less triumphal.

"No one else lost?"

"Nary a one. All on his own-io."

"Aye, aye, Sir," I said.

"Carry on, David. Ciao."

Which, being interpreted, meant they had got their, and my, man, Zkrakovic the Croat. There had been no one with him which was what they expected. But there were no weapons with him either and that, for them, for all of us, was decidedly worrying. Missiles, automatic weapons, nuclear warheads, whatever, were missing.

Since they thought, despite my raising doubts, the Croat was the principal and that he was operating on his own, perhaps they were less anxious about the weapons than I was, missiles being useless without someone to arm and fire them. I had become certain that Zkrakovic was working for Mr X and assumed that he had the weapons. *Easy: find Mr X.*

Izmet had made what sounded like a reliable identification. I had heard him on the phone again to Ankara early in the morning. Mr X was, he told me, known. His raised right shoulder had developed into a noticeable characteristic only over the last few years but his face was memorable; highly individualistic, Izmet called it, a one-off. He came from a Kurdish family in Mardin, in the extreme south-east of Anatolia, south of Lake Van, close to the border with Syria. He was called Orhan as a child but, after going to school in Erzurum, where his father, an engineer, had been working, and after completing his military service, he began to call himself Yaşar. It was, perhaps, said Izmet as we sped along, a tribute to Yaşar Kemal, the great Turkish, indeed Kurdish-Turkish, novelist, author of *Memed, My Hawk*: a tribute that Yaşar Kemal could well do without. Later he had many more names.

The thought of books, literature, made him shift direction, got him off our target.

"You know," he said, turning away from the road to give me the full force of his scrutiny, I willed him back to the windscreen, "this, the country we're driving through, is a land of myths and marvels. Ahead of us—not that there's anything left of it after the crusaders got at it—the tomb of King Mausolos, the *original* Mausoleum, at Halicarnassus which is now Bodrum. Here," he flipped a hand towards the outside world we were passing through in a blur of speed, "was the land of Lydians. It was here that King Croesus of Lydia introduced the first coins and became as rich as . . . Croesus; that the river Meander . . . meandered."

I suppose that subconsciously he had been storing up the turnings, the road signs, the resonant names, recreating childhood expeditions and adult excursions, till his natural enthusiasm exploded.

"Did you want to be an archaeologist?"

"Oh, sure," he said. "I'd have loved that but my father had other ideas. I don't know that he ever asked me. He just told me. I had a job to do—for my country—and I didn't question it. You don't, certainly you didn't, question my father."

Looking at the map, we weren't that far from the sea at any point, as we drove what was roughly due south. We had left the better-known tourist resort of Kuşadasi well behind but, approaching Bodrum, there were a lot of new holiday developments on the otherwise beautifully unspoilt coastline.

"There are kilometres and kilometres of glorious coast," said Izmet. "Marvellous, clean, deep sea; good sailing, fishing, snorkelling. A paradise for holiday-makers. And there are colonies—not for foreigners but for Turks, from Istanbul, Ankara, Izmir even—of villas. An engineers' village; an architects' village; a doctors' village. Each remote from the others, each distinct and, often enough, distinctive."

196

He was pleased with his linguistic skill. He smiled. "What do you say? A nice distinction?"

I nodded and said I thought it must be a species of hell, always being with people in the same line of business.

"The joke is," he said, "that sexual equality has triumphed at long last."

"Sexual equality?" I asked, bemused.

"Under Islam and under Turkish law," he said, "inheritance had to be equal between sons and daughters but the wily fathers got round that easily enough. They were farmers: they knew the value of land. They left the rich arable plateau land to their sons and the same amount but of stony, poor hill and cliff parcels running down to the infertile seashore to their daughters. But it was the daughters who had the last laugh. They are all now millionaires, having sold to developers, and their brothers are bankrupt. Neat.

"Right," he said, "enough of the travelogue. Back to your suspect. As Yaşar, with a variety of surnames, he went to Damascus. As Ersan somebody else he went to Lebanon, as Abdül Hamid to East Germany. By then a trained terrorist, and under the name of Yilmaz Çelik, the name he kept, he went to Cairo in 1960. He seems to have allied himself with various

Islamist groups, to have taken part in several murderous acts of terrorism and to have set himself up as an international drug and arms dealer."

"This is all good, broad brush-stroke stuff," I said. "What about specifics, details; like who he killed, when and where?"

"Why?" he said. "What for? He's wanted in several countries. No one's nailed him yet. There's no point. We—you, I—don't need to know. I—er—they will want him off our turf and won't want anything too messy to happen before that. OK?" He drummed the steering-wheel.

"OK," I said and he smiled. But he kept on drumming the wheel in sync with some tune running through his head; some maddening tune, going by the beat.

Not the easiest chap to make out. And what was this "I—er–they"? Had he got the push? Was he now free-lancing? I'd wondered why we'd gone off alone. Perhaps he was in opposition to the present government Or was considered batty. Great. That's all I needed. Not that I had any other ready option.

We had turned to the right off the main road and were now passing what looked like a lagoon and then threading our way through a populous village.

"Where are we?"

"We are going to one of those seaside communities I was telling you about."

I gave him a less than enthusiastic glance.

"This one's for psychiatrists," he said, laughing.

"That figures," I said.

"I was joking. It's an artists' and actors' community and my Uncle Feyyaz is a theatre producer. He's got a house here and at the moment he's in Prague. It'll make a useful HQ for us."

We were curving round a stunning littoral with the sea some way below, a wide bay with several inlets and coves, a clear horizon and a great sweep of cerulean sea and a paler but still vivid dome of sky. He swerved suddenly to the left on to a roughly paved road which dropped steeply, went through a kind of slalom with gradients to match, and screeched to a halt in front of a duplex, hanging over the sea, some 70 metres below.

"So far, so good," he said and got out of the car.

I wasn't so sure.

Chapter twenty-six

Bodrum, Turkey

It was now 13:30. Chuck had phoned at 11:15. He and William had taken the first boat they could find that was prepared to cross from Kos to Bodrum.

"We had the usual nonsense," he had said. "First of all no one wants to tell you where the ferry to Turkey goes from. State secret. Either that or general discouragement. Then there's the shelling out. You pay extra to leave Greece. You pay for a visa once you get to Turkey. That's apart from the fares which aren't exactly bargain basement. We did all that, went through immigration in Bodrum, paid their whack and walked along the mole looking at the yachts. Marvellous assortment from millionaire's floating gin-palace down to basic scruffy boat.

"You know the way my shoe-laces never stay done up." I said I knew. "Well, I was tying them up again, right foot placed on convenient bollard when I saw a rather small boat, some way along, well down in the water, not much free-board or whatever you call it, compared to the hulking great yachts. Two or three men unloading medium-sized packing cases, loosely covered with tarpaulin.

"It wasn't the unloading that got my attention. It was the furtive air.

That and the fact that no one else was stirring. And then I noticed the supervising guy had a tic, more of a convulsion really, with his left shoulder, which was higher than his right anyway. And I thought of your Mr X."

I had suggested that he get William to go off and rent a decently fast and reliable car, while he waited to see where the cargo went. I said I'd contact them when I got towards Bodrum. Meanwhile, please, to keep the stuff and the man under observation, if at all possible.

While Izmet unlocked the garage and tucked the Merc away, I dialled Chuck. Since he and I were both using English Vodafone circuits, I reckoned it meant going up on a Turkish local system to a satellite, thence to the UK and then back and out and back again. No wonder it took so long to establish contact. At last I heard it ringing and as it went on I got worried that it might noisily be blowing his and William's cover.

Chuck answered on the fifth ring. Everything was fine. He and William were having lunch. Mr X had gone to a house, which he could see through the window, the car was still outside and as far as they knew the packing cases, four in all, were still inside the boot. What next?

I asked where their car was. Also outside and facing the same direction, a second or two further up the road.

"Well done," I said. "You've thought of asking for the bill and having the money ready?"

"Yeah, yeah. William's good at this. In theory, any road. He's a great reader of Deighton and Le Carré and Clancy and Sebastian and Forsyth . . ."

"Fine. Izmet and I will stay outside Bodrum till we know what road they take."

"Who the devil's Izmet?"

"A friend of Sam's and owner of the Mercedes we're using."

"I'll let you know as soon as they stir. William will drive. I'll be on the phone and reading the map. Anything more?"

What could I say? The fate of the Western World depends on you? Hardly. This is our only chance to nab a murderous psychopath who otherwise will do more and more damage in both human and international political terms? So, so what? They'll do their best. We'll do ours. Neither the Americans nor the Israelis had really listened when I'd tried to expand my argument. The Americans hadn't wanted to know about Mr X. The Israelis hadn't wanted to consider the arms that the Croat had bought on Mr X's behalf.

That wasn't quite fair.

Before he saw me off to the plane, Hannan had let his hair down.

"'You've not caught us at our best," he'd said, "Indeed you've not. There's been another monumental SNAFU. Mossad has bungled an ill-considered—in all senses—assassination attempt on Khalid Mish'al, head of Hamas's Political Bureau. In Amman, for God's sake, and Khalid, you mind, is a Jordanian citizen. A pair of Mossad clowns have been arrested carrying forged Canadian passports. All hell's broken loose. Prisoners will have to be released. Kol Israel's been talking about Jordan expelling another twelve Mossad agents." He drew breath. "We know Arafat's not in control of his lot but Netanyahu, not my favourite prime minister you'll be thinking, rightly, is not only in hock to the religious crackpots and the right-wing loonies but is sanctioning dangerous adventures to keep them happy. I don't *believe* this."

He had gone on to tell me, in indiscreet detail, of other assassination missions that had been properly planned, rehearsed and carried out; that had been both militarily effective and politically useful. This abortion of an operation had been politically inept as well as a colossal balls up. He thought the time had passed for loose thinking, for ineptitude and, probably, though he wasn't going to the stake for it, for assassinations in general. Bugger the politicians, bugger Mossad.

From this I assumed him to be Shin Bet, the Israeli equivalent to MI5, the Security Service, but Sam later told me he was the boss of a joint counter-terrorism committee reporting to God, or the President, or some other Olympian.

This was the moment, probably foolishly, I'd made my bid.

"I understand," I'd said. "I chose the wrong day. A nuisance for you; having me on top of everything else."

He hadn't replied, just made a dismissive, hand gesture.

"But," I went on stalwartly, "there's a question, Hannan, I'd like to ask. Why is it that neither you nor your bright young team seem to be the least worried when I said that these psychopaths have missile launchers, possibly chemical, possibly nuclear warheads, at large in Turkey, probably aimed at ships taking part in joint manoeuvres, and more likely than not at Israeli targets?"

"Ben," he'd said, sighing heavily, "if I'd had the fluttering horrors every time I contemplated poison gas, anthrax, sarin, not to mention nuclear bombs raining down on our civilians, I'd be what they call a basket-case.

And that would be not one bit of use to me or any other living being. Of course, I worry. I worry all the time; but I have, lurking just out of vision, many a more immediate frightener at my beck and call."

He waved a sketchy farewell and was gone.

Someone, maybe Hannan, shouted from a distance. "Shalom. Good luck."

Izmet had brewed some coffee and was busy sorting out maps. He found one he liked the look of.

"Here," he said, "you'd better take this and familiarize yourself with the roads round Bodrum."

He poured us each a black coffee and pushed over a tray of sachets of milk and sugar. I pushed it back, sucked in the coffee which was both hot and strong, and perused the map. It looked new and was thankfully large enough scale to see where we were and how the exits from Bodrum were arranged.

"The chances are," he said, "they'll take 330, the road to Milas, and finally on to Izmir, the one we came on, but they won't go far. They'll nip down to some deserted stretch of coast, or to some safe house they've got ready for them, away from suspicious neighbours."

"Why do you say 'they' as though there was a team? He'll only need one helper."

"I think there'll be other people involved. As you did when it was only the Croat."

He was right on both counts.

Chapter twenty-seven

After it was all over and I was metaphorically—thank heaven— burying my dead, I wondered what Izmet had really been up to. Had he been privy to advance information? Did he know where they were going? Or was it really just copper's intuition?

At first it had seemed a stupid sort of chase, stupid and dangerous. What were we going to do, when and if we caught up with them? There were four of them in a black Mercedes, a slightly older model than Izmet's, but we would have looked as though we came out of the same stable, if there had been anyone there to see us. William and Chuck brought up the rear in their hired blue Renault 12 STW. Yilmaz Çelik, Mr X, was driving. I saw him reasonably clearly as his car shot past the intersection where we were waiting.

It was getting on for midnight. There was noise and light around and above Bodrum, great searchlights and sunbursts, and deafening music coming from discos and, notably, from a nightclub, at the top, overlooking the harbour and the town, called, with an overweening ineptitude, Halicarnassus.

Chuck had phoned the moment the front door of the house had opened. In turns, they'd dozed the afternoon away in their Renault, had returned to the restaurant for an extended light snack, and had got back in the car about half-an-hour before Çelik and gang emerged.

"Beginner's luck," I said to Izmet, but he was too busy getting out of the house and manoeuvring his Merc into position, with all lights doused and engine idling. After just under eight minutes we saw the loom of the headlights and then the car itself swept past with a map-reading light illuminating the driver and the front seat passenger. Izmet virtually slid into their slip-stream, still without turning on any lights. They, and therefore we, were going uncomfortably fast. There were enough unevennesses in the road surface, shifts in camber and bends, to make Çelik's Mercedes buck and slither, for all its solid road-holding, like a nervous stallion. Behind us, some way back, William was driving with dipped headlights.

I wished I was doing the driving but, to be fair, Izmet was well in control, hunched over the wheel, his face almost touching the windscreen in the effort to stay in touch with Çelik who, whatever the state of his shoulders, was driving like the possessed.

"Would it be sensible," I said, "to shoot at their rear tyres? I assume you want them to crash."

He bridled. "No firearms. No shooting. Maybe they'll—what's the expression?—run out of highway."

"Run out of road," I said. "Not that their crashing is going to be all that safe; but safer than letting them get away."

I got my going away present key-ring from Admiral Mike Cable out of my trouser pocket and slipped the larger ring with the keys on it back into my pocket. We were only 50 metres behind them. It might, it should work, if I could only focus on the driving mirror. I could see the mirror, just, from time to time, when we were at the right angle to the car.

"Spurts, flashes, from guns would alert them to us," he said, concentrating on a bend which was tighter than he expected. "You've sussed out who Çelik is now?"

"What do you mean?"

"He's the guy who knows you're shtupping his daughter. Make your role here a bit complicated?"

He didn't let his attention wander. We were holding tight to the car ahead.

Christ. Why tell me now? Eloïse's dad. Psychotic murderer. She'd never forgive me if I helped kill him. He was better dead. How many more Armenians, Jews, tourists, by-standers would die? The greater good. Anyway what did Eloïse feel about her father now? She might never speak to me again. But what was right? Whatever the hell that might mean. Of course, it suddenly made him human; not Mr X. mass murderer but my nearly father-in-law. What to do? Stop him. The alternative was his getting away; more deaths. He was evil. And why chase him otherwise? What else were we doing here?

As we straightened out after the bend and accelerated, I got the opportunity I was looking for and aimed the tiny red dot at the driving mirror. The effect was immediate and cataclysmic. The car went half off the road and ploughed into a rocky outcrop. In the second it took, I feared an almighty explosion which never came. I wondered too if Izmet was going to be able to hold to the road while braking. He did; he pulled up a few metres short of the tyre marks where Çelik had left the tarmac. There was an abrupt and total silence; a sense of awful peace.

Izmet broke the quiet. He was talking softly but it sounded like a trumpet blast.

"It might be sensible now to be armed. We don't know what we're going to find. Put these on." He threw me a pair of white cotton scene-of-crime gloves.

I knew quite well what we were going to find; damaged, perhaps dead, people and damaged, perhaps dangerous and unstable, warheads. I made for the driver's side, partly to release the boot, partly to see Mr X close-up for the first time. I could hear the Renault coming to a halt and two pairs of feet scurrying over to join us and then stopping some way short. I opened the driver's door, the interior light still worked. It came on and vividly lit up the carnage. It looked as though all four were dead. The steering column was stuck into Çelik's chest. There was a lot of blood. By the look of it, none of them had been wearing seat-belts but in a crash like this, they probably would have died anyway. As I bent forward to release the boot, Çelik opened his eyes and saw me. He spoke one word, with hatred but the venom was without power. He tried to spit in my face but the spittle barely got beyond his tongue. A globule, elastic-like, jiggled up and down, attached to his lower lip till a rattling convulsion shook it loose and bubbles of blood gurgled up and he died.

I took the leather document case from the door pocket beside him and closed the door. I rushed round to the boot and stared with mixed horror and relief at the wooden packing-cases which had broken open. Apart from several automatic rifles, there were three missile launchers, six missiles and one bigger package which I was pretty sure was a nuclear war-head. I passed two of the launchers and three of the missiles, one by one, to William and Chuck but took the nuclear baby gently into my arms.

Izmet was examining the back seat of the car and taking photographs.

He looked up at one point and said to me, in a remote, dreamy sort of voice, "Çelik called you 'Infidel'. He used the Turkish rather than the classical Arabic."

"Thanks," I said and turned to the others to restore my confidence. I spoke to William.

"We can't hang around," I said. "You'd better go and take a good look at the driver, Yilmaz Çelik. There's your revenge. Not a pretty sight. He's the man who killed your aunt and uncle and cousins."

He went off, reluctant but knowing his duty.

I took out my sports bag, which one of Sam's boys had picked up from the hotel, emptied out bits of uniform and pairs of socks and underpants and hid the nuke warhead beneath pyjamas and spare shirts. I asked Chuck to put the stuff I'd tipped out into his and William's cases. I removed the papers from Çelik's document case and put them into mine and then hid his leather folder beneath a jumble of rocks, off the road. I could hear William retching and Izmet remonstrating. He was saying it was time to go. If the police found any foreigners near a crash, they'd arrest them and hold them in prison for some time. And, in this case, where there were multiple deaths and no obvious reason for the accident, it would not be a good idea to be a foreigner seen hanging around the scene. Not, actually, either, a good notion for a Turk to be found nearby. "En voiture," he shouted, "en voiture."

I told Chuck to find somewhere, the other side of Bodrum, to park the car and themselves. I'd be in touch as soon as I thought it sensible. "Don't follow Izmet. I think William will need some comforting. Wait a few minutes before you set out. And then go with all decent speed. Don't call me. I'll call you."

Whatever he thought of my instructions, Chuck accepted them and carried them out; which was just as well. By the time Izmet got back to his Mercedes, I was sitting demurely in the front passenger seat, my clobber stowed away.

"I've put three of the missiles in your boot," I said. "The others are still in the other Mercedes." He seemed uninterested. He turned the car round. Chuck was helping a pasty-faced, weak-kneed William back to their Renault. Izmet gave them a fleeting glance and shot off, tyres squealing, back towards Bodrum.

Once again we turned off, seawards, on the road to what I'd discovered was called Gölköy. We followed the same route as before, ending up at his uncle's house. Before we got there, he said: "It's going to cause a rare old rumpus."

"Who were the others?" I asked.

"In the back, a neat combination; a chief of police, currently 'on leave', an appointment of the previous government, and a real hard, Turkish-Kurdish mafia boss, with fingers in every criminal pie. In the front, a connection of Çelik's, a cousin, brother-in-law, or half-uncle on his mother's side, I don't know precisely; a deputy with close Islamist links and a reputation for sailing close to the wind. Criminals, dangerous criminals."

I slipped a handcuff over my left wrist, clicked it and locked its mate on to the handle of my case. I wondered if he'd heard the clicks but the car, with the rough road and the missiles rumbling and rolling in the boot, was making too much noise. The key was inside the case. It didn't exactly make for increased mobility but the security was impeccable.

"Where are your friends?" He didn't sound that concerned.

"William was very shaken up. I expect they've gone down to Bodrum for a drink."

When we stopped outside the front door, I suggested we take a closer look at the weapons I'd removed. He didn't think that would be necessary, not at the moment. I got him to release the catch all the same. While peering at the missiles, I was groping around for the one automatic weapon I secreted, accidental on purpose like. I found it, just in time.

Izmet was fumbling with the door-key. I moved along the side of the car, until I reached the bonnet where I rested the case and took up a firing position, gun and supporting legs stable and steady. The front door sprang open before Izmet unlocked it. Ahmed, his father's steward, stumbled on the threshold and another faintly familiar figure jumped out, revolver in hand. I had it: he was one of Eleni's torturers who had escaped with Zkrakovic. I fired at his knee and he dropped to the ground. Ahmed swivelled towards me and I fired a burst over his head. He was, I realized, unarmed and mouthing something. Izmet was running back to join me, rather clumsily getting his gun out. "Don't shoot," he shouted. "They took Ahmed prisoner. There's one of them still inside."

"Get Ahmed to take the guy's revolver," I said.

Ahmed got the gun without trouble and joined us behind the shelter of the car.

"Is he Turkish?"

Izmet translated.

Ahmed said "*Evet, effendim.*"

"Yes," said Izmet.

"I'll make my way round the back," I said, "and try and draw his fire. If you hear shooting, try and get inside the house. I'll do the same from the back. Don't let's shoot each other. We'll flush him out sooner or later."

My idiocy in welding the attaché case to me with clanking chains was evident as soon as I tried to move silently to the side door. I'd forgotten there wasn't a backdoor. It was a maisonette and the back was a partitioned balcony; half to one family, half to the other. It was quite wide and deep, had roses, vines and bougainvilleas climbing up it and looked over the declension, the terracing stepping downward, mostly occupied by other houses, towards the dark, midnight sea. The slope was such that the balcony stood five metres above the path and there was no staircase. A large glass window took up the wall of the sitting room. It was this that I heard breaking as the gunman inside thrust his machine pistol out to get a decent angle on me before he opened with a sustained burst of gunfire that played havoc with the bougainvillea but missed me by a centimetre or two. I was, by then, on the ground and out of sight. I was assuming his weapon was not of the generation of sophistication that purported to fire round corners. But, effectively, I was tied down. A small area of the kitchen window was visible from my shelter so I thought, as long as my right hand held out, and it had been doing pretty well so far, I might as well create some minor counter-diversion just in case Izmet and Ahmed had decided to invest the house. I fired and took the window out with a fortissimo arpeggio. It was pretty dramatic and would have been effective, had the kitchen window been the enemy. But it did the job. There was a noisy reprise from the gunman in the sitting room and then a solitary shot and a cry of triumph. Ahmed came out on to the balcony and said, I imagined, "I've killed the bastard. Come on in. You're safe now." Big triumphal announcement, bless him.

I went in through the kitchen entrance, and bussed Ahmed on both cheeks. He gave me a thorough hug. We were comrades-in-arms; nowt better. I was waiting for Izmet to break out the champagne or, at least, the raki. In fact, I hadn't caught sight of him yet and wondered whether he'd been hurt, sympathy well to the fore.

I needn't have bothered. There was a firm nudge in my right lower back. It felt like a revolver.

"Sorry old boy," he said, "and thanks for all your help but I really do need the other warheads."

I made to turn round, to face him down, but he jabbed me again, more violently, in the kidneys and I thought I'd save the heroics for later.

"Well where are they?"

"They're in the boot of your Mercedes. I told you to check earlier and you said it wouldn't be necessary. I left some, as I told you, in the crashed car."

"It wasn't necessary until Ahmed brought the message from Adnan Bey. I don't question my father. He says there's a nuclear warhead and he wants it."

"Well. It's not here, I can tell you," I said. "I don't suppose there was one, just the missiles and their launchers."

"He wants them too. He wanted to know which model they were."

"I expect," I said, needling him, "your father wanted to know if they were SA 300s, the ones the Greek Cypriots have ordered from Russia and that your people are making so much of a fuss over."

"Rightly," he said jabbing me again, painfully rather than playfully. "The Greek Cypriots are behaving provocatively and dangerously."

"Oh, come on," I said. "This is an old story. 1974, for heaven's sake. The Greek Junta unseat Makarios, helping some right-wing, anti-communist loonies. You invade to protect, it is said, the Turkish-Cypriot minority and grab a large part of the country. And here we are still no nearer an accommodation, let alone a peace, nearly a quarter of a century later. And what's so wonderful about the SA 300s anyway?" I half turned round, and this time he made no hostile gesture. I eased a point or two of the compass.

"They're the equivalent of the American Patriots admittedly," I went on. "But you'll remember the Patriots weren't all that successful against the Iraqi Scuds in the Gulf . . ."

I swung round and used my all-too-attached attaché case to knock the gun out of his hand. I picked it up quickly and pocketed it.

"Ah that's better," I said, rubbing where I thought my kidneys ought to be, if they'd survived.

"Oh dear," he said. "I'm no good at this sort of thing. Violence, gunplay, being tough."

"No," I said. "It's overrated. I'd stick to your last, if I were you."

"You won't get far," he said, lugubriously. "Once I tell my father what happened, the whole area will be sealed off and all foreigners, including, especially, you and your friends, will be taken in for questioning. They'll hold you for weeks, however much you squawk about lawyers and consuls."

"To what end? They won't be able to find what doesn't exist. And, Izmet, I deserve better of you. Without me, you wouldn't have known who to look for, or indeed where. Nor have disposed of them so quickly and neatly."

"That reminds me," he said, changing style, eager, interested. "How did you do it? One moment they were driving fast, but managing the corners, the bends and twists, and then suddenly they career off the road and finish their lives. I was astounded. I tried to figure out what happened. I examined the car closely. Nothing; nothing that would explain the crash. Incidentally, you missed the heroin. Nearly a kilo, I guess; in two packages, well-sealed. Stashed in the back seat, under the arm of the police chief. So, tell me, how did you do it? What did you do?"

I told him I'd explain if he promised to let Chuck, William and me go free. I said we'd be out of the country before noon. I looked at my watch, it was just past two a.m.

"I can't give you that long," he said. "Adnan Bey will have the local cops, the army and probably the navy too, cutting off the peninsular in twenty minutes after I telephone my report."

"You could delay phoning in for an hour or two. If you like, I can knock you out to make it more convincing."

"Oh no," he said. "I've had quite enough violence for one night."

"Likewise," I said. "So let's have a gentleman's agreement. You give me long enough to arrange an emergency evacuation. And do nothing to stop it. I'll tell you my secret weapon. And we'll be out of Turkey as soon as I can fix our exit but, in any case, before dawn."

Easier said than done. I wandered around, mobile telephone in hand, as various numbers failed to answer. Meanwhile Ahmed, with some minor assistance from Izmet, pulling a face of distaste, was laying out the corpses. Earlier I had asked about the man outside the front door. Izmet had said he was dead. I was surprised. I thought he must be alive; I had only hit him in the leg. That, I was given to understand, was as it may be: he was certainly dead now. I didn't enquire further.

Eventually, Captain Cordier was woken up. Admiral Cable was unobtainable, away. I walked out of the kitchen door and down into the garden to be out of earshot. I explained about Yilmaz Çelik. Jim still wasn't buying the lesser role for Zkrakovic but acknowledged there must be some tie-in when I went on to detail the arms. I explained the emergency as far as I and my team were concerned and said we desperately needed a helicopter to pick us, and a sample of the weapons, up and take us somewhere—the Nimitz perhaps—to be debriefed and the dangerous stuff examined. It took him a little while to appreciate the seriousness of our situation vis-à-vis the Turkish authorities. When he did, he moved fast.

I used the house phone to get hold of Chuck and asked him to bring William and everything to Izmet's uncle's house. I gave him as exact a routing as I could remember. In the event, he only made one wrong turning and that was almost within sight of the house.

When Jim Cordier phoned back in three-quarters of an hour, I was beginning to get anxious but, in fact, he had laid on what I'd asked for, the only problem now was when and where. I had been thinking that we might have to be winched up from the edge of the sea but Chuck had been down to the bathing beach and found a large area of concrete, well away from trees or houses, which would make a perfectly good and safe helipad. Map co-ordinates were another matter. I gave a verbal description, from the map

we'd been using, and the navigator I spoke to seemed to pick up the same coastal features from his charts. I said we'd light the area with car headlights.

"We'll file a flight plan with Turkish air control, as a simulated emergency medical exercise in connection with the joint manoeuvres," he said. "It'd better be in darkness. Let's say 0415 local. Could we synchronize watches, please."

It was 0255, official. Izmet and Ahmed were giving Chuck beer and a few meze. William said he felt sick, couldn't look at food or drink. I took Izmet aside and told him about Mike Cable's present, the little laser pointer which doubled as a key-ring. The others also wanted to hear the tale. I explained the problem of focusing on the driving mirror to ensure that the driver was, at least, bothered and probably temporarily blinded. I said I'd calculated the angles but I didn't know whether it would work until I actually saw the red dot on the driving mirror and tried to hold it there and vary minutely the angle; with the result they had seen. In truth, I needn't have worried about minute adjustments: it all turned on the relative positions of the cars and it was a pure fluke. I had worked it out in theory but in practice it turned out to be a matter of chance; and I wasn't quite going to admit that.

I said that I needed to have a quiet and private word with Izmet. They moved abruptly, Chuck back to the kitchen and food and drink, William to the lavatory, neither of them saying anything, not even looking at me. I wondered if they thought I was going to kill Izmet; if that was the sort of reputation they were building up for me. I shivered. I didn't like the thought. Izmet had no such doubts. He moved over and sat beside me.

"Izmet," I said perfectly truthfully, though perhaps the emphasis was a touch misleading, "what I did take surreptitiously was Çelik's papers." He looked up, eagerly.

"Where are they?"

"In my case," I said; and we both stared at the manacles.

"Have you got the key to the handcuffs?"

"Yes," I said. "Inside the case. We can open it but first I must have your word that once you've looked at them and translated anything of interest to me, you'll give them back on the strict understanding that I'll have them sent to you as soon as I've had them copied. Unless you've got a photocopier here?"

He raised his eyes to the heavens: no.

I called Chuck back to sit beside me and carry out precisely the complex unlocking procedure. The case opened. Chuck found the key where I'd hidden it away and released me. I gave the papers, about twenty pages perhaps, to Izmet, after he said he'd abide by my terms. I expect he had a photographic memory.

Chuck brought me a beer, a few olives and nuts, relieved to see that there was to be no further violence. Izmet whizzed through the text and then went back to the beginning and took it more slowly. From time to time he gave me a précis and sometimes a nugget or two, as well.

There were three substantive sections, Izmet said, and a lot of obscene nonsense about the glory, the pleasure, the importance and the necessity of killing infidels. From time to time, he compared the experience of killing defenceless civilians to a prolonged orgasm, enhanced by the sight of flowing blood, limbs shot off, bodies mangled.

"The man is mad, criminally insane," said Izmet, "a psychopath, a monster. He relishes killing. The pages on Palestine are extreme but not illogical. He says if Jews and Arabs, Zionists and Palestinians, want the same pieces of earth, then there can only be relentless war. Peace is a dangerous illusion. Jerusalem must be a Muslim city. Islam must triumph. In a Holy War millions will die.

"He talks about the joy of seeing foreigners, westerners, Jews and

Christians, die, powerless, decadent, infected, corrupted. He justifies drug-dealing as part of the Holy War."

A long diatribe on Turkey came next and the necessity for changing the constitution, throwing out, killing, the Kemalist establishment, and reviving Turkey as a centre of Islam.

"With names?" I asked.

"With names of supporters, extremists, gangsters, who would join in this Jihad."

"You want the Turkish section," I said. "Take it. Give Sam a copy and ask him to get it to me safely."

"Thanks," he said. "Adnan Bey will be very pleased with this. Very pleased, indeed." He tapped the eight or nine pages he'd taken out of the pile and set aside.

"The last chapter is devoted to Egypt. He anathematizes the assassinated Sadat. He demonizes Mubarak. He calls for Egypt to become leader of the Muslim world, a major religious centre as well as the regional political power; a true Islamic Republic. The Christian Copts must be thrown out, or killed. The massacre of the Armenians was a great success but pressure must be kept up, violence escalated. He recommends massacres at all tourist sites. The great pyramids, the sphinx; the Nile Valley, Dendera, Luxor, Karnak, Aswan, Abu Simbel. The greater the carnage, the better: the more absolute the terror. A few thousand more infidel lives? What of it? In the end, a triumph for Islam. And there are names and organizations and plans. He tells his friends in Gamaa al-Islamiya never to countenance a cease-fire."

I almost grabbed the sheets out of his hand. We both shuddered at the blood-strewn future. I knew I had to get the material to Jeremy Sims at the British Embassy in Cairo as soon as possible. He could then filter it through to the Egyptians and brief the American Embassy through Cy Drucker.

"You must know," Izmet raised his voice, "this man is not speaking for Islam. He is a murderer, an outcast, a maniac. Even I, an agnostic, recognize he is not a Muslim, a man of religion, of faith. He is a criminal and a monster."

It was then that we heard the sirens.

Izmet said, after a curse or two, that at the moment it was only two ambulances. Someone must have reported finding the crashed car. But the police wouldn't be far behind.

212

"This isn't your doing," I said, knowing it wasn't but wanting confirmation.

"Of course not," he said, "I've got Ahmed hiding the bodies away where no one will find them. There's no reason why the police should come here. No logical reason. I hope that's right."

I looked at my watch. It was time to get down and illuminate the temporary helipad. I asked Izmet if he would pick up the hire car, return it to its office in Bodrum and settle the account. Sam, I said, would reimburse him. We shook hands, surprisingly warmly. His lanky frame loped off, back inside.

By the time Chuck, William and I got into the Renault and started down the hill, he had turned off most of the lights in the house. There was no point in attracting more attention than was necessary. The chopper would make enough noise but down on the beach.

It came in on time and surprisingly low. The pilot parked it neatly. William turned off the Renault's lights while Chuck and I took all our three bags and my attaché case on board. We were away within the minute. Among the welcoming party, greeting the three of us, were Colonel Doug Lester and the civilian Bob Pearson whom I'd met as part of Mike Cable's team back in Izmir. I undid my hold-all, wrestled and got out the bigger warhead and handed it over together with one of the smaller missiles.

"Just what we needed, David," said Colonel Lester. "Good for you."

"Yup," said Bob Pearson, "this is nuclear." Somebody's Geiger counter was clacking away. "Only the one?"

"Yes," I said.

"Brave work, Major. Brave work." He went off, carrying the nuke with him.

"The rest of the arms," I said to Doug, "are in the hands of the Turkish authorities, We couldn't spirit them away. Too heavy and too many Turks around."

"You did well, David; better than we did. We got the man but not the hardware."

They'd only got one of the men, of course, but it wasn't the time to nitpick.

When we landed on the carrier, I went straight to a cabin and slept in my clothes. They had to shake me awake for the debriefing.

Chapter twenty-eight

Larnaca, Cyprus

"I'm never," said Chuck, "going to get mixed up in something like that again. Not ever." He paused, to make sure I understood the full seriousness of his pronouncement. "Any road, I think you should have warned me."

Chuck was flying back to England in a week's time and he and I were at Larnaca airport waiting for my mother's plane to arrive from Athens. It was late. All flights were late leaving Athens Ellinikon: there was a work-to-rule by air traffic controllers.

"I'm sorry," he went on. He was in a jerkily, talkative mood today, Katie was still around, making up her mind, and William had flown back to the States. "I'm sorry Eloïse couldn't see her way to join us. Your Mum will be disappointed. She's very fond of the girl."

"Yeah," I said.

Katie had spoken to me, privately. She said she was thinking of going back to see her mother for a while. She didn't fancy another Northern Hemisphere winter. Don't tell the boys, she had said. *Boys?*

She had also said, meaningfully, that William had told her All.

"All?" I said.

"Names, details, deaths and betrayals. William sort of went off it, you know; the revenge theme. He was sickened at the end; couldn't stomach the gore. Naïve, or is it naïf, being a bloody colonial I wouldn't know, that's what William turned out to be. Dark-eyed brooding sincerity and not much guts. You might say I sent him packing. I may come back for Chuck, he's something else. Next year it would be; high summer, after the divorce. I don't think Jerra will contest anything. Nice guy but not for me. Can't imagine what came over me.

"You know Chuck thinks rather too much of you, don't you; too much for his own good. Sees you as a hero. But then sometimes so do I." She clasped me, brushed my mouth lightly with her lips. Then, on a rising inflection; almost a question: "I'm not so sure what Eloïse sees."

I alas knew quite well what Eloïse saw; a black soul, a killer's hands.

We had been back in Cyprus for nearly two months and Christmas was looming. Eloïse had, she said, suffered something of a breakdown. I phoned her as soon as the USN helicopter landed us at the RAF station at Dhekelia. It turned out she wasn't in Cyprus. She'd gone to Alexandria to stay with her mother. When I finally tracked her down, her mother said she wasn't in any state to talk to me. I phoned every day and got the same answer. Should I fly over? No! After ten days when I'd given up hope of ever hearing her voice again, she phoned me. She was back in her flat and was coming over to see me. Would five o'clock this afternoon be convenient?

I didn't suppose it would ever be more convenient. I had to tell her; tell her and lose her. What other choice had I?

She arrived, spot on time, in a chocolate brown trouser suit, looking far too thin, her eyes enormous, her adorable errant nose, pale and commanding. My heart turned over. She embraced me fleetingly and went and sat in an armchair. She was hyped up.

"What happened," she said, words tumbling out, tripping each other, "was he changed. I heard him on the ship-to-shore discussing some big deal, in French. It was heroin. Lots of it, lots of dollars. He was very excited and then he started talking about bombs, atomic bombs. More dollars, hundreds of thousands. Germ warfare. Horrible diseases. I didn't know what to do. I started to cry and he heard me. I ran down to my cabin but he followed me, put his foot in the door before I could close it. He grabbed me and shook me and pushed me and pulled me. And hurt me. He threw me on to my bed, or bunk or whatever you call it. And stood over me mouthing curses and threats. He was dribbling with fury, his eyes streaked with blood, his shoulders moving in convulsions. I thought he was having a fit.

"Suddenly he went silent. 'Listen, you little fool,' he said, speaking slowly, viciously. 'Mention one word of this and I swear I'll cut you, and your cow of a mother, to ribbons. And your boy-friend's testicles. Just one little word. I'll find you wherever you've gone. You understand?' I nodded. I remembered every syllable. He locked me in the cabin. I didn't see him again. The aunt let me out when we were in port, in Izmir. When I looked back, the yacht had gone."

She gave a little sob, stifled it and, for the first time, looked at me properly, searching my eyes.

"I was a fool," she said. "You were right. I should never have gone away with him. Better still never have met him. To fall for his tale like that. I can't believe it." Another sob escaped, followed by a tearful half-smile. "And look where I've landed in."

"Up," I said automatically.

"*Attaque de nerfs*. A breakdown. I go home to Maman. Who caused it all. And she is angry with me, with herself, with him. And of course feeling guilty she hits out at everything within reach. Which is mostly me. And I do nothing except resign from everything. I've even told them I can't examine anymore. I'm useless and I don't want to see anybody. Not even you. But I know you were right all along."

She was crying now, tears coursing down her face. I held her, kissed her tears, stroked her face gently and said, "You know he's dead?"

"I hope so," she said. "I hope he died in excruciating agony."

I could see him, all too plainly, the blood, the spittle jogging up and down like a yo-yo.

"I hope he's burning in the everlasting fires of hell," she said. "Maman read of his death in some newspaper. For a while I feared it might be untrue; that he still lives somewhere. And even now he haunts my dreams, my nightmares. Like some evil jinni. I think what he might have done to you. How could I ever have believed him loving or attractive? Oh Benjy, how could I? *Amártaine enópion Theoú kai anthrópon*."

Even I could make that out: sinning against God and man.

"I have to tell you something," I said.

She looked up, her darling face tear-stained, hopeful.

216

"I killed him." I amended it quickly, "I helped kill him."
She pulled away from me, violently.

Eleni came through customs and immigration escorted by Freddie Ericsson who was wheeling her chair.

"'Allo, 'allo," said Chuck, "what 'ave we 'ere? D'you think he's left the divine Tamara for your mum?"

"Godly Tamara," I said, "religious Tamara. Not so much of the pagan divine Tamara; not these days."

Eleni got out of her chair and walked a few careful, slightly tottering steps towards us. I ran forward and caught her in an embrace.

"See," she said, "I can almost walk. But only for a few paces. I'm still in a plaster, still in some pain. I'll probably need another trip to Athens and perhaps another op."

"Marvellous recovery," boomed Freddie. "Wonderful, brave patient. Never known anyone quite like her for determination, courage and sweetness of character."

"Get away with you, Freddie dear. You're in enough trouble with Tamara as it is, staying away for weeks, bless you, looking after me. You wouldn't know I had a son, would you. Oh I dare say he was doing something more important, like stopping World War III."

She got back into the wheelchair, I kissed her and took over the pushing, Freddie walking alongside.

Chuck obviously thought he had to say something. "You look well, Eleni," he said, "but you mustn't make jokes like that."

I shook my head violently and stared at him. He was undeterred. Fairness was all. Truth must out.

"Ben has been incredibly brave, and successful in . . ."

I hissed a venomous "Shut up!" and Freddie interposed some nicely turned phrase about there being more than one way of serving and how Eleni mustn't assume that all jobs allowed people to come and go as they, or their mothers, wished.

Eleni sniffed, a generalised disapproval. "And out of reach of a telephone too, I suppose. Because of his job. *Some* job."

I bridled at this last blast. "I've rung you every day for weeks."

"So you have," she said. "And what about the week before that?"

"He was otherwise engaged," said Chuck.

This made her laugh. "At least you have loyal friends," she said, patting my hand. "And where's Eloïse?"

No question, Eleni was back on form.

As I had half expected, Eloïse was at the hotel. She'd been helping Frosso, who had run everything in Mum's long absence, to get flowers arranged and champagne put out in an ice bucket, ready for the return.

After tearful embraces and reunions all round, Freddie as much as Eleni lachrymose and kissing everyone within sight, Eleni said to Eloïse, her eyes alert as ever for a missing ring, "So you're not going to marry him after all. I expect he treats you the same as he treats me; unexplained silence and isolation."

Eloïse didn't know what to say. She looked at the floor. I walked up and took her passive but still, I suspected, reluctant hand and said, "She's still in shock, poor love."

Eleni was contrite, sympathetic and puzzled.

Chuck and I made our escape. Freddie followed us.

"I'll just stay a day or two," he said, "to make sure she's settled in properly. And you can tell me what you've been up to."

"Right," I said and went back to the bungalow. I'd been re-organizing my life and wanted to see if the papers had arrived. Some certainly had, several thick, official envelopes.

First things first. I'd failed the medical and was out of the SBS. I'd been placed on the general reserve of officers of the Royal Marines. Another envelope, I'd been promoted Lieutenant-Colonel on the reserve list. Another, whiter, crisper; roughly speaking I'd been recommended for an OBE (Military) in the New Year's Honours. Would I accept it?

This wasn't a total surprise. The USN had made much of us, even the Admiral who was flying his flag in USS Nimitz. Captain Jim Cordier had chaired the debriefing and at the end he'd taken me aside and said, "I reckon this deserves a medal."

One of the things about being a soldier, or a marine or a sailor, is that you have to be prepared to kill and then to get pretty ribbons and dangling decorations to tell everyone that you're really a pretty good guy to do such brave and useful things for your country, and assorted allies. *It's a game, innit.*

Before the month was out, a citation and an impressive medal was on its way from Washington. When Mike Cable got through to me, he said he owed me one personally—or even two or three. I told him, all I wanted was

Zkrakovic handed over to The Hague War Crimes Commission. "OK," he said, "that's taken care of. I'll do one thing more, I'll kick British ass till they reward you suitably."

Actually, to be fair, Jeremy Sims had thanked me for the information I'd sent him, in a polite four-line letter, and Colonel Partridge, of Special Forces liaison at the SBAs, had telephoned.

"I've heard good things of you, Major," he said. "Well done. By the by, did you ever fire that undetectable, plastic gun, thingumajig?"

"No," I said. "Why?"

"Just as well. They've recalled them; a design fault, I believe."

Cy Drucker had also sent a message, somewhat later. The material had been useful, indeed valuable, to the US Embassy and, he believed, to the Egyptian government. I should be aware that Yilmaz Çelik had known I was dating his daughter and hated it, my mother being Jewish and all that. He had planned for Eloïse in effect to be kidnapped in the hope of having her converted to Islam and marrying a nice Muslim of his choice. I e-mailed back and said it was a bit late to tell me now.

The last envelope was informing me that Her Majesty had agreed that all the honours, awards, ranks and titles (*all?*) which had formerly belonged to David Ditchling could now be transferred to Benjamin Bolton in which name, I noticed, I had been gazetted a half-colonel on the reserve list.

219

A strange business: through lawyers in London I had changed my name, by deed poll, back to my real name. The time had come, I said to myself, to simplify. I was Ben Bolton henceforth, all the time. Nothing wrong with that, nothing wrong at all but I felt peculiarly bereft; a large part of my life, all the David Ditchling derring-do, the beloved SBS, had slipped almost noiselessly into the deep.

Back to work, I'd said to myself. I wondered what Ginger, our relatively silent partner in Norwich, had got lined up? Ginger, it seemed, had a little job in Burma. He'd been approached to send someone out to help one of Aung San Suu Kyi's supporters who'd been re-arrested and put in jail. Time was not of the essence, proper preparation was. Ergo I had just what I needed, he thought, plenty of time to forget everything else. He e-mailed me, in code, an outline. It sounded horrendous but he'd done his homework and found me a Burmese tutor.

I'd spent three weeks doing Burmese every day and getting nowhere. My tutor was a fairly austere Buddhist and he was at least as concerned to teach me the main tenets of Buddhist thought and belief as to instill the basics of a difficult language with what was to me an impenetrable alphabet. The one, he suggested, was impossible without the other. To this end, I had to do a meditation, every morning, after I'd finished a reading. The subject: death and the corruption of the physical body. This, he assured me, was an excellent way to subdue the lusts of the flesh; by which, mostly I think, he meant sex.

Having sunk myself in an immoderate depression, Eloïse and the memory of her father dying as he spat at me contributing, I decided to throw the whole thing over. It was never going to work. Burma was effectively an enclosed police state. I was not going to learn the language in a twelvemonth let alone twelve weeks. And above all, far from reducing sex, I wanted to increase it, promote it to the top of my wish-list.

I felt much better after that.

A few weeks after I had told Eloïse, we had lunch at a taverna and discussed her dreadful father. Slowly, painfully slowly, we re-established some kind of almost loving friendship; but it wasn't the same. Yesterday, it seemed after an eternity of abstinence, we became lovers again. But suddenly, post coitum, I seemed to see her recoiling from me, repelled by my being a killer, and in particular the killer of her father. Of course, in the end she may have feared and distrusted her father but, I was thinking, she now must feel that she had just made love to his murderer and that was a different order of relationship. She knew, she had been told, that I had killed him, violently. And perhaps she feared that violence more; violence in her lover.

"Look," I said, making what I felt would be my only bid. "First and last, I love you rotten. You're the best thing I ever met. I treasure you from the crown of your head to your splendidly elongated, ancient Egyptian hands and feet. But I hadn't known Yilmaz Çelik was anything to do with you. Not till the last minute. So in any real sense, for me, I was not chasing Eloïse's father: I was trying to stop a psychopathic murderer who had the blood of hundreds, perhaps thousands on his hands. And even when I knew who he was, and decided to go on, I didn't really know, to be honest, I was killing him, or the others. Not for certain."

"There were *others?*" she asked, in what I took to be horror.

I ignored her. "Anything could have happened. No; that's a cop-out. I knew it could, it might, end in death. But I wasn't sure."

We were in her flat. She got up and went to the kitchen; she said to make a tisane. I thought I'd better get up, and dress, and leave. There was no point hanging about. If I'd lost, I'd go off and grieve on my own. As I put on my shirt, I thought of all those mottoes; the SAS "He Who Dares, Wins" and the more subtle SBS "Not by Strength, By Guile" and decided I preferred Colour-Sergeant Malone's "Never say die, eh?"

Eloïse returned, cup and saucer in hand, as I was pulling on my socks.

"Don't be silly," she said. "Come back to bed. It's cold outside and you'll catch your death."

About the author

Austen Kark was born in London, served in the Royal Navy and then studied English at Oxford with C.S. Lewis. After writing for several newspapers and magazines in the UK, Kark joined the BBC, broadcasting and reporting on West and Central Africa and Europe and specializing in the affairs of the Eastern Mediterranean, notably Greece, Turkey, Cyprus and Israel. He later took charge of the BBC's Russian and Balkan operations before going on to run the BBC World Service in English. He was made Managing Director of the World Service and upon his retirement in 1986, he was appointed CBE.

Few writers can know and understand the passions of the Middle East as well as Austen Kark.

The fonts used in this book are from the Garamond and Stencil families.